# METTLE OF A MOUNTAIN MAN

## LOGAN MOUNTAIN MAN SERIES - BOOK 3

## DONALD L. ROBERTSON

CM Publishing

# COPYRIGHT

## METTLE OF A MOUNTAIN MAN

Copyright © 2021 Donald L. Robertson
CM Publishing

Publisher's Note: This is a work of fiction. Names, characters, and incidents are a product of the author's imagination. Locales and public names are sometimes used for atmospheric purposes. Any resemblance to actual people, living or dead, or to businesses, companies, or events, is completely coincidental. For information contact:

Books@DonaldLRobertson.com

❀ Created with Vellum

# LOGAN FAMILY GENEALOGY

**Ethan William Logan, 1779**
**Married**
**Rose Isabel Tilman, 1780**
CHILDREN
Matthew Christopher Logan, 1797
Mark Adair Logan, 1798
Nathaniel Grant Logan, 1803
Owen Lewis Logan, 1803
Jennifer (Jenny) Isabel Logan, 1812
Floyd Horatio Logan, 1814
Martha Ann Logan, 1816

---

**Matthew Christopher Logan, 1797**
**Married**
**Rebecca (Becky) Nicole Doherty, 1810**
CHILDREN
William Wallace Logan, 1834
Callum Jeremiah Logan, 1836
Joshua Matthew Logan, 1840
Katherine (Kate) Logan, 1851
Bret Hamilton Logan, 1852
Colin Alexander Logan, 1854

# 1

November 18, 1840, Independence, Missouri

Darkness enveloped the streets and alleyways, broken only by diffused shafts of light escaping from saloon windows. A cold wind whistled past the closed businesses and searched for any open collar or torn sleeve. Several late night citizens slowed their hurried steps to watch a tall rider in a thick buffalo coat. His hat was pulled low over his eyes for protection from the wind. He and his mount were momentarily illuminated by narrow shafts of light escaping from the few lit windows.

Floyd Logan, mounted on a large gaunt buckskin, led another horse and mule. After he passed, the clicking of fast-paced steps continued down the boardwalk.

It had already been a long, hard journey for Floyd, reflected in his sharp features and the tired steps of his animals. His desire to remain close to his wife, Leotie, and son, Mika, had held him too long in the Shoshone village located in a beautiful valley in the Rocky Mountains. He had paid dearly for his delay, crossing the Great Plains in chilling wind, rain, and snow flurries. He welcomed the coming warmth, as he felt sure his horses did.

Though covered in his heavy buffalo coat, he shivered in the wind.

The buckskin's steady walk brought him alongside a dark alley. Above the biting wind he heard a dull thud, much like a blow delivered to the soft part of a body, and then a cry followed by more blows.

Without a thought for himself, he wheeled Buck toward the alley and slammed his heels into the horse's flanks. Buck leaped forward while Floyd pulled a pistol from one of the holsters hanging on his saddle. Even as it was being drawn, he was cocking the hammer. In the darkness, he could barely make out the outline of three men bent over another on the ground. He could see, more clearly, their white faces turn up to him, reflecting the dim light from the street.

A pistol fired. The bullet cracked by his left ear and drove through the thin boarded wall of the store nestled next to the alley.

Without hesitation, Floyd aimed a few inches to the left of the flash and pulled the trigger. As he fired, he felt Buck slam into one of the robbers, and saw the man roll across the alley, jump to his feet, and take off like he was being chased by old Beelzebub. Floyd shoved the spent pistol back into its holster and, before leaping to the ground, drew the other.

Ears ringing from the two shots in the tight alley, he could barely hear the sound of rapidly retreating steps.

Kneeling next to the inert form, he said, "You all right, fella?"

The only response was a weak moan.

Lights were coming on in the adjacent buildings, and running feet entered the alley.

Floyd, still kneeling beside the man, turned his head and snapped, "Get a doctor."

In almost the same tone, the man carrying a lantern and running toward them said, "I am a doctor. Get out of my way."

Floyd stood and moved back, allowing the doctor access to

the injured man. Others were now pouring into the alley. Questions flew. "What happened? Is that man dead? Did the big guy in the buffalo coat shoot him?"

Seeing the people running into the alley, Floyd turned and picked up the reins for Buck.

"He's trying to get away!" someone shouted. "Git him."

Floyd spun to face his attackers, leveling the pistol, causing the several spectators who were jumping toward him to slide to a sudden stop. The reflected lantern light from his scarred face and the big .54-caliber pistol offered a huge calming effect.

The doc, working rapidly on the injured man, looked up from his patient into the excited and now fearful faces. "Settle down! This man saved this fella's life. I heard the attackers running away down the alley." He looked at three of the men who had just walked up. "Jim, you, Pete, and Jesse get over here and get this man to my office. It's open. Put him on the exam table, and I'll be up in a minute."

He turned to Floyd. "Good thing you came along when you did."

"Reckon," Floyd said.

"It's cold out here. Why don't you come with me to my office. I've got some hot coffee I fixed this morning. It'll put hair on your chest."

The older man looked Floyd up and down. "Though, I don't imagine you need any more."

Floyd shook his head. "Thanks, Doc. Reckon I've got to get these animals sheltered. They're cold and tired. Is Lucy's Boardinghouse still around?"

The doctor shook his head. "Afraid not. By the way, my name's Doc Bessel. What's yours?"

"I'm Floyd Logan." He glanced down at the injured man. "I'll take care of this feller's bill and stand you for some dinner if that would suit you, after I take care of these animals."

"Far as the bill's concerned, I'm familiar with this gentleman.

He can take care of it himself. Dinner's another thing. I need to look over him more closely, but when I'm done, I'll be right along. Why don't you meet me at the Trailhead Saloon, they fix a pretty good meal, and they do keep hot coffee."

Floyd nodded. "Know where it is."

He swung up onto Buck, touched the brim of his hat, and turned the horses toward the crowd, whom the cold wind was blowing away like last year's tumbleweeds. The few remaining split, allowing him plenty of room. He nodded and pointed Buck toward Brennan's stable. Ten years ago, he'd met Salty Dickens there. Initially, it hadn't been the most congenial relationship, but Floyd's respect for the old mule skinner and mountain man had quickly cooled his youthful temper until they were best of friends. He was looking forward to seeing Salty again.

To the right of the massive barn doors, a smaller door stood partially open, light pouring from the interior. Floyd rode close to the door, leaned over in the saddle, where he could peer inside, and called, "Anybody worth their salt in there?"

A few moments of silence passed, broken finally by a harsh yell from inside. "If yore sellin' anything, keep movin'. If yore lookin' for a place for yore horse, then get down and come on in, but don't waste no time, and close that door behind you."

Floyd grinned to himself, recognizing the voice of his old friend. *Salty must be getting close to seventy,* he thought. *He's just as rambunctious as he's always been.* Still in the saddle, he answered, "I've got some animals out here that need some shelter. I'd be obliged if you'd open your barn door."

He could hear Salty inside. Suddenly the smaller door slammed shut. Moments later the big doors started sliding on their rollers.

Floyd could hear Salty grumbling as the wide stable door opened. "It ain't decent for a body to be travelin' in this weather. Just opening this door, I might catch my death of cold."

Floyd sat silent in the saddle. With his buffalo coat on and his hat low over his eyes, his own mother wouldn't recognize him.

Salty pushed the door wide enough and stood there leaning against the frame. He waited only a second, then said, "Well, don't sit there like a knot on a limb. Get them animals in here."

Floyd remained silent. He didn't have to coax Buck to enter the warm barn. Rusty and Browny pushed up close behind, trying to get into the warmth. As the three animals passed, Salty broke out in a huge grin.

"Well, paint me white and call me a ghost. Floyd Logan. If that don't beat all. What you doin' crossing them plains this time of year?"

Floyd swung down from Buck and swept his beat-up hat off, joining his old friend in a wide grin. "How you been, Salty?"

"An almighty sight better than you or anyone who's travelin' in this weather." He stepped up to Floyd and grasped him by both arms. "Danged if you ain't growed into much of a man."

He looked at the white streak and scar left in the younger man's scalp. "Looks like them mountains ain't been a kind mistress for you."

Floyd shook his head. "You're wrong, Salty. They've been real kind. Reckon I've just had a few bumps along the way." His hand went to his head, paused at the scar, then pushed his long hair back. The white and dark brown blended for a ways, then fell, a solid brown broken only by a thin white streak, to his shoulders. "A big ole griz, who didn't like me invading his beaver stream, left me this."

"Heard about it from Jeb on his last trip here. Said you kilt that old bear and gave his hide to a medicine man."

Floyd slipped his hat back on. "Jeb talks too much."

"Maybe, but he ain't the onliest one. Why, son, you've become almost a legend around here. The local paper ran a story about yore bear fight, and the fight you had with them Blackfoot." He shook his head. "If it weren't for them scars you're carryin', I'd have to say you are a mighty lucky man. Anyone tangles with a Blackfoot ain't likely to be heard from again." He stopped to rub Browny the mule on its muzzle. "Now let's get these poor animals brushed down and fed. Looks like you been pushin' 'em mighty hard." Salty took the lead ropes for Rusty and Browny and headed toward the open stalls.

Floyd followed with Buck. "First, this has been a hard trip. Seems like that northwest wind and snow has been chasing us all the way here. I thought we were goners a couple of times, but managed to find us a place to hunker down a day or so. We've been cold and wet since we left the mountains, and it's still early. I'm lookin' for a hard winter this year."

The old mule skinner nodded. "Yep, I s'pect this'll be a bad one. I seen geese and ducks headin' south way early this year, and the horses started puttin' on their winter coats early."

Floyd continued, "I'm no legend, Salty. I've just been trying to keep my hair. The Blackfoot kidnapped a good Shoshone woman I had met, and her son. I wasn't alone in rescuing them. Shorty Zebulon, Morg James, and a Shoshone warrior, Kajika, were right there too. If it weren't for them, none of us would be here."

Salty nodded. "They were through here a while back and told us all about it. Said if it hadn't been for you, they'd been goners."

Floyd shook his head and said nothing, knowing, if he didn't put this conversation to bed, it would go on all evening.

The two men worked quickly. Salty put out corn and hay for all three animals while Floyd continued to brush. Then the younger man spoke softly to each of the animals, rubbing noses and cheeks.

"Salty, if one of those wide stalls is available, I'd be much obliged if you could keep the three of them together. They're pretty attached to each other, especially Browny. I think she'd rather be around horses than her own kind."

"Horses are her own kind, boy. At least by half."

Floyd laughed and said, "I guess you're right," and started

putting his gear together. "I'm gonna need you to take care of them for a while."

Salty rose from checking Buck's feet and shoes. "You headin' somewhere back east?"

"Yep. I want to make it home for Christmas. My folks haven't seen me for ten years. I remember some wise soul tellin' me I shouldn't wait too long to go back. Hopefully, time hasn't run out yet."

"Good for you, boy. It's already been ten years, though it seems like yesterday you fought those Pawnee and got that souvenir on yore cheek."

Through the stubble, Floyd ran his finger down the scar on his left cheek. Memories flooded back. He had been only sixteen when Jeb left him to watch over the Ryland family, on the Neosho River near the Post Office Oak. Ryland was sick, near death, when the Pawnees attacked. With help from Mrs. Ryland, he killed all the attackers except one. With bloodthirsty determination, the remaining brave drew his knife and charged Floyd. It was from the Indian's blade that Floyd had received the long scar on his cheek.

His mind snapped back to the present. "I was really a green kid, wasn't I?"

"He, he, he," Salty cackled. "You wasn't that green, but you shore was a kid. I never seen such an independent young feller in all my life, and you was almighty proud of yore shooting skill."

This time Floyd joined in the laughter. "I was, wasn't I? Jeb sure gave me my comeuppance, though he was mighty nice about it."

"Son, I ain't never seen such a natural shooter as you. You just needed experience. Now, all this talkin' is makin' me thirsty. What say you buy me a drink?"

"This stuff safe here?" Floyd said, nodding at his gear.

"Safe as if it was in a bank. Nobody with any sense would steal anything from a Hugh Brennan stable, especially yore stuff.

Folks around here know all about how you single-handedly cleaned out the Trace Porter gang, and you being only seventeen. No, no one's botherin' yore stuff."

"How'd that story get all the way back here?"

Under his dirty hat, Salty cut an eye toward Floyd, held the look for a moment, then said, "Let's go get something to eat." He stood that way for only a moment and started for the door.

Floyd rolled his eyes. Salty had been there. In fact, he had been wounded with the first shot from Porter's bunch. He shook his head and thought, *Salty's as bad as Jeb.* After latching his buffalo coat and grabbing his rifle, he followed Salty toward the door. "I'm meeting the doc at the Trailhead."

Salty shot Floyd another look. "You sick?"

"Nope, I'll tell you about it when we get there."

Salty nodded as the two of them stepped from the barn into the frigid night. Neither man said a word as, leaning into the bone-chilling wind, they trudged toward the Trailhead Saloon.

*Glad I'm not on the prairie again tonight,* Floyd thought. *There's a good chance a man and his animals could freeze to death, and this is only November. As bad as it was comin', the cold and snow is gonna be ten times worse when I head back to Leotie and Mika. I won't be able to start across the plains until February or so.*

After entering the Trailhead, the wind tried to prevent the door from closing, but Floyd pushed firmly until it latched, then turned around.

Entering the saloon was a jolt to his system. A layer of smoke lay over the room, and the warmth was almost stifling. Two potbellied stoves were pumping out heat in all directions, and when combined with the number of bodies, it was near suffocating.

But the heat was nothing compared to the smell, like someone was singeing a pile of rotten buffalo hides. Combined with the stale beer, the heat and smell almost drove Floyd back into the dark, frigid night. He was used to the smell of pines, cedars, or prairie. Even the tent saloons at rendezvous didn't smell this bad. The tinny-sounding piano banged away against the back wall, lending an irritating background to the din of voices. Floyd caught the quick movement of someone who had been sitting near the piano as the man disappeared through the back door.

Salty paused, looked around, found the doctor sitting at a table near the east wall, and headed toward him. With the doctor, sitting with his back to the wall, was a man of about Floyd's age and near as tall. He was of slim build and sporting a bandage around his head. His bowler hat rested on the table in front of him. The chairs across from the doc had been left open, so Floyd moved around to where he could lean his rifle against the wall, and sat.

"How are you, Doc?" Floyd said.

"A lot better than my friend, here." He motioned to the tall young man. "He's been severely beaten. I tried to persuade him to remain in bed for at least the night, but he insisted on accompanying me to meet you, Mr. Logan." He then nodded at Salty. "Evening, Salty."

Salty looked at Doc Bessel, then Floyd. "Now would someone tell me what's goin' on?"

The doctor turned to Salty. "You mean you didn't hear the shots?"

"Well, no, Doc. I ain't heard no shots. I was in the stable workin', and with the wind blowin', why—"

The doctor shook his head. "Salty, you're getting as deaf as a dry cactus."

Salty sat up straight and started shaking his finger at the doctor. "I ain't deaf, you good-for-nothin' sawbones! Don't be talkin' like that in front of my friend and this here young feller."

Doc Bessel, ignoring Salty's outburst, turned to the man sitting at the table and said, "Mr. Gates, this is Floyd Logan, the man you can thank for saving your life. The old fellow with him is Salty Dickens. He runs the Brennan Stable and Wagon Shop."

Salty cast Bessel a hard look at the mention of *old fellow* and started to say something else when Gates extended his hand to Floyd and said, "Thank you, Mr. Logan. Ransom T. Gates. I am forever in your debt. I was convinced my life was at an end before you arrived. I have no idea why you stepped in, but I am extremely thankful you did. Dr. Bessel also told me you offered to pay his fee, quite gentlemanly of you." After shaking Floyd's hand, Gates continued to Salty, "Nice to meet you, Mr. Dickens."

Salty nodded his head. "Howdy." He turned toward the busy bartender, waved one arm, and shouted above the noise, "Need some grub over here, Clarence."

The bartender looked between two wide-shouldered teamsters, spotted Salty, and waved back. He turned to a door to his right and shouted something that was lost in the din. Moments later, a trim young woman of about twenty-two emerged from the door, saw Salty and the doc, smiled, and headed for them.

"Salty," the doc said, "it wasn't necessary to yell like that."

The old mountain man glared at Bessel. "Mind yore own business, Doc. Ellie's comin', ain't she?"

Ellie, her long wavy blonde hair flowing below her shoulders, had to weave her way through the crowded tables, dodging, warding off advances, and slapping away grasping hands. She had a small dish towel rolled and tucked in the front of her skirt, ready for quick use. One persistent admirer felt the sting of it when she yanked it from her skirt, her pale green eyes flashing, and popped his grasping hand with the end.

He grimaced through a grin as he rubbed the back of his hand and watched her move on. Shouting, he said, "It weren't necessary for you to use that rag on me, Ellie. I ain't meant you no harm."

She stopped, only for a moment, shot one hip, placed one hand on it, and held the other out, finger pointing at the young farmer. "Tom, you know you're always gettin' too handsy. Just be glad it was only the end of my dishrag. What would you do if I told your mama? I don't think she'd be very happy with you."

Tom's grin disappeared. "Aw, Ellie, I ain't meant nothing." He paused for a couple of seconds as he realized what she had said, his eyes opening wider. "You wouldn't do that, would you?" His friends at the table and the men at surrounding tables burst out in laughter. Ellie either didn't hear his question or was ignoring him. She turned and pushed on to Floyd's table.

"Hi, Salty, Doc," she said, her eyes roving over Floyd and stopping on Gates. "Can I get you gentlemen anything?"

Gates smiled up at the attractive young woman and said, "I think we'd all like to eat?" He looked around the table as he was speaking. Doc nodded, as did Floyd.

"Ellie, alls I need is a beer," Salty said. "I'm plumb thirsty."

She flashed shiny white teeth in a friendly smile at Salty. "Coming right up. Would the rest of you like something to drink?"

"Same," Doc said.

Floyd and Gates nodded. Then Gates said, "You handled the altercation with that big fellow quite well."

She beamed at Gates. "It was nothing. I've known Tom since we were little tykes. You're not from here, Mr.?"

"Ransom Gates, but please call me Ransom, and your name is Ellie?"

"Yes, I'm Ellie—"

The front door of the saloon slammed open, and a tall, thin, clean-shaven man, wearing a bowler hat and an overcoat that almost swallowed him up, stepped into the saloon, followed by another man who looked vaguely familiar to Floyd.

Immediately the second man's arm shot out, pointing at Floyd.

"That's him. He's the leader. Him, an Injun, and two other filthy mountain men hanged my partner, Van McMillan."

## 2

———————

At the man's shout, Floyd recognized him, Henry Page. He looked much different from the last time Floyd had seen him. At that time, he had been begging for his life, in Blackfoot country. He had been the partner of the man who had beaten and raped Leotie. Now he was well dressed. A flashy overcoat was open, allowing the world to see his well-tailored suit and waistcoat, with a diamond pin in his cravat. His head was covered with a black gambler-style hat.

Floyd, outwardly calm, rose abruptly, his chair sliding back in jerks across the roughhewn floor, coming to rest against another patron's leg. His hand drifted to his pistol.

"Don't do it, boy," Salty warned in a low voice. "That tall, city-lookin' feller is a sorry excuse for a lawman, but he is the town marshal. You ain't want'n to get tangled up with the law."

Floyd had seen the marshal stiffen when his hand went to his pistol. As far as Floyd could tell, the marshal was unarmed. He removed his hand from the butt and let it hang loose. Silence had fallen on the saloon at the shout of Page. Ellie stood silent and still at the approach of the two men.

The marshal stopped on the opposite side of the table from

Floyd. His watery blue eyes, nestled in pasty white skin, seldom paused on Floyd, flitting across the saloon. Page had stepped from behind the lawman just far enough to be able to see Floyd.

"I'm Marshal Ned Cooley. Were you about to pull a gun on me, trapper?" His voice, filled with cold disdain, almost spit out the word *trapper*.

The piano player leaned against his piano, elbow striking a hard blow to the high f key. The piercing note assaulted Floyd's ears. Several men jumped, including Page and Cooley.

Floyd never moved. "Reckon when I'm yelled at by the likes of the vermin you have with you, I tend to ready myself. My friend Salty, here, says you're the marshal. If you saw my hand reach for my pistol, you also saw it move away."

Cooley's eyes continued jerking around the crowded room. "Just make sure you don't do it again." Then he glanced down at Salty and the doctor, tossing them a feeble nod of recognition.

"Cooley," the doc said, "I don't know what Page told you about Mr. Logan, but you can't believe anything derogatory. It is simply not true."

Cooley turned his head toward the doc. "I am a marshal, Doctor. I'm not a judge. I do not render verdicts, I just arrest people, and that is what I am about to do to Mr. Logan."

"Why ain't you out lookin' for those gents what beat up Mr. Gates, here?" Salty said, his thumb pointing toward Gates. "You should've heard those shots fired in the alley. Why, if it weren't for Floyd, the feller yore lookin' to arrest on the say-so of a worthless rapist—"

Page immediately shouted, his shaking finger pointed in the general direction of Floyd. "I ain't raped no woman. It was my partner, and he has been hanged by that bloody heathen. His Injun partner even shot an arrow into his belly while he was dying at the end of a rope."

Conversation erupted at the mention of rape, and men started looking threateningly at Page. Five rough-looking men, obviously from the mountains, rose from their chairs.

Page's head turned back and forth across the five, seeing and sensing the hostility in the faces turned toward him. In desperation, he shouted, "Anyway, she was just a filthy squaw!"

Little change was evident in Floyd's demeanor. A slight hardening appeared in his eyes, and the skin drew tighter at the corners. Beneath his clothing, his body tensed like that of a mountain lion before launching onto the back of an elk.

The shout from Page had barely died when the big hands of Floyd grasped the edge of the solid oak table that stood between him and Page. The table, as if with a life of its own, leaped from the floor, sailed over the heads of Doc Bessel and Phillip Gates, slamming against and then coming to rest by the wall. It hit with such force, the flimsy wall shuddered.

In one leap Floyd was across the room. His left forearm wiped the marshal from his path, driving the lawman to the floor, while his right hand closed around the thick neck of Page.

Everything happened so fast no one had a chance to make a move, if they'd had the inclination. Eyes were divided between watching the disliked marshal slide across the floor, knocking over spittoons, picking up splinters from the rough-cut floor, finally coming to rest against booted legs, and watching Floyd attack Page.

Floyd had never felt the rage now consuming his body. When he was younger, before coming west, he had a temper that could flash at the least provocation, but his Philippine teacher, in Santa Fe, had showed him how and why to control it. What he felt now was nothing like anything he had ever felt. Even in fights to the death, this kind of emotion had never filled his body.

He felt cold and determined to crush the life from the evil presence before him. The words "just a squaw!" kept crashing through his mind. It was an unknown but all-consuming emotion that had taken hold of him. His vision closed in as he focused on

Page. He could see the marshal, but only as an obstacle to be brushed from his path, in his unrelenting desire to destroy.

Floyd felt the thick muscle in Page's neck, felt the racing heartbeat. The man's eyes bulged, appearing as if they would explode from his head. He could hear loud voices. Some shouting, "Kill the rapist," but others shouted, "Stop," and grabbed at his hand. He fought them off with his free arm, but they kept coming back.

Floyd stared into the panicked eyes and squeezed harder. His voice, hard and determined, said, "I should have hanged you with McMillan."

The world exploded. He tried to tighten his grip, to end the worthless life of the animal who stared with hate and fear at him, but his hand was weaker. He caught a glimpse of a fist coming fast. The room disappeared.

WHEN FLOYD REGAINED CONSCIOUSNESS, he was lying on a bed, and light was flooding through the window above him. He moved his head to look around. Pain slashed from his neck to his head, stopping the movement. But he had moved enough so that he could see the bars and, on the other side of them, Salty.

"Good," the old man said in relief. "I had to stop you. The marshal had already unlimbered his sleeve gun, a double-barrel derringer. He was about to blast you. I had to step in. Were it up to me, you could have choked the life out of Page and the world would've been a better place."

Floyd's head throbbed with each beat of his heart. He reached back and rubbed the lump on the right side of his head, just above his neck. "You hit me?"

"Had to, boy. If'n I ain't, that worthless marshal would have plugged you for sure. There weren't nothing else to do. Several of the other boys were trying to pull you off Page, but I knew they'd never git 'er done in time. You woulda snuffed him out like a match, so I had to hit you."

Salty held up his hands and shook his head. "I didn't want to. You've got to believe that. But it saved your life."

Floyd, his cot up against the cold, thin wall at the back of the jail, slid his legs off the bed, sat up. He stared at Salty seated straight in front of him on the other side of the locked cell door. His headache worsened.

"What'd you hit me with? An axe handle?"

Now the older man looked hurt. "Why would you say that? I told you why I had to do it, and no, I didn't hit you with an axe handle. I hit you with this." Salty reached inside his unbuttoned coat and pulled a pistol from behind his waistband, holding it by the barrel with the butt turned toward Floyd.

"Is that blood still on it?"

Salty jerked the weapon up to his face and peered, examining the butt of the weapon. While looking at it, he said, "There ain't no blood on it." Then he gave Floyd a sharp look. "You're funnin' me."

"I saw a fist just before I blacked out."

"Page. After I—" Salty hesitated and rubbed his beard, as if trying to figure out how to describe the blow, then looked back up at Floyd "—uh, had to stop you, when you was fallin', Page hit you."

"How is he?"

"He ain't dead, but he shore enough has yore big ole finger marks around his neck."

"He's twice lucky," Floyd said.

"Not to hear him tell it. If you was to listen to him, he went through a real ordeal trying to get back to civilization."

"Good."

The older man eyed Floyd. "You wasn't just tryin' to scare him in the saloon?"

"Salty, if you had left me alone just a few more seconds, Page would never have taken another breath. He was with the rotten pigs who beat and raped my wife. Then, after I caught up with them and hanged McMillan, he smooth-talked me into turning him loose. I should've strung him up right next to his partner. Like I said, he was lucky I let him go."

Salty looked around the room and toward the closed front door. "Son, for what those fellers did, they should've all been kilt. Out there in those mountains, you've got to be yore own law. But back here, we're gettin' all civilized. Shoot, in town, here, stealin' a man's horse don't even git ya hanged anymore. You go around talkin' like that and this here marshal'll git you sent off to prison right quick."

Floyd looked at Salty in disbelief. "Salty, you'd have done the same thing."

Salty nodded his head. "I would, and there's a bunch of men back from the mountains around town who would've too. In fact, several of them jumped the marshal and kept you from gettin' shot in the back with his hideout gun. I'm surprised they ain't in here. He's probably afraid of 'em and their friends." Salty took a big breath before continuing.

"But that ain't the point. Yore the man in this here jail, and you don't want to be talkin' like that, or you'll be staring through bars for a bunch of years."

Floyd shook his head. "I can't go to prison. I've got to see my parents and get back to Leotie. That's my wife's name. I didn't want to make this trip now, but she insisted."

"I know her name, son. Jeb told me all about you and her. She sounds like a fine woman."

"She is, Salty. She's strong. She came through all of her trials, never complaining. She's quite a woman."

"If'n you want to see her again, then you'd best listen to me. You've got quite a few friends here. Floyd Logan is a well-known name in this country. They're talkin' to the mayor right now. I've already had a few words with him. I told him that Hugh Brennan would be pulling his business out of Independence and moving it to Westport if they allow that marshal to pursue this. That's got him thinkin' pretty strong. But he likes Marshal Cooley's ideas, so he could go either way."

Floyd started to say something, and Salty held up his hand, continuing, "The point is, you've got to keep yore mouth shut about Page and stay away from him. He showed up here four, five years ago. He's a respected, if not well liked, trader here in Independence. He's always seemed shady to me, so if he's like you say, he'll end up dead sooner or later. It don't have to be you killin' him."

Floyd could hear the last words Page had said again playing in his mind. "After what he said, Salty, I don't know if I can ride out of here knowing Page and I are breathing the same air."

Salty slammed his fist on his knee. "Dang it, boy. You can and you will. That is, if you git a chance. If Page has anything to do with it, you'll end up in the new pen east of here, and that ain't where no one wants to be."

The young mountain man nodded. "I hear you, Salty. I guess a lot has changed in the time I've been gone. It's good that the country is more civilized. I imagine that families are safer now, but harboring a lowlife like Page turns my stomach. After his filthy remark about my wife, I know what I intended to do, and I feel no regrets. If he had said that to me in the mountains, I would have sliced out his liver."

"Well, just remember, sayin' that to the marshal or the judge, if it goes that far, will git you ten years. Boy, you don't want to spend that much of yore life in prison." Salty sighed and stood. They'll be bringin' you something to eat fore long. Remember, keep yore mouth shut." He looked at the door. "I've got to go take care of the stable."

Salty turned to head for the door.

Before his friend opened it, Floyd said, "Thanks, Salty."

The old man nodded and shuffled out the door.

Floyd stretched out on the hay-filled mattress. The cell was no more than six feet wide, two bunks stacked to one side. He lay on the lower bunk and stared at the rock ceiling. *I wonder,* he thought, *if I should have stayed in the mountains. So far, this has all the signs of a hard winter. Leotie will need me, and what about Mika?* His Shoshone wife, who also functioned as the tribe's doctor, would have her hands full if this was a severe winter. She used many remedies that Floyd's mom had used, but also had a number of others that she had learned from her own mother. He worried about her, knowing she would never think of herself, only those of her village and her son, Mika.

The door slammed, jerking him from his reverie. He cut his eyes toward the tall figure striding toward the desk. The marshal never spoke or looked toward Floyd until he had slipped out of his overcoat, hung it on the makeshift coat rack on the wall behind his desk, straightened his jacket, and seated himself behind his desk. Once seated, he removed the bowler hat, placed it on the desk in front of him, rolled his chair back far enough to allow him to rest his legs on his desk, leaned back, and said, "Floyd Logan, the famous mountain man."

Floyd lay on his bunk, hands behind his head, silent, watching.

"Harumph," the marshal said, clearing his throat, and, not unpleasantly, though his eyes refused to meet Floyd's for more than a second or two, said, "How does it feel to find yourself behind bars?"

Floyd watched him for another few moments, then said, "Not my favorite place to be."

"No, I would think not, but I doubt you will be here long."

Floyd felt a glimmer of hope rush through his body. He wanted to be home by Christmas. If the marshal released him soon, he might still make it. He knew his folks would be excited to see him, and he wanted to see them and all of his brothers and sisters. It would be a good Christmas present for everyone, if he could just leave Independence soon.

The marshal continued, now with a cold smile on his face, "Yes, I think you will be out of here soon." He turned his head so he could see a calendar hanging next to the gun cabinet. He studied it for a moment. "Let me see, today is Thursday, November the eighteenth. Why, yes, you are in luck. The Right Honorable Judge Norman Needles comes to our fair town, from St. Louis, every third Friday of the month, and tomorrow is the third Friday." He cast a smug look toward Floyd that bode no good.

Floyd's heart sank. He felt sure whatever this lawman had planned, it didn't bode well for him.

The door, released from its latch, slammed open, banging against a chair sitting behind it. The crack of the door hitting the chair, and the sudden burst of frigid wind, caused the marshal to drop his feet to the floor and shout, "What the blue blazes—" Only to stop when he saw the bundled form of Ellie rushing through the door with a basket in one hand and a coffee pot in the other. She stopped and pushed the door closed with one hip and turned toward the marshal.

"I'm so sorry, Marshal," she gasped as she placed the items she was carrying on a chair. She then proceeded to unwrap the long wool scarf from around her face and neck and slip out of the heavy coat she was wearing, hanging the two on a hook by the door.

Turning back to the marshal, she said, "There was a big gust of wind, and the door got away from me." Her face was red, whether from the cold or the shock of her entrance, it was hard to tell.

The marshal had immediately risen, when he saw Ellie, and smiled. "Why, Miss Ellie, please come in. It is always a pleasure to see you."

Picking up the bucket and pot she had brought in, she said,

"Thank you, Marshal Cooley. I brought some breakfast for Mr. Logan." When a frown crossed the marshal's face, she rushed on to say, "Mr. Worth, at the saloon, told me to bring it over for the prisoner, but I thought of you and brought something along I know you like."

Now the marshal beamed, cleared his throat, and said, "That is most kind of you, Miss Ellie. I could certainly use some fresh coffee. Goodness knows, that would be most pleasant."

From the tin, she withdrew a piece of pie and filled the marshal's cup.

Even in his dire situation, Floyd was having a hard time keeping a straight face at the entertaining way Ellie was manipulating the marshal.

As he watched, she smiled into the marshal's eyes and said sweetly, "Marshal, may I see Mr. Logan? You wouldn't want me to get in trouble with Mr. Worth, now would you?"

The marshal cleared his throat again. "Of course you may, and I certainly would not." He stepped around his desk, grabbed the keys to the cell door, opened it for her, and placed a chair inside.

"Oh, Marshal Cooley, would you mind moving that little table in here for me? It would be so much easier for me to leave the food, and I *must* take these things back with me or Mr. Worth will be upset with me." She held the pot and tin bucket up. "And do you have a clean cup we could use?"

Cooley rushed over to the coffee pot, picked up the cleanest of the two remaining cups, and held it for a moment as he looked first at the cup and then the small table.

Ellie, holding the pot in her left hand, extended her little finger, smiled radiantly at him, and said, "You can hang it here."

The marshal held her eyes for a moment and looked away. He smiled in relief, gently slipped the ring of the cup onto her finger, unlocked the cell door, and followed her in with the table. He set it next to the chair and stood uncomfortably watching Ellie as she placed the tin bucket on the table and started taking out the food. "Is there anything else you need, Miss Ellie?"

She looked up and said, "No, Marshal, this will do."

He turned, exited the cell, and locked the door, the big iron key making a grating sound as it turned in the lock. "Sorry, Ellie, procedure. Let me know should you need me."

She rolled her eyes at Floyd, turned to Cooley, smiled sweetly, and said, "You are so nice. Thank you, Marshal."

## 3

E llie pushed her chair against the bars and started to pick up the table to put it between her and Floyd.

Floyd stood from the bunk, a wry grin on his lips, and, while lifting the table, said in a low voice, "You've certainly got him eating out of your hand."

Almost imperceptibly her head shook twice, and she said in a near whisper, "I cannot stand the man. I think he likes me, but I feel like he undresses me every time he looks at me, and he never looks a person in the eyes. It is curious that he was given this job, but I've heard he and the mayor are friends. Now, let's get you fed."

Floyd seated himself on the bunk, leaning forward to keep his head from hitting the frame of the upper bunk. Ellie poured Floyd's cup full of still hot coffee. "I didn't bring any cream. Salty said you drink it black."

Floyd grinned back at her. "Yes, ma'am, I surely do." He took a long sip of the steaming liquid and watched as she laid out the food.

She took the cover from the tin. Immediately the aroma of food filled the jail. Floyd felt his mouth start watering. There hadn't been time for him to eat last night before he was slugged and thrown into jail. He had been on the trail for over a month, pushing hard to get home before Christmas. This was the first actual meal he'd had since leaving Fort Bent. His last day of travel, he had pushed hard to reach Independence, eating jerky only when he stopped to rest the horses.

He watched Ellie take the three plates placed carefully on top of each other in such a fashion that allowed the top to be pushed down on the tin bucket, sealing in the heat. Each plate was heavy laden. She unwrapped the plates, for they were wrapped separately in heavy towels, as she took them out. The first had been placed on top to protect its contents. When she opened it, he could see, resting on the plate with heat still rising from them, huge apple dumplings covered in brown sugar, cinnamon, and broken pecans. He looked up at Ellie, hoping she had brought utensils, but even if she hadn't, he was ready to go aboard the dumplings.

"Just wait," she said, "there's more to come. I know you're hungry, and being the size man you are and how long you've been on the trail, I imagine you can put away quite a lot of food, but you'll be glad you waited."

After placing the second plate on the table, she unwrapped the cloth from around it, exposing to Floyd its delicious-looking contents. A thick slab of fresh ham lay in the middle of the plate, surrounded by five eggs fried just the way he liked them, whites firm, and the yellows runny. Scattered around the outside of the plate were big puffy biscuits.

This time, Ellie stopped, pulled a knife and fork from the bucket, and handed them to him. "Guess I shouldn't torture you any longer."

He gave her a quick grin, cut an egg with a fork and slipped it on the tines. He felt the rich flavor of the yolk in his mouth, but only for a second. Much like a hunting dog, he swallowed it almost as quickly as it passed his lips. Quickly the eggs disappeared, as did the ham and biscuits. With the remaining biscuit, he sopped up the remaining juices from his plate and looked at the dumplings and at Ellie.

During this short period of time, Ellie had said nothing, watching the ravenous man devour the food. When he looked up at her after glancing at the apple dumplings, she shook her head, not yet. Even before she had unwrapped the second plate, the aroma of fried chicken assailed him. Balanced on one side of the plate was a bowl of gravy, with additional biscuits resting on the plate.

The ham and eggs had taken the immediate edge off his hunger, and now he savored each bite of chicken. While he ate, Ellie leaned forward and began speaking in a low voice. "The Trailhead has an agreement with the city to feed the prisoners, though there usually isn't much business. Salty and Mr. Worth, the owner, are good friends. Before I brought the meal over, Salty stopped in. He asked me to give you a message. He says things aren't looking good. That there's something going on. It seems Page is . . ." She stopped, as if trying to assemble her thoughts.

Floyd, following up a large bite of chicken, dipped the edge of a biscuit into the gravy bowl.

"Oh, yes," Ellie continued, "he says he saw Page coming out of the mayor's office when he was on his way to talk to him. The mayor didn't seem too pleased when Salty came in. He told Salty . . . Let's see, I want to tell you exactly what Salty said. He told Salty he would not interfere with the law, and justice must be served."

Floyd took a sip of the coffee, swallowed, wiped his hands and mouth with the towel that had been around the chicken, and said, "That doesn't sound good. This wouldn't be the greatest place to spend Christmas."

Ellie looked at Floyd with sad eyes. "I can't imagine they would do anything to you for defending your wife's name. A lot of the men in the saloon would have gladly taken Page behind the woodshed and left him there. That was awful."

"Thanks, Ellie, I appreciate you saying that." Floyd finished the chicken and biscuits, slid the plate aside, and pulled the apple dumplings over. "Did Salty say anything else?"

Ellie shook her head. "I'm sorry, that was all."

Floyd nodded as he worked on the dumplings.

The marshal's sharp voice split the calm in the jail cell. "Aren't you about finished, Ellie? I have to say, I don't remember you bringing that much food to any other prisoner."

She turned and threw a smile the marshal's way. "He'll be finished in just a few minutes, Marshal."

Brusquely, he responded, "Well, don't you be taking too long. He's a dangerous man."

"Thank you, Marshal."

Floyd had finished the dumplings, refilled his cup, drank, and sat looking at the girl. "Tell Salty I'm obliged for the information. Also tell your boss I owe him for this meal. I feel sure this was way more than a regular prisoner might get, and I'm obliged to him too." He started stacking the plates.

"Here," Ellie said, "I'll take care of these." She folded the towels, placing them on the bottom of the bucket, set the dishes on top of the towels, and the utensils on top of the plates. Then she shoved the lid back on top of the bucket, giving it an additional nudge to push it into place. When she was finished, she looked up at Floyd. "Mr. Worth remembers you when you came west, as a boy. He's proud of the name you've made for yourself. He said to tell you that if you need anything else, let him know." She stood.

Floyd rose to his feet, his size overwhelming the jail cell. He picked up the table and moved it so Ellie could get by. "I'm in your debt, ma'am. You've been very kind to bring me this food and the information. If you would tell whoever cooked all this, it was delicious."

Ellie blushed. "Me and Ma fixed it. I'm glad you liked it. Good luck, Mr. Logan."

She turned to the door.

Cooley was unlocking the cell. "You don't usually go in the cells with the prisoners."

"Oh, I'm sorry. I didn't realize that was a problem. I just had so much to carry, I thought it would be easier. Please forgive me if I've done anything wrong, Marshal."

Floyd took another sip of his coffee and watched, laboring to keep a grin from his face. *She really knows how to disarm this useless marshal,* Floyd thought. He watched as the man fumbled through his response, then hurried to lock the cell door and get to the front door ahead of Ellie. He made it, unlatched it, and, resisting the wind, opened it for her. She smiled up at him one last time and exited the jail with a swish.

Cooley watched her for a moment longer than would be respectable, closed the door, making sure the latch caught, and strode back to his desk, looking at Floyd. "You mountain men think you can come into town and raise Cain anytime you like. That's coming to an end. Independence doesn't need the likes of you."

Floyd bit his tongue, remembering what Salty had said. He finished his cup of coffee and watched the marshal sit, pull his chair up to his desk, and reach for a stack of papers. "Marshal, I appreciate the use of this cup, but I've finished with it. Would you like to take it, or do you just want me to keep it with me?"

Cooley let out a huge sigh, pushed his chair back, and marched to Floyd's cell. Floyd extended it through the bars. "Thanks, Marshal."

With only an irritated look, Cooley took the cup and returned to his desk. Floyd, satisfied and hunger satiated, took the few steps to his bunk and stretched out. His mind started going over possible outcomes. The wind rattled the door and the closed shutters over the cell windows. Whoever had built the shutters must have been in a hurry, for no plank fit tightly with the other. Though there was a potbelly stove in the marshal's office, the heat labored to make it back to the cells, and with the wind wrapping around the rock building, the heat escaped promptly from the cell area. Floyd wrapped his buffalo coat around himself, thankful Salty had brought it along.

*How long will I be here?* he thought. *How are Leotie and Mika doing? This is going to be a long winter. I sure hope I'll make it home before Christmas.*

The shutters rattled, and the wind gave a low ominous moan across the buildings. The bark of a lone dog echoed faintly into the jail. *I know you're cold out there, pup, but I'd change places with you in a heartbeat if I could.* Floyd lay quiet on the bunk, a frown of worry across his scarred face.

HE HAD HOPED he would be released with a fine or a couple of days in jail, but here he sat, a trial, and the city attorney had brought *attempted murder* charges against him. The judge was supposed to be in Friday, but hadn't shown up until the following Monday, and set the trial date for Tuesday. Now, they sat in another saloon, the Rolling Wagon, which most people simply called the Wagon, west of the Trailhead. Salty, not one to usually object to any saloon, had told him it would've been best for Independence if the Rolling Wagon had kept on rolling. The seedier types gravitated to its dark interior.

Today, light, which seldom found its way inside, worked diligently to brighten the surroundings. Heavy drapes over the windows had been opened, and through one, Floyd could see the clear blue of the sky. There was no moan of wind or bang of loose boards or shutters. The storm had passed through, leaving a pleasant, though still cool, day.

A table had been set up just in front of the bar, at which Judge Norman Needles sat. Before sitting, he had taken a coffee cup from his case, and what looked like a flask, Floyd thought, even though the judge had tried to hide it. He poured an amber liquid in his cup, slipped the thin, flat object back in his coat pocket, turned, placed the cup gently on the table, and sat. He looked more the part of an undertaker than a member of the judicial branch, a gaunt stooped man, in his late forties. Dressed completely in black, with the exception of a stained white shirt, his wrinkled brow and downturned mouth bode no good for anyone who might come before him.

Sitting at the table to the judge's right were Floyd Logan, Clarence Worth, the Trailhead owner, and Floyd's attorney, Jason Naylor. There was an empty chair next to Floyd for Salty, but he hadn't shown up yet. To the left of the judge, the table was occupied only by the city attorney, Foster T. Albright III, and Henry Page. Farther to the left of the judge and against the wall were six chairs occupied by four men from the town.

Both attorneys sat straightening papers, awaiting Judge Needles to strike his gavel against the small sound block he had placed on his table, and bring the trial to order. Floyd glared past Naylor at Page, who caught the look and immediately frowned in pain, rubbing his neck. Floyd held the stare until Naylor poked him in the ribs. When he turned back, he saw the judge frowning at him. Disgusted with himself, he thought, *Smart. Salty's right. If I don't watch myself, I'll end up in prison, and who knows when I'll see Leotie or my folks.*

At that moment, the judge slammed the gavel on the sound block, bringing the low roar of conversation, for the saloon was packed, to an immediate halt.

"Uh-hum," Judge Needles said, clearing his throat, the frown never leaving his face, "this trial will come to order. I am Judge Norman Needles"—everyone knew who he was—"and on this day"—he looked down at his notes—"the twenty-fourth of November, eighteen forty, this court will come to order. He banged the gavel again and laid it flat on the table. "Are the attorneys present?" he asked, though he knew both men.

Naylor and Albright III both stood and, in unison, said, "Yes, Your Honor," then sat.

"Good. Let's get this show on the road. I've got to be getting back to St. Louis. The stage leaves bright and early in the morning, and I intend to be on it." He looked pointedly at each attorney. "Now, Mr. Albright, what is the case I am hearing?"

Albright III stood again and said, "It is an attempted murder case, Your Honor. The heinous act was perpetrated in front of numerous witnesses right here in our town. This is brought against a trapper whose name you may know, Floyd Logan."

For the first time, the judge turned and examined Floyd, and the look was not promising. Floyd gazed back at the judge until Albright cleared his throat.

The judge, with lips pursed, turned back to the city attorney. "Yes, Mr. Albright?"

"Your Honor, our case is ready, and you need to be on the morning stage."

"You're right." Judge Needles cast what, in his estimation, must have passed as a smile, but looked more like a grimace, toward Albright. "Thank you, please begin."

"Thank you. Your Honor, this crime—"

Immediately Floyd's attorney, Jason Naylor, rose from his seat. "Your Honor, I object to the use of the word crime. Mr. Logan did not perpetrate, nor has Mr. Albright presented any evidence of, a crime."

The judge's eyebrows pulled together, and his eyes became slits. "Mr. Naylor, you aren't going to waste the court's time with time-consuming objections today, are you?"

"Your Honor, with all due respect, I have found that legitimate objections are not a waste of time."

The judge picked up the gavel by the mallet, turning the end of the handle toward Naylor. "Now you listen to me, young man. First, do not take it upon yourself to lecture me." Naylor was near the age of the judge. "Second, I have a stage to catch in the morning, and it is a long and dusty ride. I plan to be rested when I get on it. Do you understand?"

"Completely, Your Honor. Now may I ask about my objection?"

The judge released a long sigh. "Objection sustained. Mr. Albright, make your case before convicting Mr. Logan."

Albright called Henry Page to the stand, which was a chair between the judge and the jury, facing the audience.

The man stood, adjusted his waistcoat, and stepped regally around the table between him and the witness chair. He inclined his head respectfully to the judge, lifted up the back of his coat slightly, and seated himself in the witness chair.

Dripping with sympathy toward his witness, Albright said, "You are Henry Page?"

Page nodded and said, "Yes."

"You are a well-known businessman here in Independence?"

Page turned his face toward the judge, addressing him when he said, "Yes, I am."

"Now, Mr. Page, can you tell us what happened on the evening of November the eighteenth of this year."

"I sure can," Page said. Arm suddenly outstretched, he stabbed a finger toward Floyd. "That man tried to kill me. He fully intended to kill me. My face was within inches of his. He tried to squeeze the life out of me." At that point, Page ripped the scarf from around his neck, exposing to the judge and the audience the wide, blue marks from Floyd's hand around his throat.

The women in the audience gasped and leaned forward in their chairs, hoping to get a better look at the bruised neck. Then almost in unison, they turned their eyes toward Floyd and glared.

"But thanks to Mr. Salty Dickens, a friend of Logan, I survived. He slugged him over the head with his pistol. If he hadn't done that, I wouldn't be here today."

Again Page's attorney gazed at him in exaggerated sympathy and turned to surveyed the jury and finally the audience. "That trapper, Logan"—now Albright pointed at Floyd, his face turning into a hard glare of anger—"was choking you to death, until his good friend had to smash him on the head to get him to stop."

Page's head bobbed up and down like a woodpecker. "That's right, and I could see it in his eyes. He meant to kill me, until Mr. Dickens knocked him out cold."

Albright's head canted slightly, anger disappearing, his expression that of a man sincerely seeking enlightenment. "Mr. Page, did you do anything to instigate the trapper's action toward you?"

# 4

To Floyd, the silence in the courtroom rivaled that of the deep mountain forest. It was as if everyone was holding their breath.

After a moment, allowing the silence to thicken, Page said, "I'm afraid I did."

Immediately there was a loud intake of breath as each of the observers inhaled. Even the judge, having also been pulled into the moment of drama.

"I was afraid for my life when I saw Logan. Seven years ago, in the western mountains, he hanged my partner and sent me packing into the wilderness amongst all them bloodthirsty savages."

A shout from the back sounded. "Tell 'em what you did, you worthless—"

The shout was cut off by the banging of Judge Needle's gavel. His head twisted and turned as he tried to locate the guilty party. Unable to figure out which of the mountain men standing against the wall had shouted, for they were all glaring at him, he waved the gavel at the entire group. "Do not disrupt my courtroom! I'll have the next person in jail for such an outburst." He turned to

Cooley, who was sitting just behind the prosecutor's table. "Marshal Cooley, you will arrest the next person who interrupts this proceeding."

Cooley nodded to the judge and took a quick look at the back wall. The mountain men were now glaring at him. He looked away quickly.

The judge turned back to Page. "Continue, Mr. Page."

"As I was saying, Your Honor, Logan, there"—pointing again at Floyd—"hanged my friend. I thought he was going to hang me, but one of his friends talked him out of it, and he turned me loose. It took me a week of starving—"

"Your Honor"—Naylor had risen—"I object. Not only did this happen a thousand miles from here, but ten years ago. This has no bearing on this case whatsoever."

The judge leaned forward as Naylor was speaking. "It may have no bearing on the case, but I want to hear it." He turned back to Page. "Continue, Mr. Page."

Once his attorney was seated, Floyd leaned over and said, "He's making out like I hanged McMillan out of meanness. That's an out-and-out lie, and *I* made the decision not to hang him, no one prompted me. In fact, they were for hanging him too. Look at the jury. They're believing him."

"Don't worry, Mr. Logan, I've been doing this for a long time. We'll get our turn."

Page continued with his tale of woe, explaining how he had managed to slip through thousands of Indians and make it down to the rendezvous, where several mountain men were still camped. His story droned on until the judge finally had had enough.

"All right, Mr. Albright. We've heard enough of this tale. Have your witness stick to what brought us to this courtroom today."

"Yes, Your Honor." Turning back to his client, Albright said, "In conclusion, Mr. Page, you feared for your life?"

"I certainly did. I think anyone would with that animal's big hand around their neck. I knew I was dead, and he was killing me right there for the whole world to see."

"Thank you, Mr. Page.

"Your Honor, I'm finished with this witness."

The judge turned to Floyd's table. "Mr. Naylor, your turn."

Floyd's attorney was a man who, in a group, might not be recognized as a lawyer. Standing, he could look Floyd in the eye, and the sun had baked his face and hands almost as much as Floyd's. He was obviously not a man who feared physical labor, for his well-fitting suit rested comfortably across wide shoulders.

Without responding to the judge, his eyes locked on those of Page, he strode toward Logan's accuser. Coming to a stop no more than three feet in front of Page's chair, he stared down at the man. "Mr. Page, have you ever killed a man?"

Immediately Albright was on his feet, shouting, "Objection, Your Honor. Mr. Page is not on trial here today."

The judge nodded. "That is very true, but I allowed you quite a bit of leeway, and I'd be interested in hearing Mr. Page's answer. Also, Mr. Albright, do not shout at me in my courtroom.

"Go ahead, Mr. Page, you may answer."

"Remember," Naylor said, "you swore to tell the truth, and you can go to jail for lying."

Albright had started to rise again, but the judge waved him down before he was to his feet, and he dropped back into his chair.

Page looked at the jury, licked his lips, and dusted unseen lint from his trousers. "Reckon I did, but it was a long time ago, and it was in self-defense."

"When did it happen?"

"Like I said, it was a long time ago."

"So long ago you can't remember when? Wouldn't you consider killing a man a hard-to-forget event? At least you can remember what year it was."

Page thought for a moment more and said, "Likely, umm, eleven, twelve years ago."

"Where did it happen?"

Page nodded. "I can remember that. It was in Mexican territory, up near Taos. I barely got out with my life. Them Mex soldiers chased me a long way."

It was Naylor's turn to nod. "So do you think you should be tried today for what happened in Mexico eleven or twelve years ago?"

"Shoot no, that Mex had it coming. If he'd . . ." Page stopped and looked at first the prosecutor, who was shaking his head, and then the jury.

"Good," Naylor continued, facing the jury, hands clasped behind his back, and standing to his full height. "Just like you should not be on trial for what happened eleven or twelve years ago, a thousand miles from here, neither should my client, Mr. Logan, as your testimony suggested." He turned sharply back to Page.

"But there's one more important point I believe has been missed. You did say that my client hanged your partner?"

"You'd better believe it," Page said.

"Can you tell me why?"

Page licked his lips and again looked at the hard faces of the men in the jury. In a low voice, he said, "My partner bought an Indian girl from the Blackfoot and had his way with her for a while."

"I'm sorry, Mr. Page, I feel sure the jury couldn't hear you. Would you speak a little louder?"

Page started again, but his voice was still too low for the jury or the audience to hear.

Naylor's booming voice echoed through the saloon, so that even the judge jumped. "Louder!"

Page also jerked in his chair before saying, sufficiently loud for all to hear, "McMillan bought and raped an Indian girl."

"Did you take part?"

"I did not. No, sir, I did not."

"You were in the same cabin with your partners. There were others, weren't there?"

"Yeah, there were two others. They helped themselves." He looked around the saloon. All but a few of the men were staring hard at him, and the women were shaking their heads. "But I didn't. I swear I didn't. I don't treat women like that, not even Indians."

The attorney turned to the jury. "Not even Indians." Still facing the jury, he said, "Now that we've cleared that up, can you explain to me what you said to my client before he tried to—" he paused and tapped a long brown finger against his cheek "—let's see, how did you say it, oh yes, 'squeeze the life out of me'?"

Page fidgeted in his seat.

"I'm waiting, Mr. Page, and let me remind you, I have several witnesses who will be more than happy to testify to exactly what you said. And please speak up this time."

Page shifted in the hard wooden chair, pulled again at the edges of his waistcoat, and looking at his boots, but loudly enough to be heard throughout the saloon, said, "I guess I called her a filthy squaw."

Naylor boomed out again, "A filthy squaw."

The attorney shook his head. He first looked at the jury and then across the audience.

"When you said that, you knew this 'filthy squaw' was and is the wife of my client?" He pointed at Floyd and turned back to Page.

"Well, I reckon. But I was afraid for my life and wanted the marshal to arrest him."

"You were afraid for your life. You were afraid of the man who hanged your partner and released you?"

Naylor let his statement hang in the air for a moment, then, changing the subject, he asked, "Mr. Page, what do you do now?"

Puzzled, Page said, "Pardon?"

"I said what do you do now? You know, what is your line of work? How do you obtain your income?"

Page pulled himself together. "I'm a successful businessman."

"Doing what?"

"I'm a trader."

"What do you trade?"

"Trade goods. Linens, thread, tools, canned goods."

Naylor had been pacing back and forth in front of Page during the questioning. He stopped and whipped around to face the witness. "Guns?"

Albright again rose and, in a voice dripping in frustration, said, "Your Honor."

Judge Needles waved Albright down. "Yes, yes, I know, Mr. Albright, but this question interests me, too." The judge turned to Page. "Mr. Page, please answer the question."

"I do sell guns, but there are many other merchants who sell guns. There's nothing wrong with that, nothing at all."

Naylor continued. "You also trade guns to the Indians, do you not?"

At this, Page paused, then said, "I do, Mr. Naylor, but that is all perfectly legal."

Naylor turned to the jury. "Legal? Yes, but frowned upon." He returned to Floyd's table, acted as if he were about to sit, straightened and turned back to Page. He locked eyes with the witness, held them only for a moment, and said, "Mr. Page, you were constantly with your partners and the future Mrs. Logan, and you were in that tight mountain cabin all of the time before Mr. Logan came to her rescue. If you despised the actions of your associates *so much,* why didn't you stop them?"

Page broke eye contact with Naylor. He started to say something, then stopped. He looked at the jury, who were staring back at him with loathing.

Naylor shook his head and said to the judge, "Your Honor, I

have no more questions for this witness," and dropped into his chair.

"Good," the judge said, "Mr. Page, you're finished."

While Page walked back to his seat alongside Albright, Judge Needles said to the prosecutor, "Do you have any witnesses?"

"Yes, Your Honor. I have a list of witnesses," Albright said, holding up a sheet of paper.

The judge rolled his eyes. "How many witnesses do you have there, Albright?"

The lawyer examined it for a moment and replied, "I have fifteen witnesses who can testify to what took place."

The judge took a deep breath and slowly pulled his watch from his waistcoat pocket. He opened it, checked the time, closed it, unfastened the chain that hung across his narrow middle, and placed it on the table in front of him.

"Mr. Albright, we do not have time for fifteen witnesses. I will allow you three if you make it quick."

Albright started to argue, but Judge Needles held up a hand. "Don't argue with me, Mr. Albright."

The attorney pressed on, "But, Your Honor, these are eyewitnesses. They saw—"

The judge shook his head. "I told you not to argue. Your witness list is now down to two. Do you have any further argument?"

Albright was exasperated. He stared at the judge, his mouth opening and closing like a fish out of water. Finally, making up his mind, he said, "No, Your Honor."

"Good, let's get started. Call the first of your *two* witnesses."

Albright called each of his witnesses, and both of them testified to the violence of the attack by Floyd Logan, his flinging the table across the room, striking the marshal to the floor, and almost squeezing the life out of poor Mr. Page. As he was finishing, Salty dashed through the door, behind the audience, and up the aisle created when the chairs had been set out under the direction of the judge. He reached Jason Naylor, leaned over, and whispered something in his ear. Then he moved to the empty chair next to Floyd and sat.

Albright had turned to watch Salty, looked at the judge, who was trying to frown at Salty and Naylor, and said, "No more questions."

As the witness was leaving the stand, the saloon door opened again. A large man, not as large as Floyd or Naylor or some of the other men in the room, but with a self-confident air, strode into the room. His heavy wool coat, boots, hat, and thick leather gloves, which he removed as he was entering, were covered in trail dust. Many of the town's residents' faces brightened when they recognized him. The mountain men became animated. They erupted in friendly laughter. When he reached them, they were shaking his hand, slapping him on the back. Words and phrases like, "Crazy, this time of year, freezing weather," sailed across the room.

Judge Needles banged his gavel twice. When silence returned, he again pointed it at the mountain men. "I've already given you men one warning. If there is another outburst, I will clear you from this proceeding." His face softened as he addressed the newcomer. "How are you, Hugh. Don't you know better than to be traveling in this sort of weather?"

Hugh grinned at the judge. "Norman, I mean Judge Needles, I've gotten older, but not much smarter. When this is over, I'd be happy to buy you dinner down at the Trailhead."

"I look forward to it, Hugh." The judge looked at the marshal, his expression changing to a frown. "Marshal, didn't I tell you to arrest the next mountain man who disturbed my courtroom?"

Cooley started to rise, his face reflecting his displeasure with what he had been told to do. "Well, I guess you did, Your Honor, but—"

The judge waved him down. "Sit down, sit down. You don't need to arrest anyone. Just make sure order is kept back there."

Relieved, Cooley dropped back to his chair, a few short barks of laughter coming from the trappers.

"Now," Judge Needles said, "let's get on with this. Mr. Naylor, do you have any witnesses?"

"I do, Your Honor. I had several, including my client, but since observing your expeditious method of dealing with Mr. Albright's list of witnesses, I have reduced mine in like manner. Therefore, I have only my client, plus two witnesses."

A patter of laughter drifted across the courtroom, and even Judge Needles registered a passing smile. "Good, Mr. Naylor. See, you're never too old to learn. Call your first witness."

"Your Honor, I'd like to start with a character witness, Mr. Hugh Brennan."

The judge's eyebrows rose. "Proceed, Mr. Naylor."

Hugh had removed his coat, gloves, and hat. Now, a red wool shirt was barely visible, collar and upper portion of the placket peeking from beneath an outer handsome, pale buckskin war shirt that hung to his hips. He strode confidently to the stand, was sworn in by the marshal, whom he barely looked at, and seated himself in the chair. He rested his arms on the armrests, fully exposing his scarred and sunburned hands. He turned and grinned at the judge, then gave Naylor a nod, as if to say, "I'm ready."

Naylor nodded back and began. "Mr. Brennan, first could you give us a little background on yourself so the jury will know who you are?" As if a second thought struck him, he said, "And please make it concise, Judge Needles must leave in the morning, so he would like to get this trial finished today."

The judge looked at Naylor, his face reflecting the suspicion that Naylor was pulling his leg, but said nothing. Naylor's face was unreadable as he stepped back to stand by his table, giving Hugh the floor.

"I'm a trader. I have an office here in Independence. I also have offices in Santa Fe and Taos, Mexico. I do quite well. One of the reasons is I am fortunate enough to know men and only hire honorable men who are hard workers." He nodded toward Salty and Floyd. "Many of you know Salty Dickens. He has been with me for quite a few years. He is an excellent, respectable man of great knowledge and know-how."

Salty rubbed his eye and whispered, "Dang it, got somethin' in my eye."

"The young man sitting next to him is one of the most honorable men I have ever known, and I have known many, including Jedediah Smith, Jim Bridger, and Kit Carson, all good men. Floyd Logan may not yet have the knowledge of those three, though he has much, but I would trust him with my own family. In fact, I have. On his first trip west, and I am proud to say this trip was with me, he single-handedly saved a family from a Pawnee attack. In fact, that was how he received the knife scar to his face. An amazing fact is that he was only sixteen years old."

Hugh had been addressing the jury and the audience, but now he turned to the judge. "Your Honor, he worked for me, almost a year. I trusted him with everything I own, and he never let me down. Did he hang the contemptible Van McMillan? Yes. But he had good reason after what McMillan did to the woman who would become Floyd's wife."

Now Hugh paused, then suddenly turned toward Page and addressed the man, his words cutting like a razor-sharp bowie knife. "And I will tell *you* this. I don't know why he allowed you to live. If I had been there with him, you would have hanged, and the other night in the Trailhead, after what you said, I would have shot you dead where you stood!"

An uproar broke out in the saloon, and Albright leaped to his feet. Page, his face white with either anger or fear, gripped the arms of his chair. From the mountain men in the back came a yell, "Finish Floyd's work. String up the varmint now."

Page turned to stare at the rough-looking men staring back at him.

The judge banged his gavel repeatedly, calm finally returning to the courtroom. He leaned toward Hugh, an elbow bracing against the arm of his chair, shaking a bony finger at the witness. "Hugh, don't you go disrupting my courtroom, or I'll throw you in jail along with the defendant. Do you understand me?"

Hugh nodded, casting a rueful look at the judge. "Sorry, Your Honor, I swore to tell the truth, and I wouldn't want anything to happen to one of the finest men I know."

"Are you finished?"

Hugh coolly surveyed the jury. "Yes, Your Honor, I believe I am."

"Then step down."

## 5

———

Hugh Brennan rose from the witness chair and started to walk to the back of the room, but Clarence Worth, who had been seated at Floyd's table, rose and nodded at his chair, then moved to another seat. Salty moved over, allowing Hugh to sit next to Floyd. When Hugh stepped to the chair, Floyd stood and thrust out his hand. Hugh grasped it. They held the grip for a moment and then sat.

Albright was still on his feet, trying to object. Jason Naylor also stood. The judge waved both attorneys down, but Naylor did not sit.

"Mr. Naylor, do you insist on interrupting my courtroom and delaying this trial further?"

"No, Your Honor. I only wanted to say I have my other witnesses, including Mr. Logan."

"Yes, yes, I'm sure you do. Now sit."

Naylor stood for a moment longer, then slowly eased himself into his chair. The judge waited, surveying the audience, until both attorneys were in their chairs. Then he turned to the jury. "Thank you, gentlemen, for doing your civic duty, but you will no longer be needed for this trial."

At the judge's statement, a buzz went through the courtroom, but ceased immediately when he reached for his gavel. The jurors looked at each other and started to rise from their seats.

"Keep your seats, boys," the judge said. "It's not necessary to move. This won't take long."

The two attorneys looked at each other, but with a glance for each from the judge, they remained seated.

"Now," the judge said, "I am going to issue a verdict, for it is clear to me what has taken place in this town. I've seen it happen before over my many years on the bench."

Floyd sat tall in his chair, awaiting a verdict he fully expected to go against him. The trial had gone longer than he expected, and except for his attorney's cross-examination of Page and Hugh's character testimony, everything else pointed to a long stay in the Missouri Penitentiary.

"Towns have growing pains. You want to bring peace and justice to your towns, and that's understandable. However, sometimes as peace is pursued, justice is trampled. That has happened here today.

"Ned," the judge said to Marshal Cooley, "you went too far." The judge turned his hawkish face toward the city attorney. "And you, Mr. Albright, added your enthusiastic stamp of approval. Now I'm not saying that Floyd Logan was in the right, choking Page here near to death, but there was certainly provocation."

Floyd felt a glimmer of hope.

The judge turned back to the marshal. "Ned, you were definitely in your right to arrest Logan. He indirectly assaulted you in the process of getting to Page. But to push for an attempted murder charge—" here the judge stopped and shook his head "—that's ridiculous. How long has Mr. Logan been in jail?"

Marshal Cooley thought for a moment, stood and said, "Six days, Your Honor."

Judge Needles nodded and turned to glare at Page. "Mr. Page, I do not like you, nor your kind. It is my opinion that you are a very lucky man. You have escaped death twice that I am aware of. I hope you are an honest businessman and have put evil ways behind you. But if you have not, I must warn you for your own good, in the future never appear as a defendant in my court."

Page looked at Albright, as if expecting him to object, but the attorney remained seated, staring straight ahead.

Now the judge turned to Floyd. "So what am I going to do with you, Mr. Logan? First, I want you to know I have heard of your exploits, and I must admit to being surprised when I found it was you who was the defendant in an attempted murder trial. I also expected you to be older."

The judge stopped, cleared his throat, and continued. "What you did is a crime. It may be justified, but it is still a crime. You are no longer in the mountains, where I clearly understand the necessity of sometimes taking the law into your own hands. You are back in the United States, where there are laws against such acts. Please remember that in the future. Now, to the verdict."

Judge Needles sat a little straighter, banged his gavel twice, and began. "I find the defendant, Floyd Logan, guilty of assault. Mr. Logan, you are sentenced to six days in the city jail. Since your sentence has already been served, you are free to go." With his last statement, the judge banged his gavel once.

The bartender stepped to the bar and yelled, "Bar's open."

With that pronouncement, the many women who had been in a courtroom, now turned back into a saloon, hurried toward the door.

Floyd turned to Naylor and extended his hand, saying, "Thank you, Mr. Naylor. I sure appreciate your work here today. What do I owe you?"

"You owe me nothing. I have already been compensated generously by Mr. Gates," Naylor said, and nodded to the man who had stepped up beside Floyd.

Floyd turned as Gates stepped closer. "Thanks, Mr. Gates, that's mighty nice, but I pay my own bills."

"Certainly," Gates said, "I would expect no less, but please let me do this, and consider it a way of me demonstrating my gratitude for your saving my life. Had it not been for you, I'm sure I would be pleading my case to Saint Peter."

Floyd grinned and replied, "Well, that's mighty nice, thanks.

"Let me introduce you to my good friend and teacher. As you heard him testify, he took me west when I was a snot-nosed, know-it-all kid." He turned and put his hand on the shoulder of Hugh Brennan.

"Hugh, this is Ransom Gates. Mr. Gates, Hugh Brennan."

The two men shook hands. "Nice to meet you, Mr. Gates," Hugh said.

"My pleasure, Mr. Brennan, but if it is agreeable to everyone, may we dispense with the misters? I find it much simpler when doing business, though I will admit, it is sometimes smarter to keep certain gentlemen at a distance. You, sir, I do not believe are one of those."

"Thank you, Ransom, I do agree. Maybe you and Ned"—he nodded to Naylor—"could join us for supper. I've been eating trail food for six weeks, and I'm ready for a good meal." He turned to Salty, and the older man nodded. "Floyd?"

The crowd was dwindling except for the men who had moved to the bar. Through the one window and the occasionally open door, Floyd noted the waning light. *I need to get a room for tonight,* Floyd thought, *get cleaned up, and head east if I'm going to make it home before Christmas.* Hugh's question pulled him out of his thoughts. "That's a good idea, Hugh. But as much as I'd like to, I can't stay long. I'm trying to get home before Christmas and then get back to Leotie as soon as I can."

Hugh clapped his protege on the shoulder. "We all understand. If you boys'll give me just a moment." He turned and stepped up to the judge, hand extended. In the din, the conversation couldn't be overheard, but it was obvious the two men were pleased to see each other. After a short conversation, Hugh returned with the judge.

The jurist stepped up to the group, and Floyd extended his hand. "Thank you, Your Honor. I was pure worried there for a while."

"It's nice to meet you, Floyd. Your exploits have reached me in St. Louis. I am, of course, good friends with Hugh and also several of the traders in the mountains, including Bill Sublette, who speaks highly of you."

The judge's eyes glanced toward the door, where Ned Cooley, along with two tough-looking men, was escorting Page from the saloon amidst the glare of remaining mountain men. Floyd turned, his eyes following the judge's. At the sight his face hardened.

The judge saw the look. "Floyd, remember you're not in the mountains. You cannot take justice into your own hands."

Floyd nodded, and though he knew his feelings, he said, "Thanks, Judge."

Judge Needles continued, "Also, I know men. You need to watch out for Henry Page. He has friends, many of questionable background, but some of them are influential. That man will never forget this. Keep your eyes open." He shook hands all around. "Hugh told me about supper, but I have a previous appointment with the mayor and my nephew, the marshal." He gave everyone a wry grin and said, before striding away, "This should be an interesting supper."

THE TRAILHEAD SALOON was just as hot and smoky as before, but Floyd hardly noticed. He was free. He listened as Hugh regaled him with the news he had of his business, family, and what he had heard from the mountain men in Santa Fe. The trapping business was still going, but beaver was down below two dollars a pound. One of the things Hugh told him was that there was going to be a huge market for buffalo hides. Floyd felt a chill of apprehension pass through his body. *What would that mean,* he thought, *for the buffalo and the Indians who depend on the big hairy animals?*

Finally, it was time for him to leave. He said his goodbyes, and, as he was leaving, Ransom Gates joined him. The two men stepped outside the Trailhead, and both took a deep breath.

The night was still, and the sky clear. The fresh air smelled sweet, as their breath hung stationary before them.

"Floyd," Ransom said, "how long will you be in Limerick?"

Floyd thought for a moment, feeling the welcome cold on his cheeks. "I think I've still got a chance of getting home before Christmas if nothing happens. Assuming I do, I'll be leaving no later than the second week of January."

"Good, I'm planning on being in Nashville early in January for only a few days. Do you think you could meet me there?"

"Sure, as long as you don't hold me to a firm date. You never know what will happen when I get home. If I need to stay longer, I will, but I am anxious to get back to the mountains."

Ransom nodded. "I can understand that. I'll be staying at the Broadway Hotel. Look me up when you get there. If for any reason I've already left, I'll leave you a message."

The two men stared up at the stars for a few moments. Then Floyd said, "If I'm heading out in the morning, I'd best be going."

Ransom turned to Floyd and extended his hand. "I can never repay you for what you did. I owe you my life. Hopefully your family will be doing well."

"Glad to help," Floyd said, taking Ransom's hand. After a brief, firm handshake, the two men turned and headed in opposite directions, Floyd to the stable, and Ransom to the hotel.

The brisk air nipped at Floyd's cheeks as he strode to the stable. Opening the barn door, he stepped in and called to Buck.

At the sound of Floyd's voice, the two horses and the mule looked up, their heads turning toward the door.

Floyd moved to the animals, spending time with each. Then he went through his supplies, repacking for the morning stage. Once finished, he stretched out on the hay next to Buck. Sleep overtook him quickly.

~

IT HAD BEEN A LONG TRIP, all of it cold and wet, as if winter was following him home. He chuckled to himself, thinking, *If I ever make this trip again, it will be in the summertime.*

He had passed through Limerick a short time ago and was now turning up the lane to the homeplace. As he neared home, through the falling snow, he could see lights beckoning from the windows. The snow muffled the horses' footsteps.

He swung down from the back of the sorrel he had rented in Dyersburg, and tied the two horses to the hitching rail. They were good animals, but still not Buck or Rusty. Those two, with Browny, his mule, had become a part of him, though, he knew the break, in Independence with Salty, would do them good.Taking a deep breath, he stepped to the door. Singing could be heard from the inside, punctuated with laughter. Grasping the door latch, he pulled. When it released, his big hand swung the heavy door wide open, and he stepped into the lighted room.

The singing and laughter halted, and everyone turned to stare at the apparition standing in the door. He hadn't shaved since stepping off the riverboat in Dyersburg. He was clad in his beat-up old slouch hat, worn boots, and heavy buffalo coat. His beard did little to cover the knife scar down his left cheek.

"Well, isn't anyone going to welcome a weary traveler home?"

His youngest sister, Martha, let out a squeal of delight and bounded toward him. "It's Floyd!"

Pandemonium broke out, and he was mobbed. Ma and Pa

stood back, their faces wreathed in smiles, while Floyd's brothers and sisters hugged, kissed, and pounded him on the back.

Jennifer, his other sister, was the first to step back. Holding her nose, she said, "Floyd, you stink!"

Everyone roared.

Matthew, his oldest brother, said, "She ain't wrong, Floyd."

His ma stepped forward, opened her arms wide, and said, "Come here to your ma, you stinky boy."

Brothers and sisters stepped aside as Ma stepped forward and Floyd grasped her in his arms. It had been a long time, but she still smelled the same. The soft aroma of cooking enveloped her. He could smell the flour, smoke, and the soft hint of soap he remembered as a boy. Though at times she could be downright frightening, he had never doubted her love for him or his siblings. Most of all, his parents had always demonstrated an abiding love for each other.

"We've missed you, son," she said as she pressed her lips to his bearded cheek. She stepped back and ran her hand over the old scar.

He could see the concern in her eyes, but she said nothing. Holding him at arm's length, she surveyed the son who had been gone for ten years. "My, you have definitely become a man."

His pa stepped forward, and Ma, still holding onto his left arm, moved to the side. Pa stood taking in the son he had entrusted to a stranger all those years earlier, eyes finally locked on Floyd's. "Like your ma said, you have become much of a man. Looks like you lost a little hide in the process. Now, give your old pa a hug."

When Pa stepped back, and just before his brothers and sisters rushed him again, he reached up and removed his hat, exposing the scar and white streak. "More than you know, Pa."

With the exposure of the bear scar, questions flew, everyone speaking at once.

From outside the group, Pa called, "Give the boy a break. I'm sure he'll answer each and every question that you all have."

With Pa's statement, the questions came to an abrupt halt, and everyone stepped back.

"Pa's right," Floyd said. "I'll answer everybody's questions, but first I need to put up my horses." He looked around the room at all the smiling faces and said, "By the way, Merry Christmas."

Laughter again burst through the room as Christmas wishes flew. After the bedlam died down, Matthew said, "Come on, Owen. You and Nathan help me take care of Floyd's animals."

Floyd looked up at his brother, who stood a good two inches above him, and said, "Thanks, Matthew, but I can take care of my horses myself."

"Not tonight, brother. We'll take them to the barn, give 'em a rubdown, feed, and water. It won't take long, and we'll be right back."

"That's right," Ma said. "It's time you took that filthy coat off and get a bath." She turned to Martha. "Draw up some water, and get it heating." To Jennifer, she said, "Get some towels and lay them out in your old bedroom. I think we have some of Nathan's old clothes here that should fit you," she said to Floyd as he was taking off his coat.

"That's not necessary, Ma. I've got clothes in my gear."

"Fine, son. You can wear what you want tomorrow. Tonight, you wear what Jennifer lays out."

Floyd grinned at his ma. "Yes, ma'am."

He handed Ma his coat, and in so doing turned toward the large Christmas tree that was standing in the corner. Alongside the tree were six children of various ages staring wide-eyed at him.

Floyd turned his head quizzically and said, "Now who might these youngsters be?"

It was obvious to all the adults in the house that the children were awed by the man standing in the doorway. Several even looked frightened. But two of them stepped forward, and the oldest said, somewhat confidently, "I'm William Wallace Logan, but everybody calls me Wallace." He placed his left hand on the younger boy's shoulder. "And this is my brother."

The younger of the two, no more than four years old, spoke up, two broken front teeth causing a slight lisp. "I'm Callum." His bright blue eyes were wide with curiosity. "Who are you?"

Floyd grinned at the two boys and extended his big hand. "I'm your uncle Floyd, and I'm mighty glad to see you."

The two boys, now sporting wide grins, stepped up to their uncle with small hands extended. Floyd, beginning with Wallace, took each of his nephews' little hands in his. "Now, tell me this, who do you men belong to?"

Callum, the smallest of the two boys, pointed to a trim woman with auburn hair, sparkling blue eyes, and a big smile. "She's our ma."

Floyd glanced over at the auburn-haired woman and said, "Why, Callum, I've known your ma way before you showed up. She's a real nice lady."

Still with wide eyes, but now with interest and curiosity, the other children moved toward Floyd. The oldest of the group, a tall girl of about ten years old with long brown hair, stepped close to Floyd.

"Are you really our uncle Floyd?" she asked. "My pa says Uncle Floyd is way west in the mountains."

"You're looking at him, in the flesh."

At his response, the girl, having moved very close to Floyd, wrinkled her nose. "Aunt Jennifer was right. You do stink."

Floyd's ma, hearing her granddaughter's comment, stepped forward and said, "All right, that's enough. Floyd, I'm sure the water's ready back there. It's time you get cleaned up before you stink up this whole house." Her comment was softened by the tender smile to her son.

———————

## 6

F loyd eased his tired body into the tub. The hot water immediately started relaxing tired muscles. *Pa must've splurged,* he thought, looking at the porcelain tub. Though the tub was longer than a regular washtub, it still wasn't long enough for his long legs to stretch out, so his knees protruded above the waterline.

He relaxed against the sloping back of the tub and felt the soothing hot water work its magic on his muscles, then started scrubbing with the coarse cloth his ma had left him. *I'm home,* he thought, listening to the excited conversations and laughter coming from the main room. He could hear the front door open, footsteps, and its closing. Matthew, Nathan, and Owen were back from taking care of the horses. They were laughing at the fact that Ma had made him wash up.

Floyd grinned. It was nice to be home, and he immediately thought of Leotie, his grin disappearing. *It must be miserable right now in those mountains,* he thought. *No telling how deep the snow is. I just hope they were able to put away enough wood to last.* One thing he was thankful for, the buffalo-hide teepees were surprisingly warm. It took only a small fire inside to warm the interior, keeping the occupants toasty.

He closed his eyes and could see Leotie's face in front of him. Her dark brown eyes sparkled in the fire's reflection. One of her two long black braids fell over her slim shoulder. Her cheeks were soft and round, the left one showing the faint two-inch scar left by McMillan. The dark moment was chased away when he remembered what she had said to him while caressing his facial scar with her long fingers, and using his Shoshone name, "Igasho, we match."

Floyd's thoughts were interrupted when his brother Matthew walked in. Matt closed the door behind him and leaned back against it. "It's good to see you, brother, but if you don't hurry up and get yourself out there, the party's going to move in here. You're a mighty sorry sight with those knobby knees sticking out of the water."

Floyd grinned back at his brother. "Then I'd best get moving. I sure wouldn't want everybody in here." Using the big block of lye soap, he took a few more minutes to finish washing his feet, then looked up at Matthew. "How about handing me that towel?"

Matt walked over to the bed, picked up the towel, and tossed it to Floyd. When Floyd stood and stepped out of the tub, Matt got a good look at the other scars across Floyd's back. "Looks like you've had a tough time."

Floyd looked back over his shoulder at his brother and said, with grim humor, "Ain't near as bad as they look. Anyway, I'm still here, and the other fellers aren't."

He finished drying off, squirmed into the long johns, and pulled on the pants. They were the right length but a little large in the waist. Next he slipped the wool shirt over his head, tucked it into his pants, and pulled the galluses over his shoulders. He turned to his brother and said, "How do I look?"

The Logans, for the most part, including Matt, were clean-shaven men. "Other than that fuzzy face, you'll do."

Floyd sat on the edge of the bed and pulled on the clean boots. He stomped them on, turned to his brother, and said, "Give me a hand, and we'll get this tub emptied. I'm sure no one will care to follow me in this water."

"You planning on shaving?"

"I am, but figured we needed to get out of here as quick as possible."

Matt nodded. "Tell you what. I'll get Nathan to lend a hand, and you can whack off that beard."

Floyd laughed. "All right, brother. I'll get it done." He walked over to the dresser, where a pitcher, washbasin, razor, and shaving soap, along with a shaving brush resting in a cup, were laid out.

While he was building the lather, Matt opened the door and called, "Nathan, give me a hand."

Nathan came in, saw the tub, and grinned at Matt. "Seems like we've been carrying water for this young-un his whole life."

Floyd laughed. "And well deserved, I might add." He continued scraping the mass of black hair from his face, being especially careful as he cut the white strip around his scar.

His brothers left, and he continued to carefully remove the remaining portion of his beard from his neck. The razor was extremely sharp, and he was able to cut the stubble quickly. Finished, he rinsed his face, dried it, and, while looking in the mirror above the dresser, rubbed his hand across his scar. The scar never really bothered him. It only concerned him now because of his mother. He'd have to keep his shirt on so she wouldn't see the rest, and hopefully, Matt wouldn't mention them.

Quickly dressed, he turned and, catching a glimpse of the leaner man staring at him from the mirror, walked through the door into the kitchen. The main room and kitchen joined, forming one long room, and everyone was gathered waiting for him. When he stepped from the bedroom, there was loud applause.

"Join us, brother," Nathan called.

The family was arranged in a semicircle facing ma and pa, who had an empty chair between them. "Sit here," Pa said, patting the chair.

Floyd eased himself into the chair next to Pa. He looked at the happy faces full of anticipation and said, "I want to start this off by letting you know that I met the most wonderful woman I've ever known." He quickly turned to his ma. "Besides you, of course, Ma."

She waved the compliment away and said, "Tell us about her, son."

The room had quieted down in anticipation of Floyd's news but, with his announcement, burst into excitement, everyone peppering him with questions. Finally Pa held up his hands and, once quiet had returned, said to Floyd, "Go ahead, son."

Floyd nodded his thanks to his pa. "She is a mighty pretty woman, and she saved my life. I'll tell you about that part later. She's Shoshone, and when we met, she had a five-year-old son. His name is Mika."

"Well, don't keep us waiting, son. What's her name?" Ma asked.

"Sorry, I guess I just forgot to mention that."

Laughter filled the room while Floyd grinned self-consciously. "Her name is Leotie. She was born on the prairie during a buffalo hunt, and, as the story goes, her folks thought she was a beautiful baby. Her name means Flower of the Prairie."

"What does Mika mean?" ten-year-old Anna Marie asked.

Floyd smiled at his niece. "That's a mighty fine question, Anna Marie. Mika means Inquisitive Raccoon. His pa named him that because he was getting into a lot of things."

Ma said, "We have so many questions, son. How old is Mika? Where's his father?"

"From what I understand, his pa was killed in a fight with the Crows. Mika is twelve years old." Floyd smiled at his ma. "I know you didn't ask, Ma, but yes, we're married. We were married by a preacher at Bent's Fort. It's located on the Arkansas River, just east of the Rockies."

Ma gazed at Floyd with her searching blue eyes. "Are you happy, son?"

"Ma, I'm happier than any man has a right to be."

Through tear-filled eyes, she asked, "Why didn't you bring them with you?"

A flicker of concern crossed over Floyd's face before he spoke. "I wanted to, but she couldn't leave. She is one of the tribe's doctors, and she's very good. I know she wanted to come, but felt too much responsibility to those families. The tribe is located in a beautiful valley between the Sangre de Cristo and the Greenhorn Mountains. Though the country is beautiful, you wouldn't believe the amount of snow and the cold that the people have to deal with in the wintertime. There's a lot of sickness in the winter, and she feels those folks need her."

Floyd looked across all the serious faces. "And I hate to say it, but deep in my heart, there was a spot of relief. With her people, she is respected and loved, but she and Mika would have to face a lot of hate and ridicule had I brought her back with me."

There was a long silence in the room. Pa, in a softer voice than normal, was the first to speak. "It's bad, son. I have to agree with you, but I hope you know that she and Mika are always welcome in our home."

Floyd placed a hand on his pa's shoulder, turning to look at the man he loved and respected. "I know that, Pa." Then he removed his hand and looked around the room. "So that's my news. Who's ready for some stories?"

A chorus of cheers and yeses echoed across the room.

He couldn't help but grin. All of the kids were battling with molasses candy. The dark toffee was sticking to their teeth, giving each of the younger ones a momentary case of lockjaw. However, while they battled diligently with their candy, they stared at him with rapt anticipation.

"All right, but there's not a lot to tell."

Floyd's brother Matthew, sitting next to his wife, Rebecca, spoke up. "Floyd, that's sure not true. I saw all those scars on your body. If you just told us how you got each one of them, we'd be here all night. So why don't you start with the one on your cheek."

Floyd immediately looked at his mother, who was watching him with a mixture of melancholy and happiness. *Might as well,* he thought. *The cat's out of the bag now.* Floyd began his story with the shooting match between him and Jeb so many years ago.

Time passed quickly as Floyd told his stories and answered questions. The children had moved closer, around his feet. Two of them, Wallace and Callum, had usurped his lap, while the oldest, Anna Marie, stood leaning against his left shoulder. When he told the story of his facial scar, her small soft hand caressed his cheek tenderly.

The fireplace, no longer blazing high, now cast a steady warmth from the low flames. Pa looked over at the old clock on the wall and said, "Son, though we're all anxious to hear more, as you well remember, Christmas comes early in this house."

"Yes," Ma said, "we must get these children to bed."

Wallace frowned and turned to his ma, but the stern look on his pa's face silenced his protest. He turned back and looked up at his uncle Floyd. "Will you tell us more tomorrow, Uncle Floyd?"

"Sure, Wallace. I'll tell you all I know about the mountains."

Matthew stood, little Josh sleeping in his arms, and said, "Come on, boys, bedtime. You keep listening to your uncle Floyd, and you're liable to be wanting to leave here and go back to the mountains with him."

Wallace slid from Floyd's lap, but before Callum slipped to the floor, he turned, threw his arms around Floyd's neck, and whispered in his ear, almost whistling with his lisp, "I want to go to the mountains with you, Uncle Floyd."

Pa stood and to all of his grandkids said, "Give your uncle Floyd a hug and then get to bed, or St. Nicholas may not stop by."

With his words, everyone scrambled toward the pallets spread on the floor while Floyd was spinning his yarns. Nathan moved to the fireplace and laid a large log on the back of the coals.

Floyd stood and turned to Pa. "I don't think I've talked this much since I left here."

While the women quickly got the children to bed, the brothers had joined Pa and Floyd.

Floyd continued. "But it's sure great to be home."

Pa put his hand on the shoulder of his long-missing son. "I can't begin to tell you, boy, how good it is to have you back. This is one of the best Christmases we've had in quite a few years."

"I'll second that," Matthew said. "It's really good to have you home. I've got a growing horse business, and I could sure use a partner. Maybe you'll think about staying and joining me."

"Matt," Floyd replied, "that's mighty nice of you. But I've made a home in those mountains. I've found a place I love, and if I can work it out, there's room for all the family to live a great life there."

From one of the pallets near the fire, the sleepy voice of Callum spoke up. "I want to go, Pa."

All the adults chuckled, and Matthew turned to inspect the lad, a tiny lump beneath the heavy blankets pulled up to just below his mouth. His bright blue eyes gazed sincerely at his pa. "Son, the only place you're going is to sleep." Matthews eyebrows rose, and he gave Callum what was known among their family as the look.

Callum pulled the cover up farther around his nose while snuggling a bit deeper, and from beneath the cover a small, "Yes, sir," could be heard.

"And with that," Floyd said, "Callum isn't the only one headed to sleep. It's been a long day, and these bones need some rest."

Floyd felt an arm go around his waist, and he looked down at his little sister. He put his right arm around her and squeezed. "It's really good to see you, Martha, but it's a real adjustment for me to think that you're married and have a daughter."

She looked at him, her large green eyes tearing up. "It was hard for a long time after you left. I was surprised at just how much I had come to depend on you. You were always there for me, but, in my heart, I knew you had to go to the mountains."

"Yep, he was always your protector," Owen, another of Floyd's brothers, said, "except when he was gone, gallivanting around the Tennessee hills."

Floyd laughed. "Well, that's true. I spent many a day trapping, hunting, and exploring those hills. But I learned a lot out there."

A young man, so far a stranger, moved up beside Martha. Floyd stuck out his hand and said, "I'm guessing you must be the lucky fella who managed to corral Martha."

As the two shook hands, the young man said, "I sure am. I can't say it was easy with all of her brothers protecting her." He laughed an easy laugh. "But I managed to convince her."

Martha spoke up. "Floyd, this is my husband, Thomas Edward Jackson. Everyone calls him Tom, and I'm the lucky one."

"Pleasure to meet you, Tom. You've got a fine woman here."

Ma stepped up to the group. "All right, let's knock off the jabber. It's way past bedtime." She looked at Pa. "Like *you* said, it's Christmas in the morning, and there's a lot of work to do tomorrow." She grabbed Floyd's arm. "Come on, son. I've got a bed for you made over here on the floor."

Floyd shook his head. "No, Ma. I can sleep in the barn."

"It's cold out there," she said.

"With the animals' heat, being inside and in the hay, I'll be warm as toast. I've been sleeping mostly outside for these past ten years, so this won't be cold at all."

"No son of mine is going to sleep in the barn when there's room for him in this house."

Floyd looked down at his ma. The set of her shoulders, the stern look on her face, and the flashing eyes were all familiar. He knew, before even getting started, that he would be wasting his time trying to argue with her. "Yes, ma'am."

## 7

F loyd rode Pa's bay gelding along the road toward Ezra's house. Pa had told him that Ezra and Elizabeth Graham had married the following spring after Floyd had left, and they had four boys. As he rode, he thought back to this morning.

When Martha accidentally bumped one pot against another, his eyes jerked opened. Instincts kept his muscles still while he surveyed his unfamiliar surroundings. For the last ten years he had been sleeping under a canopy of trees and stars, or inside a teepee, but recognition had come quickly.

Christmas morning had been exciting for the kids. The stockings were hung from the sides of the fireplace mantel and filled with apples, candy canes from the store, cookies and homemade carvings of guns and animals. Floyd had brought gifts from his Shoshone family for his Tennessee family. Ma especially loved the soft, white deerskin dress that Leotie had made for her, adorned with blue beading, with fringe around the sleeves and at the hem. He had also brought back a hand-carved ceremonial pipe made by Chief Pallaton for Pa. Unaware of why he was making it, Floyd had seen the chief work for hours in his effort to finish the pipe before Floyd left. It was of great importance to the chief and to Floyd. He also brought assorted tomahawks, knives, headbands, and moccasins, made by his Shoshone friends, for the other family members.

He had to smile at the thought of the reactions of his family over the gifts. Pa didn't smoke, but that morning he made a place of honor, next to his old rifle that was mounted above the fireplace mantel, and hung the pipe. The rest of the family had also been excited over their gifts.

FLOYD WAS LOOKING FORWARD to seeing his old friend. In their youth, Ezra had given mouth service to going west with Floyd. When Floyd's opportunity arose it had not included Ezra. At first his friend was angry. However, after cooling down, he admitted to himself and Floyd that Liza had stolen his heart and he could never leave her. The buffalo coat Floyd was wearing felt good this morning. Though the overnight snow accumulation was small, the chill wind was piercing.

The gelding strained at the reins. "All right, boy, it'll be cold, but if you want to run, we'll run." The gelding needed little urging. Floyd leaned slightly forward, bumped the gelding in the flanks, and they were off and running. The wind pulled streams of tears from Floyd's eyes, but he let the big horse have his head. It felt good. *I guess we both needed some exercise,* Floyd thought.

He met a family, in their wagon, headed towards town. It was loaded with the husband and wife and six kids bundled up in the bed. They all waved as he raced by. "Boy," Floyd, leaning forward near the gelding's head, said to the horse, "they must think we're crazy, but doesn't it feel good."

From Pa's directions, he figured Ezra's house should be just past the second bend in the road. He had no sooner slowed his horse than three riders rode out of the trees just ahead and turned toward him, spreading across the road.

Floyd only had time to visually check his two pistols in scabbards hanging from the pommel of his saddle. Both had the leather loop slipped over their hammers. He knew the pistol on his right hip was loose, for he always carried it ready, under his heavy coat. Though the coat was fastened, he could access it through the pocket in his coat. The arrangement had saved him before, but now each of the men had rifles, and those rifles were laid nonchalantly, but ready across their thighs. If he did anything with his hands, the next thing he'd feel was a .50-caliber ball slamming into him. Maybe if he could cause a distraction, if he needed them, he could get his guns in action, but he had to figure that at least one of them would get lead into him.

He examined the men. They all wore scraggly beards that looked like they'd never seen a brush or comb. Their clothing was unkempt. Stained slouch hats barely controlled the mass of hair that threatened to explode from beneath them. The only things that showed care and concern were their weapons and horses. He had seen these types before. Thieves always had the best horses because their lives depended on their mounts.

*If they're not intent on robbing and killing,* Floyd thought, *it isn't because they haven't done it before.* They were scoundrels who crossed the line when it was convenient for them.

Floyd pulled his horse to a halt when he was only a foot from the man he figured was the leader. He was a huge man, his wide chest almost bursting from his coat, thin cruel lips barely visible through his thick, food-strewn beard. "Howdy," Floyd said.

One of the men leaned over and shot a stream of tobacco juice at the ground. The leader looked Floyd up and down, then said, "I don't know you."

"That makes us even," Floyd said, examining the leader closely. Older, hair and beard shot with white, his clothing was relatively new, but filthy. The eyes were what held Floyd's attention. Thick, unruly, black and white eyebrows crawled above narrow slits set in a wide, puffy face. He had known men like this in the mountains, cruel, overbearing men who took what they wanted and killed anyone who might stand in their way.

"What's yore name?" the big man demanded.

"What's yours?" Floyd shot right back at him, noting, if it was possible, the man's eyes narrowed even more.

The younger fellow spoke up. "We-uns is from Alabamy. We—"

The big man cut in, never taking his eyes from Floyd, his voice low and threatening. "Felix, shut up! I told you about talkin'. There ain't no talkin' from you. I do the talkin'." He continued to stare at Floyd, then said, "Unusual getup yore wearin', young-un. You sound like you're from this here country, but you don't look it."

Floyd said nothing, eyeing each of the three men.

Finally, the leader tried on what was supposed to be a smile, though it more resembled a sneer. "This here is Felix Barnam, t'other feller is Leroy Tatum, and I'm Rufus, Rufus Johnson. I'm the chief. Now what's yore name?"

"Chief of what?" Floyd said.

Rufus Johnson leaned forward over the action of his rifle, eyes narrowing to mere slits, and said, in a low conspiratorial tone, "We be slave-catchers."

In the first couple of minutes, Floyd had evaluated these three. The leader was a big intimidating man. He'd just as soon beat you to death as give you a howdy-do. The type who got his pleasure from beating a man to death. Floyd figured they were all bullies, used to lording it over the poor folks they chased and caught.

Felix Barnam's hat was on the back of his head, allowing a huge tangle of red hair to hang loose, into his eyes. Pimples and freckles were warring across his chubby face, but it looked like the eruption of pimples was winning. He couldn't yet be twenty.

They might be great woodsmen, but they sure weren't trackers. They'd been searching since Alabama and hadn't yet found their quarry.

Floyd turned his horse slightly to keep an eye on Tatum. Of the three, he was the most dangerous. He didn't have the brute power of Johnson, but the same cruelty radiated from his cold, blue, calculating eyes. He sat his horse easy, with a humorless smile exposing rotten and broken teeth, and the muzzle of Tatum's rifle was casually pointed within inches of Floyd's chest. Just a twitch, and he could send a ball into Floyd.

In a low firm voice, Floyd said, "The name's Floyd Logan."

Tatum, never taking his eyes from Floyd, said, "Rufus, there's a lot of Logans in this country. He may be related to 'em."

"Right as rain, Tatum," Floyd said, nodding, watching Johnson but using his peripheral vision to keep a close watch on Tatum. "I'm related to all of them. In fact, my folks live just back up the road a ways."

Now the three slave-chasers looked at each other. Barnam's oversized Adam's apple traveled up and down as he swallowed. Johnson spoke in a much less belligerent tone. "Well, Mr. Logan, we is lookin' for some runaways. Two of 'em, a man and a woman. They done took off from a fine Alabama family, and that family would like us to invite 'em back."

At that, Tatum spit and said, "Yeah, we aim to give 'em a real fine invite."

Floyd, holding the eyes of the leader, Johnson, said, "I don't hold with slavery. Neither does my family."

"Well, I know there's folks what don't hold with it up here in the north, but you see, we being paid to bring those folks back home, so we got it to do. Now, if you'll just tell us if you seen any folks like that, and we'll be moving along."

"I have not," Floyd said.

"Any suggestions where we should look?"

Floyd stared at each man, then came back to Johnson. "How about *Alabamy*?"

Even as slow as Felix Barnam was, he picked up on the sarcasm in Floyd's voice. Now, three rifle muzzles turned toward Floyd.

He leaned forward in the saddle and spoke, his voice as cold as the snow on the ground. "You boys have the drop on me. You could kill me right here, but you're on a main road. I've friends and family all around these hills who will hear the shots. You won't make it five miles before someone gives you a mighty fine invite to your own necktie party. Trust me on that."

The muzzles held steady for what seemed like hours to Floyd, but in reality were only a few seconds.

"Put yore rifles down, boys," Johnson said, and two muzzles lowered. Tatum still had his long-barreled rifle trained on Floyd's chest. Johnson turned to Tatum. "Not now. Lower yore rifle."

Tatum held it steady for a moment longer, then slowly eased the muzzle away from Floyd's chest, and the hammer down. A cold grin exposed his disgusting teeth again.

Johnson, showing a hurt expression to Floyd, said, "You got no call to be unfriendly, Mr. Logan. We'll be movin' on." He kicked his horse, and the animal jumped forward, followed by Barnum and Tatum.

Passing Floyd, Tatum leaned toward him, and as he spoke, a foul odor surrounded Floyd. "'Twas up to me, mister, I'd kill ya and haul yore body off in those woods."

Floyd knew he would, and felt sure there were others who had crossed this man, their bodies now probably lay in the dark forest. He stared at Tatum as he passed. After the trio had disappeared, he took a deep breath to clear his nostrils of the stench and urged his horse forward. He would be at Ezra's soon, and there was no reason to upset Liza. He'd keep this run-in to himself.

Rounding the bend, he could hear an ax striking wood. Only

a short distance farther, a house appeared from behind the trees. It was solidly built with a large barn. A man was chopping wood in the yard, with three boys working diligently stacking logs and picking up chips while staying well clear of the swinging ax. One of the boys looked up, saw him, pointed, and said something to the man. As soon as he looked up, Floyd recognized Ezra. He could see a big grin break out on his face as he made a final swing of the ax, sticking it into the log he had been chopping.

Floyd pulled the horse up to the hitching rail, leaped down, and tossed the reins across the rail. As he turned, Ezra was on him, throwing his arms around him. They alternately hugged and pounded each other on the back. Stepping away, Floyd said, "Ezra, you haven't changed a bit."

Ezra looked Floyd up and down, his eyes stopping on his cheek. "Well, old son, I wish I could say the same for you. Looks like you got in the way of someone's knife blade."

The three boys, standing back at the woodpile, were watching, mouths open, aghast at the big man in the slouch hat and buffalo coat whom their pa had just hugged like he was family. Ezra turned to them, beckoning. "Come on over here, boys. I want you to meet Floyd Logan, the mountain man I talk about so much."

The three boys ran over and stopped. The biggest said, "Are you a real mountain man, Mr. Logan?"

"Reckon I am, son." Floyd examined the boy. He had blond hair that hung over his ears but was even around the back of his head. Whoever was cutting his hair was using a bowl. He also had the greenest eyes Floyd had ever seen. Even though he was very young, his shoulders were wide and his arms were thick.

"Who are you?"

"I'm Clarence, Mr. Logan." Then he gave Floyd a big grin. "But everybody calls me Bull."

"How old are you, Bull?"

"Almost six."

Floyd tossed a questioning look at Ezra.

"He's right," Ezra said as he tousled Bull's thick, curly hair. "He gave his ma a real hard time when he was born. That boy came out weighing twelve pounds. I know. I weighed him on the scale in the barn. She was stove-up for two weeks after that."

"Pa," Bull said, "you ought not be telling that. That's mighty personal."

Ezra threw his arm around the boy. "Son, this here is a good friend of not just me but your ma, too. She won't mind at all."

The two other boys stood quietly scuffing the toes of their shoes in the snow. Ezra noticed and said, "This other tall, good-looking feller is my oldest son, Sam. He's a fine boy and just about as good with the mules as I am. Now the youngest one here is Jesse. He ain't but three, but I'm right proud of Jesse. He's already a hard worker."

All three boys beamed up at their pa, basking in the praise.

Floyd shook hands with them, saying to each, "Glad to meet you." Then he looked at Ezra. "I thought you had four."

"We do," a feminine voice called from the back porch.

Floyd looked up to see Liza Mason standing on the back porch, wearing a flour-spotted apron and holding the hand of a little tyke. She looked as cute as the day he had left.

"Floyd Logan, you handsome man, you get yourself up here and give me a hug."

Grinning, Floyd, accompanied by Ezra and the boys, strode to the bottom of the porch steps. "Liza, you're just as pretty as when I left," Floyd said.

"Don't you try to sweet-talk me, Floyd Logan. I know you tried to take my Ezra to the mountains with you."

At that, Floyd shook his head and looked up at the attractive woman. "I'll have to admit, I did, Liza, but poor old Ezra was already stricken by you. Why, ten years ago you were all that boy had on his mind."

"I wish he still felt that way," Liza said. "All he's got on his mind these days are those danged mules. Now, get up here and give me a hug."

Before climbing the three steps to the porch, Floyd looked pointedly at the little boy whose hand Liza was holding, then at the other three boys. "I don't know, Liza, it looks to me like he's had other things besides mules on his mind."

Ezra slapped his knee and broke out in a cackling laugh as Liza's face turned a bright pink. "Looks like he's got you there, honey."

In response, obviously finding nothing to say, she threw her arms around Floyd.

Ezra, barely able to speak for laughing, said, "Floyd, boy, I swear, I ain't seen her speechless since we got married."

After the hug, Liza stepped back, concern in her soft, brown eyes as she examined Floyd's face. "You've had some hard times, Floyd."

"No more than most, Liza, and less than many," Floyd said, a little embarrassed.

Breaking the serious moment, Liza slapped Floyd on the arm and said, "I've put some coffee on. You two come back in about fifteen minutes." She stopped, sniffed, wrinkled her nose, and looked down at her little son. "Make that twenty minutes. Ezra, why don't you show Floyd your mules." She turned and led the small boy back into the house.

"Come on, Floyd, I've got something to show you." Ezra spoke to his sons. "You boys clean up around the wood, stack up what's cut, and then go in and see if you can talk your ma into giving you a piece of Christmas pie."

The three boys turned back to the woodpile while Floyd followed Ezra to the barn.

Examining the building, Floyd said, "You've got a nice barn here, Ezra. It must have taken quite a while to build it."

"Naw, it didn't. I had a lot of help. This barn was built in two days. My folks, Liza's folks, and your folks, plus other neighbors, including your brothers, showed up, and we had it built in no time."

Ezra swung the barn door open. "Come on in, quick. I want to keep it as warm as possible in here."

Once inside, Floyd looked around. The barn had six stalls on one side, opposite an enclosed shed and an area for harness storage. But what got Floyd's attention was the third stall. Inside was a mare and her mule filly that couldn't be more than two days old. The filly looked like she was composed only of legs and ears.

Floyd walked over to the stall and leaned against the top rung. "Well, isn't she cute, but if you took away those legs and ears, there wouldn't be much left." Floyd turned his head toward Ezra, who had just joined him. "Pa said you've gone into the mule-raising business. He also said you're starting to produce some excellent working stock."

"Well, thank you, Floyd. That's a fine compliment coming from your pa. Yes siree, been working hard over the past few years to develop good mules, the best. I like mules. They're smarter than any horse that walks, and they'll outlast a horse every day of the week."

"I have to agree with you, Ezra. In most ways a mule is mighty good. But everybody knows that they're just not as fast as a horse."

After chuckling, Ezra said, "Yes and no, Floyd, yes and no. Most times they're not, but trust me, sometimes they are. I've got one little jenny that's produced some fast mules. Yore brother Matthew is doing some mighty fine horse breeding. He's come up with several fast ones, and he's let me breed my donkey to a couple of them. I think, here pretty soon, I'll have something that'll outrun a horse. Now won't that be something."

Floyd shook his head and said, "I'd like to be here to see that. If you can do it, you'll have plenty of takers willing to bet their horse is faster than a mule. Speaking of money, how are your animals selling?"

The little filly came up to Ezra, nuzzling at him through the bars. He scratched behind her ears for a bit. Then she walked back to her ma and started eating.

Ezra brought a foot up and rested his boot on the lowest rung. "Well, Floyd, I'll shoot straight with you. If it wasn't for the farming, in the beginning, we would've been in bad shape, but nowadays, the mules are starting to sell pretty good."

Floyd had been leaning against the top rail. Now he turned to face his friend. "You've got a good reputation, Ezra. Matthew says that when he goes to Nashville, the stockmen up there talk about how good your mules are."

Ezra looked down at his boots, wiped them on the back of his trousers, looked at them again, nodded, and looked up at Floyd. "Well, that's mighty nice. It's taken time and work."

Ezra was about to say something else when Floyd heard a noise from the shed. He spun around, his right hand flew into the pocket of his buffalo coat en route to the pistol he carried on his hip.

"Did you hear that, Ezra?"

## 8

"Pshaw, Floyd, that ain't nothing but them dang rats. Since the cold's moved in, it's like whole populations have taken over my barn."

Floyd stood watching the shed, his right hand resting on the butt of his pistol. "That sure sounded bigger than any rat."

"I got some big ones in here."

At that moment, Bull opened the barn door and stuck his head in. "Pa, Ma says to come on in. The coffee's ready."

"Thanks, Bull. We're coming right now." He turned to Floyd. "Come on, there ain't nothing out here. Let's go get some coffee."

After the first sound, Floyd had heard nothing else. He gradually relaxed, turned, and said, "You must have some big rats, Ezra." He removed his right hand from the butt of the pistol and from his coat pocket. His friend was watching him. "In the mountains, sometimes you've got to be quick."

Ezra nodded and started for the house. "Well, I'm ready to be quick about surrounding a piece of pie and a cup of coffee. Let's go."

As Ezra started off, Bull disappeared from the door, and his feet could be heard running toward the house.

Floyd watched Ezra secure the barn door, and then the two walked toward the house. He looked around the well-trimmed yard, noticing the snow disappearing. Through the trees, now skeletons with their leaves picked by the shorter days and the cold weather, the sky was a clean deep blue. He hoped the weather was this good back in the mountains. Passing his horse, Floyd stopped, rubbed his hand around the edge of the saddle blanket, and it came away damp. He shook his head and reached for the reins. "I oughta be shot. I ran this boy before we got here, and then left him out here in the cold without a rubdown." He looked over at Ezra. "I've got to take him into the barn and do what I should have done when I first got here."

Ezra's forehead wrinkled for a moment, and then he turned and yelled to the house, "Boys, come on out here and take care of Floyd's horse."

"I can do that, Ezra. It's my fault he was left sweaty in this cold. Anyway, your boys are mighty young for a horse this big."

The kitchen door swung open as Sam and Bull, carrying a large covered basket between them, came out the door, followed by little Jesse. Sam said, "Mr. Logan, we'll take good care of him. We help Pa with his mules all the time."

"Give them the reins, Floyd. They can handle it."

Reluctantly, Floyd handed Sam the reins. "That's a big load you got there. Are you sure you can handle it and the horse?"

"Yes, sir," the two older brothers responded in unison.

After pulling his rifle from the scabbard, Floyd watched as Sam, reins in his left hand and basket handle in his right, led the horse to the barn. Bull, on the opposite side of the basket, grasped the handle in his left hand and Jesse's hand in his right.

"That's quite a sight, ain't it, Floyd. Those boys take good care of each other—" Ezra chuckled "—when they ain't fighting." Then he clapped his friend on the back. "Relax, Floyd, they'll be fine. Come on, let's get that coffee."

Ezra led the way into the kitchen and pulled up a chair at the table. Floyd leaned his rifle in the corner alongside Ezra's shot-gun, removed his old hat, exposing the white streak in his hair, and hung it on the back of his chair.

Liza was standing at her kitchen stove when Floyd and Ezra entered. She picked up the coffee pot and turned just as Floyd removed his hat. Her eyes widened as she focused on the white streak in his hair surrounding the scar. "Goodness, Floyd. What happened to you?"

Floyd grinned at her. "An ole grizzly bear decided he didn't like me. Fortunately, he lost the argument."

"It looks like to me," Liza said, "he came pretty close to winning."

She poured the coffee and nodded toward the bowl of cream and the sugar sitting on the table. "Help yourself, that's fresh cream, and I'm about to take some biscuits out of the oven."

Floyd shook his head. "Goodness," he said as Liza opened the oven, and, with the end of her apron acting as a hot pad to protect her hand, she pulled out a pan of golden brown biscuits and set them on top of the stove. "Liza, if I'd known you could cook that good, Ezra would've had some competition."

Ezra balled up a fist and punched Floyd in his right shoulder. "If you don't stop flirting with my wife like that, you ain't gettin' nary a biscuit."

The three of them laughed just as they had as kids, and Liza placed the steaming biscuits on the table. Floyd picked up one, broke it open, and spread some of the fresh butter Liza had just placed on the table across the biscuit. He inhaled the sweet aromatic blend of bread straight out of the oven and fresh-churned butter and took a bite. After chewing, he took a sip of his coffee, swallowed, looked over at Liza, and said, "That's delicious, girl."

Liza had seated herself at the table across from her husband. Floyd sat at the end between the two of them. She picked up one of the biscuits, separated it in half, first spread butter on one side, then blackberry jam she had canned on the other, closed the biscuit, and looked seriously at Ezra. "Is everything all right?"

Ezra, who had just taken a long sip of coffee, nodded his head several times, swallowed, and said, "Shore is, honey. The boys are giving Floyd's horse a good rubdown right now."

Floyd, puzzled at the loaded basket the boys had been taking to the barn, noticed a conspiratorial look pass between the couple, but said nothing. There was something going on here he wasn't aware of, but it wasn't his business.

Liza turned to Floyd and said, "Thank you. I've got some apple pie if you'd like some."

Floyd shook his head. "Liza, I don't see how I could pass up these hot biscuits, even for your great apple pie, but thanks." He reached for and buttered a second biscuit.

The three of them sat and reminisced. Liza persuaded Floyd to explain how he had received the scar on his face and the one along his scalp. He also shared the news of his marriage to Leotie, which was followed with a barrage of questions. Before they knew it, an hour had passed. Suddenly, the three older boys burst through the kitchen door.

They saw the diminished stack of biscuits and charged toward the table, their tumult waking the baby. Liza rose and headed into the bedroom to get Ben. As she was disappearing through the door, she called back to the boys, "Wash your hands before you touch those biscuits."

The two older boys slowed, looked at each other, and turned toward the washbasin. Little Jesse, ignoring his ma, stood on his tiptoes, grabbed the edge of the table to brace himself, and stretched a dirty hand toward the biscuits.

Ezra, his warning voice halting his son's reach, said, "Boy, you touch those biscuits before you wash yore hands and, I allow, when yore ma is through with you, biscuits will be the last thing on yore mind."

Jesse looked up at his Pa. Floyd watched the youngster weigh the punishment versus the reward. Finally the hand slowly came away from the biscuits, and he headed for the washbasin.

When the boy had turned away, Ezra grinned at Floyd. "See what you got to look forward to."

Floyd laughed softly. "Yeah, Ezra. I see how your boys look up to you. I think your bark is a lot tougher than your bite."

Liza walked back into the kitchen with Ben, and Floyd grew serious. "I need to tell you two about what happened just down the road a ways."

Liza, with Ben, came to the table and sat. A questioning look wrinkled her brow.

The three boys, finished with washing their hands, gathered around the table, each grabbing a biscuit.

"You boys," Ezra said, "take your biscuits and go check on the new filly."

"Yes, Pa," Sam said as the three charged back outside.

Once the reverberations of running steps and slamming door died, Liza smiled apologetically. "They never walk anywhere."

Floyd grinned. "Neither did we."

"So what happened?" Ezra asked.

"Funny thing, maybe a quarter of a mile from your house, back towards our place, three scruffy-looking heathens stepped their horses into the road. They came out of the trees from the north side."

Floyd caught the concerned look Liza gave Ezra. "After blocking the road, they proceeded to question me about runaway slaves. Said they were slave-catchers. I figure they're more like chasers than catchers. They didn't look like they could catch anything or anyone, though I feel sorry for anyone they caught. What they lack in aptitude, they make up for in pure meanness."

Ezra had been listening while absently running his thumb and forefinger around the edge of his plate. At the mention of slaves, he stopped and looked into the concerned eyes of his wife.

This time, Floyd did not let it pass. He looked at Liza and then

Ezra. "All right, what's going on? You two've been acting funny since I got here."

Seconds passed as the couple continued to stare at each other. Finally Liza said, "Ezra, you've got to tell Floyd. Maybe he can help."

Floyd's friend continued to stare at his wife and then, making up his mind, turned to Floyd. "How do you feel about owning slaves?"

Floyd responded with a surprised look. "What do you mean, Ezra? You know how I feel. You know how all the Logans feel. We've never owned another human being and never plan to. It's wrong, and I'll tell any man that, anytime, anywhere."

Liza gave her husband a pleading look. Ben started crying. Liza sighed and said, "I've got to feed him," and stood. Carrying the crying child, she walked from the kitchen.

Concerned for his friends, Floyd waited silently.

Ezra's eyes followed his wife as she carried their son into the next room, then turned to Floyd. "Have you ever heard of the Underground Railroad."

Floyd nodded. "Heard of it. Don't know much about it."

Ezra's brow wrinkled, and he thought for a moment. "I'm not sure who started it, but I think it was them Quakers over in Friendsville, at least here in Tennessee. I met one of them when he was passing through town. The long and the short of it is, they help slaves to escape."

"That's good," Floyd said, "but what's that got to do with you?"

"We're part of it."

Floyd's brow wrinkled. It didn't surprise him. Liza and Ezra, even when they were little, had always been kind to other folks, no matter their color. So it wasn't like they had made a big change. "I see, so you *know* why those three are hanging around, and you're about to tell me."

Ezra nodded. "Over the past couple of years, we've helped several escape. Most times, we have no idea where they were from, nor where they're going. It's just our job to hide 'em and protect 'em and move 'em on." He eyed Floyd for a long moment. "I swear, you was always quick. Those weren't rats in the barn."

Leaning back, Floyd said, "I thought that sounded too big for a rat. So, you're hiding folks in your barn?"

Ezra shook his head. "No, that's too dangerous. One of the folks who guided them here came down to get some food."

Floyd nodded. "The basket."

"Right," Ezra continued. "Hopefully those chasers or catchers, whatever you call 'em, won't find him or his tracks. They're hid in that cave on the south side of the mountain. You know the place, located behind a thick stand of dogwood. Many's the night we camped there. I don't think anybody else knows about it to this day. At least, I sure hope not." Ezra stood, walked over to the stove, and picked up the coffee pot, holding it toward Floyd. "Ready for another cup?"

"Sure," Floyd said. He watched his friend pour the coffee, take the pot back to the stove, set it down, then drop back into his chair. "I don't need to tell you that you could lose your place and end up in jail, so I won't. But what I need to know is how can I help?"

Ezra sat silent for a moment, blowing on his coffee. He looked up. "Are you sure? I can guarantee you this is dangerous."

Floyd fired a short laugh. "Ezra, I've been living amongst the Ute, Comanche, Pawnee, and Blackfoot. I think I can handle three two-bit slave-chasers. So, where do you want me to take those folks, and how many are there?"

"They's two, man and woman, who'll be going with you. The other feller is trying to make sure everything is arranged before he sends them on their way. Once they're gone, he'll head back down to Alabama, but there's a catch. The woman's pregnant."

Floyd thought for a moment. *Her being pregnant could be a problem, but maybe not. She almost assuredly works hard and is prob-*

*ably in good shape. If they've been fed well, they'll be able to handle the travel. They've made it this far.*

"You know if they've been eating well enough?"

"They're all lookin' haggard, but who wouldn't be if they was being chased for their life?"

"All right, so where are we taking them?"

"There's the problem," Ezra said. "We've got to get 'em to Friendsville."

Floyd leaned back in his chair. "That's a long way. By wagon, we're talking at least five, maybe six days, and that means traveling on busy roads with those slave-chasers out and about."

"Since you know this country so well," Ezra said, "I was thinkin' you could take 'em across the valley, through the foothills and the mountains. I know that'd take longer, but with you guiding them, they'd have a good chance of slipping through the net."

Astonished, Floyd stared at his friend. "Ezra, you're talking about rough country. Men on foot and in good shape might make it in a week, but with a pregnant woman? That's bordering on crazy. We couldn't take horses. Some of those trails would be impossible for horses. They'd just slow us down. Then it'd take another week to get back, and this is winter.

"It'd be miserable for them out there. What if we get another snow? I'm thinking cutting across country is nigh on impossible this time of year." Floyd shook his head. "The only way we have a chance of getting them there fairly quickly is by wagon."

"What if you had mules?"

Floyd leaned forward, thought for a moment, and said, "Mules might make it. I know of a couple of trails that might be suitable for them. It would still mean that, for some of the way, those folks would have to walk."

"I raise mules, Floyd."

"Yes, but do you have enough mules you could spare, suited to either pack or saddle?"

It was now Ezra's turn to pause. Finally, he nodded. "Yep, I do."

"It'll be at least eight mules, because we need at least two additional men with us who are good woodsmen."

"I'm one of them."

Floyd shook his head. "No, my friend, you are not. You are a good breeder of mules and a good fighter, but you are no woodsman. When we were boys, you sounded like an army coming through the woods. Ezra, I saved you from getting lost on more than one occasion."

Ezra swallowed his objection. "Who would you take?"

"I don't know yet. I have a couple of people in mind, but I have to check with them first. We also have to put together supplies, and we can't be buying a load of supplies in town, or people will start getting curious. Do you have any surplus?"

"When Liza and I started doing this, we started gradually building up our larder, but we don't have enough to last the whole trip."

Floyd took a sip of his coffee, swallowed, and said, "My family can help."

Ezra shook his head. "No, I don't want to get them involved."

"They're already involved, Ezra, with me joining you, so don't worry about it. They'll want to help."

Liza walked back into the kitchen and let out a sigh of relief. "Would you believe it? After he ate, Ben went right to sleep. Of course, with him sleeping now, he may keep us awake all night."

She stopped at the opposite end of the table, grasped the back of the chair, and looked from Floyd to her husband. "You told him, didn't you?"

Ezra nodded. "I did. And he's going to help."

Her eyes filled with tears. She blinked quickly, holding them back, and said reverently, "Oh, thank God. Floyd, you are sent from God. I have been so worried. We want to help all of them, but when you mentioned those chasers, I could just see us losing our place and Ezra going to jail."

Ezra got up, quickly moved to the end of the table, and took his wife's hand in his. "Don't worry, honey. It'll be all right. We get these folks to Friendsville, and it'll be over."

Floyd could see the love between his two friends and felt their courage. His heart ached with longing for Leotie.

"No, Ezra," Liza said firmly. "This won't be over until this horrible system is ended."

"You're probably right." Ezra rubbed his forehead with the fingers of his left hand, then looked into the eyes of his wife. "But we'll do what's right no matter what happens."

The sound of horses invaded their solemn moment.

"It could be the men I told you about," Floyd said, rising from the table and turning for his rifle.

## 9

E zra nodded. "I'll check, but it could just be our neighbors. It is Christmas Day."

"You check, but have that shotgun close." Floyd nodded toward the shotgun standing next to his rifle. "I'll be right behind you."

"What about the boys?" Liza asked.

Ezra was opening the door. Floyd glanced back and said, "Don't worry, we'll watch out for them and make sure they stay safe."

Ezra moved the shotgun from the corner to where it now leaned against the doorframe, just inside the door. It was within easy reach for him. Floyd reached for his rifle and checked to ensure his pistols were loose and ready.

When Ezra opened the door, Floyd recognized the three who had stopped him. Ezra stood leaning against the doorframe, his hand inches away from the shotgun.

"Howdy."

Floyd recognized the gravelly voice of Rufus Johnson.

"Morning," Ezra said. "What can I do you for?"

"My, my, they're some mighty sweet smells coming from inside your house on this fine Christmas morning. Reckon it would be right neighborly if we was invited in for some coffee and sweets."

"Reckon it would be right neighborly if you'd state yore business," Ezra said.

Now, the voice of the leader became harsh. "Mister, we're doing government business. My name is Rufus Johnson. I'm in charge, and we're looking for some runaway slaves."

"You won't find any here, so be on about your business," Ezra said.

"Now listen, mister, as I said, we're on government business. We require food and some of that there coffee I smell, and we're getting it." Emphasizing his point, Johnson started to swing his leg over the saddle to dismount.

Ezra reached back, picked up the shotgun, and moved to the side as Floyd stepped through the door. Both men eared back the hammers of their weapons. The appearance of Floyd, Ezra's shotgun, and the sound of cocking hammers, in the cold crisp air, caused Johnson to freeze with his right leg halfway over the back of his horse.

"Howdy, boys," Floyd said. "I thought I'd seen the last of you. Johnson, why don't you just swing that leg back over your horse, and you boys turn around and do like my friend said. Ride right on out of here."

Johnson slowly dropped his leg down, slipping his booted foot into the stirrup. All three men sat stock-still, but Johnson was flushed with anger. "Logan, you're makin' a big mistake. You ain't a-wantin' to mess with me."

A cold smile pulled at Logan's lips. "Johnson, there's two things working against you. Number one, I don't like you, and number two, I don't miss. Any time you feel a desire, look me up. But for now you're going to turn your horses around and ride out of here peaceably."

Ezra swung the muzzle of the shotgun to cover Johnson. "You fellers best turn your horses around and get off this property."

Johnson growled, "Let's go," and yanked the reins of his horse, jerking the animal toward the road. His two silent partners followed suit.

Floyd noted none of the three men had any desire to go up against the barrels of Ezra's ten gauge, or the odds with both of them already drawn down and ready. But he could also see they weren't leaving from fear, but because they didn't like the odds.

He watched the three disappear behind the thick trees and listened as they turned onto the road, hoofbeats gradually fading in the distance toward town. That would put them passing the entrances to his family's places.

Ezra lowered the hammers on his shotgun and dropped the butt to the porch. "Whee," he said as he expelled the air trapped in his lungs. "I'm glad that's over. I ain't never shot a man, and I sure wouldn't want to."

Floyd, his face still hard from the confrontation, said, "A man does what he has to do, Ezra. It isn't fun, but sometimes it's necessary."

"Hadn't thought about it," Ezra said, "but I reckon it's been necessary in the mountains."

Floyd just looked at his friend.

The sound of running feet from around the side of the house preceded the appearance of the boys. Breathless, they pulled up at the porch, and, looking up at their pa, Bull said, "What was that all about, Pa?"

"Weren't nothing you boys need to worry about. Those fellers lost their way and just needed a little urging. Why don't you sprouts go on in and get cleaned up for dinner."

While the boys dashed by and banged into the house, Floyd said, "Walk with me to the barn, Ezra. The roads are still muddy from the snow, so I'll be able to track them easily. I want to see where they turn off, if they do."

"Why don't you stay for dinner," Ezra said.

"No. Those three are up to no good, and I need to get on their tail." Floyd stepped off to the barn with Ezra alongside. He had slipped the buffalo coat on just before stepping outside, but now he realized the day was warming quickly, as was he under the coat. He pulled it off, draped it over his arm, and continued with Ezra.

"Fill me in, Ezra. I need to know when you'll be ready and where you want to meet."

Ezra swung the barn door open, pushing it near the wall, and flipped a piece of looped rope through and around the hasp to hold it open. "Well, I got no word yet as to when we should be leaving. I'm waiting for word from Friendsville."

Floyd moved to the first stall, where his horse waited. The bay was contentedly chewing on hay the boys had left for him, his saddle still in place. Floyd wasn't surprised. His gear was too heavy and the horse too tall for them to get the heavy saddle back in place once they pulled it off. He tied his buffalo coat behind the saddle.

"Ezra, if there's any way you can hurry it along, I'd be obliged. I need to be getting back to my wife and family. When I head west, it'll take me a good part of three months to get there. That's figuring with no trouble."

"I'll see what I can do," Ezra said as he was slipping the bridle back on the bay. "These things are hard to rush because everyone's got to be in place. One messed-up stop might cause whoever's being moved to get caught, and those folks who are tryin' to help."

Floyd took the reins from his friend and backed the horse out of the narrow stall. Once out, he swung into the saddle. "Look, Ezra, I don't want to rush anything or anybody. The last thing I want is to be the reason some folks get caught. Just see if it can be moved along. If it can't, I'm fine. I'll stay as long as I need to, but the sooner the better." He leaned over and shook his friend's hand. "Tell Liza I'm sorry about leaving so abruptly. It was really great to see you, her, and your boys."

He walked the bay out of the barn and turned up the path to the road. As the horse walked, Floyd examined the tracks of the chasers. By the time they reached the end of the path, he knew the tracks and would recognize them anywhere. The men had turned left upon reaching the road. That would take them toward his brothers' farms and his folks. The brothers should be home by now. They had celebrated Christmas early and would leave shortly after breakfast, as farm duties would not wait for a holiday. He bumped the bay into a trot, his rifle resting across his saddle, pistols ready.

His mind worked feverishly on the immediate problem. *Should the chasers decide to stop, hopefully,* he thought, *they won't be stupid enough to try to search the farms. I know they have the law behind them, but my folks don't care for slave-catchers and wouldn't look kindly on anyone trying to search their property. I don't think those three would do anything but bluster unless they found someone they could bully, and that won't be happening at any of the Logan farms.*

He continued to trail the men toward town until they passed the last family turnoff, Matthew's.

Floyd left the road and trotted the bay toward the small house at the end of the lane. The house, taller than a single story, was not large, but it wasn't as small as it had been before he left. Still, the nearby barn was more impressive than the house.

Nearing the yard, Wallace and Callum came racing out of the barn, both yelling, "It's Uncle Floyd!" Floyd slowed the bay to a walk as the boys, faces animated, ran up and began fast-walking alongside the horse, Callum's little legs almost in a run.

Callum, his face turned up toward Floyd, said, "Uncle Floyd, are you going to tell us some stories about the mountains?"

"Why, I reckon I can, but first I need to see your pa."

Wallace spoke up. "Pa's in the barn."

Reaching the barn, Floyd shoved his rifle into the scabbard and swung down from the horse. His foot hit the ground as Matthew came walking from the barn. His brother was at least two inches taller than Floyd, with the same wide shoulders, thick arms, and big hands all of the Logan men displayed. But now, for the first time, Floyd noticed the gray peppered through his brother's thick brown hair.

"You're just in time, Floyd. I've got the wagon already loaded. You can give me a hand repairing the back fence in the horse pasture."

"Sure thing, Matt. Let me water Pa's horse and get this gear off him, and I'll be raring to go. Had any strangers around this morning?"

"Nope. Why do you ask?"

"We can talk about it while we repair your fence."

Matthew shot Floyd a questioning look but said nothing. The men and boys walked the horse over to the trough, let him drink, and led him into the barn. Floyd unsaddled, Wallace grabbed the blanket, Matt removed the bridle, and Callum closed the stall door once they were out. They hung the tack, and Matt turned to the boys.

"You boys need to stay here while your uncle and I repair the fence." He was met with glum faces. "I know, but there's work to be done both here and at the fence. I need you boys to fork down some hay for the cows so they'll have feed when they come in for the evening milking. Once you're finished, go check with your ma. I bet she might be able to find a sweet taste for you boys."

Floyd watched the boys' faces light up at the mention of food. He shook his head, thinking, *Logan boys never change when it comes to food.* He tousled both boys' hair. "I'll tell you what, when we get back, I'll tell you a story about Blackfoot Indians in the mountains. How does that sound?"

Callum, now with a big grin on his face, looked up at Floyd

and said, lisping past his broken teeth, "That thounds great, Uncle Floyd."

Everyone laughed, and Matt said, "Let's get a move on. We're burning daylight."

The two men turned to head out toward the wagon, Floyd pausing to pull his rifle from the scabbard. "You have your rifle with you?" he said to Matt.

"In the wagon. Even if I didn't, you're armed well enough for both of us," Matt said, glancing at the rifle and two holstered pistols.

"Never know when we might get attacked by those dangerous milk cows you have," Floyd said, climbing into the wagon.

The two men rode in silence through the pasture. The herd of horses grazing at the east end of the pasture watched the wagon pull out and raced after it. They circled it, two young colts prancing and kicking up their heels with youthful exuberance.

Floyd watched them as they ran. "You've got some nice-looking animals here, especially that gray mare." He pointed to the mare leading the herd.

"She is," Matt said. "The frisky black colt is out of her. She's a real improvement to the herd, a Morgan. I had to go to Nashville, and a farm I was passing had a sign up, horse for sale. So, Floyd, you know me, I can't pass up anything having to do with horses, so I pulled in and talked to the gentleman."

Once the horses had figured out there was no feed to be had from the wagon, they went back to grazing, except for the two colts. They continued chasing each other, but now around the herd.

"He," Matt continued, "could barely get around. Said he'd hurt his back and was unable to work, so he put a couple of his horses up for sale. He'd already sold one and would've sold this Morgan, but the man said he wasn't interested in a horse that small."

Matt pulled the wagon to a stop next to the split-rail fence.

Floyd looked the fence over and said to Matt, "Your fence looks in good shape."

"So it is, but since I got the Morgan, it's a little short. She's already gone over it once, but we're not building fence today, we're splitting rails."

Floyd looked at his brother. "This might make me mighty hungry."

"Then you're at the right place. Rebecca is about as good a cook as Ma."

The two men went to the bed of the wagon and picked up the tools, metal wedges, two sledgehammers, and two axes. They walked them to the fence, bent over the top and laid them on the other side. Matt climbed over the fence while Floyd walked back to the wagon, reached in, and removed both rifles.

Matt watched him as he strode up to the fence. As Floyd handed him the rifles before climbing over, Matt said, "You expecting trouble?"

Floyd crossed the fence, took his rifle from Matt, walked over to a log, and laid his rifle across it, the muzzle pointing away from where they would be working. "Not really expecting anything, just like to be prepared."

"Those mountains have made you a sight more cautious."

Floyd picked up a wedge and a sledgehammer and walked to one of the twelve-foot logs. "You want to start with this one?" he said.

"Looks good, but don't forget to speak to it first."

Floyd first examined the log. Spotting the knot halfway down, he grasped the log in his two big hands and rolled it a quarter turn. He eyed it again, nodded in satisfaction, and picked up the wedge and hammer. Tapping the wedge lightly with the hammer, he scored it across the base of the log, then looked at his brother. "That good enough for you?"

"I guess you haven't forgotten what I taught you about

speaking to the log before splitting it," Matt said to his younger brother, a grin across his face.

"I hate to break your heart, brother, but it was Pa who taught me, not you," Floyd said as he drove the first wedge into the end of the log. With a pop, the log split along the line he had set, extending along three feet of the log.

Matt watched Floyd closely, examined the split, and, placing his wedge along the fine crack that extended past the split, he tapped it once to drive it into the log just far enough to hold it, swung the sledge and, with a grunt, drove it through the log. The split sailed easily past the knot, and the end wedge fell out. Floyd picked it up, leapfrogged Matt, and repeated Matt's set and swing. The split log fell open, held together only by a few strands of wood and bark.

Matt switched from sledge to ax, making quick work of the strands, and the two halves fell apart. The sweet smell of the white oak drifted up to them. Now it was necessary to split the two halves to make the rails. While Matt separated the halves, Floyd moved to the end of one of them and was scoring the wood to split that half.

"So what's this important thing you couldn't mention to me in front of the boys?" Matt asked.

Floyd drove the wedge into the end of the log, watched it split, and looked at his brother. "I might need your help for a couple of weeks." While they continued to split rails, Floyd explained the situation to Matt.

"Of course I'll help," Matt said. "For this time a year, the farm's in mighty good shape, so Rebecca and the boys can take care of it while I'm gone. Tell me, how long are you planning to spend with us before heading back to the mountains?"

Floyd, using the ax, separated two halves they had just split. He stopped, looked at his brother again, and said, "Matt, I'll tell you. I really need to get back to my wife. I figured on being here for a couple of weeks. But this trip to Friendsville is going to put a big crimp in that plan. I might even need to leave directly from Friendsville."

While Floyd was talking, Matt moved to the end of one of the rails they had just split, but set down the wedge he was about to use, and rose, sliding his hat back. "Floyd, you don't have any idea how much the folks have worried about you, especially Ma. They need more than just a couple of days with you. They need you to spend some time here. They're getting older, and there's no telling when you can get back here, if ever."

Floyd mimicked his older brother, sliding his hat to the back of his head. He rested both hands on the end of the ax handle. "I can see that, Matt, but what would you do if you were in the mountains and Rebecca and the boys were back here, during a harsh winter with massive snowstorms?"

Matt looked up to the clear blue sky and watched a couple of turkey buzzards sail gracefully over the trees. Finally, he turned back to his brother. "I see your problem, Floyd, and I've got to tell you, sitting here, right now, I can't say what I'd do. I only know your leaving so soon could break Ma's heart."

Floyd stared at his brother, a myriad of thoughts crowding his mind. *What is happening to Leotie and Mika? How is the tribe making it through the winter? How deep is the snow now?* He lifted the axe, unconsciously scraping his thumb perpendicular across the blade edge to check the sharpness. *And what about Ezra? What about that family who needed to escape to freedom?* A large wood chip lay on the ground. He stared at it, then, drawing his right foot back, kicked it all the way to the trees. He loved his ma and pa, but he loved Leotie and Mika too.

After watching the wood chip fly into the brush, Floyd looked back at his brother. "We'd best be getting busy if we're going to finish this today." With that, he walked over to the log Matt was working on, and waited for Matt to start the crack.

They worked through the rest of the afternoon, finishing the trees Matt had cut and prepared for splitting. Once all the logs were cut into rails, they stacked them near the fence. Laying the last rail on top of the stack, Matt stepped back and dusted his hands together. "Thanks, Floyd, you've been a big help today."

"It felt good," Floyd said. "I've been needing some hard work."

"I'd say you got it. You hungry?" The last was said with a grin.

Floyd looked at his older brother. "You ever seen me when I'm not?"

"Then let's get the gear loaded, and head for the feed bag."

The two men, loading their tools first, came back for their rifles, looked over the results of their labor one last time, walked back, and stepped up into the wagon. By the time they'd made it to the barn, the sky had turned from azure to deep indigo with the hills to the east darkening and shadowed. Wallace and Callum had already taken care of the cows and horses and gone to the house. Now, their pa and uncle parked the wagon, oiled and stored the tools, and fed and watered their two horses.

The boys must've been watching, for as the two men stepped from the barn, the door of the house slammed, and they came racing toward them. The bright sun of the afternoon had turned the mud to dry earth, which already puffed barely visible dust with each of the boys' steps.

# 10

They slid to a stop, and Wallace, looking up at his pa, said proudly, "I rode Bessie over to Grandma and Grandpa's while you were gone. Ma said to go tell them Uncle Floyd was here and would be eating supper with us." He looked up at his uncle and grinned. "She said she didn't want them worrying about you."

"That was mighty kind of your ma and you, Wallace," Floyd said.

The foursome headed for the house. Callum, walking next to Floyd, slipped his tiny hand into Floyd's. Surprised, Floyd looked down at his nephew, who was concentrating on his steps in the growing darkness. He glanced over at his brother, who winked at him, and felt the tug at his heartstrings. He and Leotie would never know this because of the rogue mountain men who had bought her from her captors and then assaulted her. The happy chatter of the two boys quickly drove away the brief cloud of melancholy.

Entering the house of his brother, he felt the warmth of this Tennessee home. The house was similar to his folks', but somewhat smaller, except for the loft that ran the full length of the house and extended almost halfway above the room below. A hanging ladder provided access. The primary living area was a long space divided between the sitting room and kitchen.

Rebecca, Matt's wife, hurried from the stove at the far end of the kitchen. She wrapped Floyd in a big hug. "You have made it a wonderful Christmas surprise for everyone. I'm so glad you are here and still alive. Your ma has been telling us not to worry, but I could see she was concerned."

She stepped back, and Floyd said, "Rebecca, you're even prettier than when I left. I don't know how my ugly brother could have ever persuaded you to marry him."

She laughed. "If truth be told, I had to persuade him. Now you four wash up and gather at the table. Supper's ready." She turned, pushed an auburn curl behind an ear, and led them toward the washbasin and moved past to a large pot on top of the iron stove.

Matt laughed as she reached for the lid, and Rebecca shot him a stern look.

Callum, looking pouty, said, "It's not funny, Pa. I liked Prince. He was my friend."

Having moved over to the table, the two men sat, the boys joining them. Matt said to Callum, "Son, what have I told you about making friends out of farm animals, especially those that will get sold or eaten?"

"I know, Pa, but he was a good rooster."

"Callum," Rebecca said, "you know you'll get in trouble for lying."

"But, Ma, he was good to me."

She turned from the stove with both hands on her hips. "You were the only one that murderous rooster was good to. He killed two of our hens, and I told you what would happen if he killed another one. And, young man, when I found his latest victim, he made the mistake of coming at *me* with those spurs. I think that rooster was crazy. Anyway, he'll be very tasty with these dumplings."

She filled Callum's plate and set it down in front of him. The boy sat there for a moment looking at the plate of chicken and dumplings. After filling each plate, she took hers, sat at the opposite end of the table from Matt, and gave him a nod. He looked at his sons, bowed his head, gave a short blessing on the food, and once finished, everyone picked up their forks. Callum, after a long resigned sigh, stabbed a bite of Prince.

Floyd, with an empathetic gaze, watched his nephew. He wasn't so old that he couldn't remember his pig. A little older than Callum, Floyd had made friends with his little pig. *Old Henry,* he thought. *I still feel a twinge of pain when I think about him.* His pa had told him the same thing Matt had told Callum. But he, like his nephew, hadn't listened. The pig followed him everywhere, like a dog. And Henry kept growing. Until that fateful day Pa and Matt killed, hung, and butchered Henry. Floyd could still hear the squeals as his pet was being dragged to slaughter. He had sworn he wouldn't eat a bite of Henry, but the smell of the fresh ham cooking, combined with the appetite of a growing boy, and he, along with the rest of the family, enjoyed, though Floyd not at first, Henry's offering.

After dinner they retired to the chairs around the fire. The rocking chair was reserved for Rebecca. She had taken Josh from his crib and placed him on the floor. He was crawling rapidly, hands and knees almost a blur, around the room. He came to Floyd, grabbed a leg of his pants, and pulled himself up. Floyd reached down and lifted him, setting him in his lap.

"You're a mighty big boy."

Josh looked at Floyd with serious gray eyes.

"Looks like he's gonna be another big one," Matt said. "Just like his brothers."

Rebecca joined in. "Like all the Logan men." She looked over at Floyd. "Why, Floyd, I think you're the shortest, and you're still tall. These Logans grow to be big men, but they also greet life as big babies. It makes it hard on the women."

"I wouldn't know about that," Floyd said, "but it sure gets tiresome looking up at all of them."

Josh stared at Floyd a few moments longer, then pushed away and slid down his leg. Once on the floor, he headed straight for his ma. Laughing, she leaned over and lifted him to her lap, where he wiggled for a moment and then settled down, finding his favorite position.

Once Josh left Floyd's lap, Callum crawled up. "Uncle Floyd, you promised you would tell us a story about Indians."

Wallace also moved forward and leaned against an arm of his uncle's chair.

With Callum in his lap, Floyd looked at his other nephew standing next to him. "I think there's room for both you boys up here."

Wallace showed a wide grin, moved to the front of his uncle, and began to climb up. Floyd shifted Callum farther to his left, making room for Wallace. With an arm around each boy, he began. "There I was, crossing the Missouri River. You boys know where the Missouri River is?"

Both of them nodded their heads vigorously, and Wallace said, in one breath, "That's the river that runs west from the Mississippi that Captain Lewis and Mr. Clark traveled almost all the way to the Pacific on." Then he took a big breath.

"Why, Wallace, that is very good. Who taught you that?"

Proudly, Wallace said, "Ma."

Floyd smiled at his sister-in-law. "You're teaching them mighty good, Rebecca."

She smiled at her brother-in-law. "I try, Floyd." She reached across to her husband and patted him on the arm, the rocker continuing to rock, and said, "Since they are boys, I find it difficult to keep them still for any length of time. Especially with all their distractions."

"I can see where that would be difficult," Floyd said. Then he looked back down at the boys. "So you boys ready for me to get on with the story?"

Both boys eagerly nodded their heads. Callum said, "Yeth, please, Uncle Floyd. Tell uth about the bad Indians."

"Well, Callum, there are bad Indians. Just like there are bad white men. But my wife is an Indian." Now he grinned at both boys. "And I think she's a mighty good Indian. In fact, she belongs to the same tribe the lady who guided Captain Lewis and Mr. Clark belonged to. You boys remember that lady's name?"

Both boys shook their heads.

"Her name was Sacagawea. In fact, my wife, whose name is Leotie, knew her." He watched their intent faces. "But you two wanted me to get back to my story. Am I right?"

Again, the vigorous nods.

"All right, crossing the Missouri. There I was, on a sandbar, my pards still behind me on the high riverbank, when a bunch of Blackfoot rose up on the other side, all painted for war . . ."

Floyd found, at least in his own mind, he was a great story-teller. He watched the boys as he spun the yarn. He could tell they were lost in the river bottom of the Missouri, their faces both excited and desperate at times.

". . . and that is how I was saved by Kajika, Shorty, Morg, and Leotie. I reckon if they hadn't been there, your uncle wouldn't be sitting here, by your nice warm fireplace, telling you this story."

Callum gazed into his uncle's eyes. "When you go back to the mountains, Uncle Floyd, can you take me with you?"

Floyd didn't laugh at his young nephew's request. He said, with a serious expression, "You've got to grow some, Callum. And there's a lot of learning ahead before you're ready."

"Time for bed," Rebecca said.

The reactions from the two boys were immediate. They had been concentrating intently on their uncle's face. At the declaration from their ma, they both spun around. Wallace said, "Please,

Ma, can't we hear just one more story? We'll go right to bed when it's over."

"Yeth, Ma, right to bed."

"Boys," Matt said, "do what your ma says. Maybe Uncle Floyd will be able to tell you another story before he goes back to the mountains."

Both of them whipped back around to stare into their uncle's face. "Will you, Uncle Floyd, will you?" Callum asked.

Floyd grinned at his nephews. "Boys, I'd love to. I don't think I've ever had as good an audience as you two."

Callum threw his arms around Floyd's neck and squeezed. "Good night, Uncle Floyd. I love you."

Floyd, a man who never cried, felt his eyes fill. He looked down into his lap and fiddled with a trouser leg for a moment before looking up. Both Rebecca and his brother had been watching him.

Wallace followed, giving Floyd another hug. "Good night, Uncle Floyd. I love you, too."

The boys jumped down, gave their ma and pa a hug, telling each one good night and that they loved them, and dashed toward the ladder at the end of the kitchen wall. One boy pushing, the other pulling, they moved the ladder to the opening in the loft floor. Wallace waited while his little brother scrambled up the ladder, then followed.

Rebecca stood to put Josh to bed. He had fallen asleep halfway during Floyd's story. Carrying him in her arms, she walked into the back room. After only a few moments, she returned.

Matt waited until his wife had seated herself in the rocker, and said to Floyd, "So, tell me about your plans with Ezra."

Rebecca, after sitting down, had started lightly rocking. At Matt's statement, she stopped and gazed at Floyd with interest.

"Be glad to," Floyd said. "There's not a lot more to tell, but I'll bring Rebecca up to date." Floyd explained what Ezra and Liza had been doing, and what their plans were for the family they were hiding. Initially, Rebecca had looked shocked, but as Floyd continued his story, she began nodding in agreement.

When he finished, Rebecca, her face pale in the firelight, said, "Don't they know Ezra could go to jail, and they could lose everything?"

"Reckon they do," Floyd said. "But they flat don't care. They're trying to help them folks, and more power to them. Now that brings me to what I'm here for. Matt, like I told you in the field, Ezra wants me to take those folks to Friendsville. With the slave-chasers out looking for them, he's concerned about using the roads. I agree, but what that means to us is that we're going to have to cut straight across the hills to Friendsville. That's where you come in."

Floyd had been sitting with his legs crossed, his left ankle resting across his right thigh. Now he dropped one big foot to the floor and lifted his right one, laying it across his left leg. After pulling the sock down slightly, he scratched his leg just above his boot. "Dang mosquitoes. I swear, they're worse here than in the high mountains, by a long shot. Even in cold weather these little gnawers can drive a man nuts."

He looked up and grinned sheepishly at his brother and sister-in-law. "Sorry, I don't like those little devils. Now where was I?"

"You were saying," Rebecca said, "that's where Matt comes in."

Floyd nodded. "Yep. Brother, I need your help." Floyd continued, explaining the need for his brother's skills and expertise with mules.

At first, especially when he mentioned it could be ten days to two weeks, Floyd could see Rebecca's face darken with concern. But as he continued, her tightened jaws relaxed, forehead smoothing.

He waited after asking Matt if he thought two men could

handle the mules, and, if he didn't, whom he'd recommend to join them.

Before Matt could answer, Rebecca spoke up. "Matt, I want you to do this. This is the perfect time of year. We have enough wood cut to last us for at least two months, even if it turns cold again. All of the stock is in good shape, and the boys can help me take care of everything else. If we need help with anything, your pa is just down the road. Nothing is more important than getting those folks to Friendsville."

Floyd smiled to himself. Rebecca was an independent woman who had no problem speaking her mind. He had respected her since the first time Matt introduced her.

Matt extended his right hand to Rebecca. She took it, and they both squeezed. Then turning to Floyd, he said, "I'd recommend Owen. He's not quite as skilled as Nathan, but Nancy's pregnant, and Nathan doesn't need to be gallivanting across the Tennessee countryside. He needs to be home with his wife."

"What about that poor woman in those caves. I can't imagine being left out there in the winter. What is Ezra thinking?" Rebecca asked Floyd.

Floyd shook his head. "It's not as bad as it sounds. I know the cave they're in. It's spacious and warm. The entrance is small, but it opens up into a large room, which keeps the wind out. They're a lot better off than trying to hide in someone's house where the slave-chasers might search and find them."

She held her palms out to the warm fire. "I still can't imagine what it must be like for her."

"Rebecca, I was a prisoner of the Blackfoot, fully expecting to die. I imagine being a slave is much like that, and I reckon they'd rather be living free in that cave than under someone's thumb on a plantation."

"When put in such a manner, their situation is brought into much better focus. Thank you, Floyd."

Floyd stood. "Reckon I'd best be on my way, or Ma and Pa

will be wondering what's happened to me." He nodded to Rebecca. "Thanks for your hospitality. The rooster and dumplings were mighty good." Turning to Matt, Floyd said, "Reckon we should have supplies for nine days. I'll get some from Pa. If you and Owen could donate a bit and haul them out to Ezra's, I'd be much obliged. We should be leaving in somewhere between two to five days. And you'll let Owen know? I'd like to get by his place and ask him myself, but, like you reminded me, I really need to spend some time with Ma and Pa."

THE LAST THREE days had passed quickly. Floyd had slipped easily back into the role of son, working at whatever his pa needed doing around the farm. He had also spent a great deal of time with his ma. There had been some repairs needed in the kitchen, which provided him the opportunity to share about his life in the mountains.

His ma asked many insightful questions. His answers reflected his great care to filter the dangers he faced on a daily basis. But he knew his ma, and he knew she was a frontier woman. She and Pa, along with all of the other pioneers who opened up this country, had faced many dangers during their life. The Cherokee had been deadly when his parents first moved here. In fact, their home had been burned to the ground twice and rebuilt.

So Floyd knew that she was familiar with the dangers he faced. But he could also tell she was glad to have him home. As was he glad to be back. The three of them had just finished supper when a horse was heard trotting up the lane. Floyd stood, moved to the coat tree, where his pistols were hanging, and drew one from the holster.

When the knock came, he opened the door, the pistol at his

side. It was Ezra, his eyes immediately sliding to the pistol in Floyd's hand.

"Come on in, Ezra," Floyd said, stepping back to allow his friend through the door.

"Why, good evening, Ezra," Ma said. "Come in, and sit a spell."

Once through the door, Ezra quickly removed his hat, shook his head, and said, "Sorry, Mrs. Logan, Mr. Logan, I can't stay. I just needed to let Floyd know." He turned to Floyd, and said, "It's time. I just got word. The folks in Friendsville are ready. You leave in the morning. The messenger also said the slave-catchers have been seen by several people along the road."

After Ezra's last statement, Pa spoke up. "Guess that means you're going to have to cut cross-country, like we talked about."

"You're right, Pa, but we've planned for it and were expecting it." Floyd turned back to Ezra. "Do Matt and Owen already know?"

"Naw, I wanted to tell you first."

"Ezra," Pa said, "come sit down, son. We got some questions before you leave."

## 11

E zra hesitated only for a moment, then moved to the table and, after hanging his coat on the back of his chair, sat. He placed his hat next to him and looked expectantly at Pa.

Ma rose, removing the teapot from the stove. Without asking, she poured a cup of steaming tea for Ezra and slid the cream and sugar toward him.

He nodded his gratitude and said, "Thank you, ma'am. It's warmed up after that cold snap, but it's still pretty chilly outside. This'll hit the spot." He poured a dollop of cream into the tea and, after adding two heaping teaspoons of sugar, stirred the hot tea, and took a sip. "Mrs. Logan, that tastes fine and feels good all the way down."

Floyd, after slipping his pistol back into the holster, rejoined them at the table and said, "Did you get all the supplies?"

Ezra took another quick sip of the tea before responding, "I did." He turned to Pa again. "Thank you, Mr. Logan. Those supplies came in yesterday and will be right handy."

Pa nodded.

Ezra turned back to Floyd. "Got supplies from Owen and

Matt, too. Way more than enough. What's left over we'll bring back as soon as we get our guests on their way."

Floyd shook his head. "Not necessary, Ezra. I think I can speak for all of us. What you and Liza are doing is worth more than supplies. You keep them and use them as you see fit. Now, tell me, is everything ready? Most importantly, are your two *guests* ready and able to travel?"

Ezra laughed, and his head bobbed. "Yes siree, I think they're more than ready. From listening to them talk, I'm guessin' they're pretty educated, and I figure they ain't much used to outdoor livin'. Reckon they've had as much of that cave as they can stand."

Ezra finished his tea, stood, slipped on his coat, and picked up his hat. "Much obliged for your hospitality, but I'd best get moving. I still need to let Owen and Matt know."

Floyd rose from the table and met Ezra at the door, extending his hand. "Thanks, Ezra. Tell them I'll meet them at your place before daylight. I want to get those mules away and into the timber before it's light enough to be seen from the road."

The two men shook hands, and Floyd remembered the last time he shook hands with his good friend, much like this. It was just before he left for the mountains, over ten years ago. Looking into the eyes of his friend, he could tell Ezra was also remembering that time.

Ezra cleared his throat and said, "I'm the one who oughta be thanking you and your brothers. I should be doing this."

Floyd clapped his friend on the back. "We both know your main concern is your home and family. You never know when Johnson and his outlaws might show up at your place. You need to be there in case they do."

Ezra nodded, turned to Ma and Pa, and waved. Floyd followed him out the door. "You take care, Ezra. I'll see you in the morning."

Already mounted on his gray mule, he raised a hand in salute, turned the mule back up the path, and slowly disappeared into the darkness. Floyd stood quietly listening to the soft moan in the treetops as the limbs of the hardwood skeletons rattled against each other in the breeze.

THE FAMILY WAS in bed early, and Floyd, snuggled under a stack of blankets, immediately fell asleep and slept like a baby. He was roused by a light hand on his foot, shaking gently.

"Son, it's time to get up."

His eyes popped open to see his ma standing at the end of the bed, smiling at him. The light from the fire flickered across her soft cheeks. He returned her smile. "Thanks, Ma."

She turned and walked from the room, saying as she left, "Water is in the pitcher next to the basin. Your pa took your things out to the barn and is saddling your horse. Breakfast will be ready in ten minutes."

"Pa didn't need to do that," Floyd protested, jumping out of bed.

From the kitchen, his ma replied, "Yes, son, he did. He knows he's not a young man any longer and can't do the things he used to. However, he can help, and you need to let him. I know I don't need to tell you to be grateful."

Floyd quickly poured cold water into the basin, lathered his face, and made a few rapid strokes over it with his straight razor. Though the razor was extremely sharp, in the cold water, it dragged and pulled across the thick stubble, but he hardly noticed. His mind was on the task ahead. He rapidly dressed and stepped into the kitchen.

He watched his ma as she worked efficiently at preparing breakfast. Floyd always marveled that everything was ready at the same time. Sure enough, she pulled the biscuits out and set them on the top of the iron stove while finishing up the ham and eggs. Moments later, she placed the platter of biscuits on the table.

"Ma, you never stop teaching me."

The door had opened mid-sentence, and his pa stepped in, closing the door behind him. "What's she teaching you now?" he asked.

Floyd had to think fast, for he didn't want to hurt his pa's feelings, and, if his pa had been younger, Floyd knew he would have been a huge asset to this trip. Floyd had learned so much of his woodcraft from him. He grinned at Pa and said, "She's still teaching me that if I want hot biscuits, I'd better get to the table quick." He knew that was weak, and watched his pa look at him, then at his ma.

"So what were you up to so early, Pa?"

His pa looked down at the plate Ma had set before him, then up at his son. "Took most of your gear out there and saddled your horse. It's Blackie. She ain't much of a horse anymore, other than having about the sweetest disposition on this earth. She's getting pretty old, but since you're only riding her down to Ezra's, it won't make much difference."

Ma placed the eggs and ham in front of Floyd and Pa and sat across the table from Floyd. Once seated, she nodded to her husband, and all three bowed their heads.

Pa began the prayer. "Lord, we thank you for the food we have on this here table. We thank you for our family that continues to grow. We ask you to watch after our sons and the folks they are protecting, and keep them all safe. One more thing, we ask you to be with Floyd as he travels back west. Keep him safe, and keep his family, back there in the mountains, safe. We're much obliged for all you give us. Amen."

Breakfast passed with little conversation. Floyd's mind was on his journey. He had been through the country they would be traveling many times as a youth, and knew almost every nook and cranny along the route they would be taking. Fortunately, if there had been any changes, Matt or Owen would know.

Finishing, Floyd looked at his ma and said, "A fine meal, Ma. I'll be looking forward to another good one when we get back."

His ma and pa looked at each other, and then Pa spoke. "That's something we need to talk about, son. We know you got to be leaving here fairly quick, but your ma and I need to talk to you before you get on your way."

"Sure, Pa," Floyd said, looking at his pa first, then glancing at his ma, surprised to see tears in her eyes.

"We've surely enjoyed having you home again. It's been a prayer that we said time and time again over these past years, and you have no idea how much it means to both of us for you to be here, especially this time of year. Your timing couldn't have been better."

Pa shifted in his chair and cleared his throat, but before he could speak, Ma said, "Son, it has been a real blessing for you to come home."

"Yes," Pa said, "but we can't expect you to spend a lot of time here. The time you could've spent is being used up by taking those folks to safety."

Floyd took a breath to speak, and Pa held up his hand. "I know it's necessary. Those folks, just like all of us, deserve to be free. You're doing a righteous thing, and we're proud of you. However, the fact remains that you have a family out West."

Floyd listened closely. What was Pa leading up to, and why was Ma tearing up? Ma was a strong woman, and he had seldom seen her cry. He puzzled over it as Pa continued.

"Ethan," Ma, a sharp edge to her voice, said, "can't you see the boy's confused? He needs to be leaving now. Get on with it."

Pa, a patient and concerned look on his face, continued, "The point is, son, we think it best if you head straight back west after you drop those folks off in Friendsville." Pa took a deep breath and let out a long sigh.

Floyd looked back and forth between his parents. Both were

nodding their agreement. He took his ma's nearest hand in both of his. "Are you really sure, Ma?"

She gave him one of her sweet smiles he was so familiar with, as he looked into her tearful, brilliant blue eyes. *Sixty years old,* he thought, *and still a kind and lovely woman.*

With her free hand she patted his and said, "Yes, Floyd, you have a family back there who depend on you. You need to be there. You've always had a kind heart and a willingness to help others, but the others you need to help now, once you get those folks safely away, is Leotie and Mika. I know it's a long, hard trip back, and the winter is going to make it worse. You need to get started as soon as you can."

She took a hankie from a pocket and dabbed at each eye. "And, son? I know you've been terribly worried about them."

"So," Pa said, rising from the table. "What gear you've left here, we'll send with Nathan. He'll meet you in what used to be a wide spot in the road. It ain't much better now, but they call it Smithville. Now don't argue with us. You've got to get moving."

*I love my folks,* Floyd thought, *but they're right. Once this job is done, I need to be getting back to Leotie.*

His ma walked around from the other side of the table, and they embraced. *I wonder if this will be the last time I ever hold my ma.*

She stepped back and placed her hand on his scarred cheek and said, "May God be with you, my sweet son, and with your wife and boy. Thank you for making that long trip here. Travel safely, and don't worry about us. We are truly satisfied, knowing you're safe and that you can obviously take good care of yourself."

Floyd could feel himself choking up, but he controlled it. His pa took him by the right hand and placed his big left hand on his shoulder. "I'm proud of you, son, and I thank you for coming home. I have seen with my own eyes that you are Logan strong, though I always knew it. You go back to the mountains you love, and live a good, honest life. Don't worry about us. Like your ma said, seeing you has been all we need." Pa cleared his throat, threw his long arms around his son, in a brief, giant bear hug, and stepped back. "The time is here. You'd best be going."

Floyd nodded and croaked, "Thanks, Pa." He swung his pistols on before stepping out the door and pulled on his buffalo coat, noting how clean it smelled. Blackie was at the hitching rail, waiting patiently in the cold. Pa had thrown a blanket over her, which he now yanked off. Floyd swung up into the saddle and looked at his ma and pa for one last time.

In the thin, flickering light from the fireplace, his parents looked old, and he had a foreboding thought. *This is the last time I'll see them.* The thought was so strong that he felt almost a physical force pushing him out of the saddle to give them one last hug, but he resisted. It was time to move on. Daylight would be on them soon enough, and they would need to be out of sight, in the trees, before the light caught them.

He raised his hand in goodbye and swung Blackie up the lane. Among the trees, the light from the cabin disappeared quickly. Reaching the end of the lane, hoofbeats were approaching rapidly. He eased Blackie under the trees, slipped his rifle from the scabbard, and sat, waiting in the darkness. As they grew closer, he could make out the sound of two riders. Approaching the lane, the two horses slowed to a walk. Floyd figured it was his brothers, but held his peace until he could make out the distinctive figure of Matt. "Morning, boys." They both jerked.

"Gracious sakes alive!" Owen said. "You near scared us to death." He and Matt reined up at the entrance to the lane.

Floyd could see their heads turning as they strained to find him. He chuckled, sliding his rifle back in the boot. "Thought you boys were woodsmen."

Matt spotted him first. Floyd turned Blackie, allowing him to walk out from under the tree he was standing near. "You had your rifle out. You might have shot us."

Floyd could see Matt's teeth shining as he grinned. Floyd

laughed again. "I wouldn't have shot you, Matt, but as many times as Owen beat me up when we were kids, there's always a chance there."

All three of the men laughed now. Owen said, "You wouldn't need to shoot me. I about suffered a heart seizure when you spoke up."

The three brothers bumped their horses simultaneously and continued down the road to Ezra's place. The short trip was uneventful. After their initial meeting, not a word was spoken until they arrived at Ezra's barn.

Liza stepped out of the barn as they swung down from the horses. Speaking softly, she said, "Leave your horses out here. Ezra will take care of them after you've left."

Floyd and his brothers nodded and followed Liza into the barn. Owen, who was bringing up the rear, closed the barn door. It was obvious Ezra had been up for hours. Though his barn was large, now it was crowded with mules, either loaded with packs or saddles.

When Ezra saw Floyd and his brothers, his face lit up. "Morning. I got to admit, I'm mighty glad to see y'all." He looked at his mules and continued. "I'm thinking everything is loaded, and these fine fellers are ready to stretch a leg." He affectionately slapped the nearest mule on its shoulder. The mule swung his head around and gently nipped at Ezra's hand, causing his owner to take a moment and rub the cheek of the animal.

The brothers walked up and down the line of mules, rubbing, patting, and talking to each one of the eight animals.

Floyd looked back at Ezra. "Did you even go to bed last night?"

"No, he did not," Liza said. "Since the message yesterday, he's been up."

Floyd shook his head. "Ezra, you should've gotten us. We could've helped."

"No, I shouldn't have. You boys are going to be riding for the next seven to ten days, maybe even more. You needed a good night's sleep. I'll have plenty of time for sleeping. Now, you'd best be getting your gear, and let's get it fastened on these boys so you can be on your way."

Floyd nodded and, with Owen and Matt, went back out to their horses. Each one removed his personal gear, leaving the saddle and bridle on the horse, since horses' saddles wouldn't comfortably fit mules.

"Liza," Ezra said, "show Matt and Owen to their mules and introduce 'em. I'll take Floyd to his."

The mules were lined up in the barn. Ezra took Floyd to the second mule in the line and patted the animal on his shoulder. "This here fine feller is Jasper. He's about the most peaceful, sure-footed mule around. You treat him right and he'll do the same for you."

Floyd stepped up and scratched Jasper behind the ears. The mule twisted and lowered his head to get Floyd's fingers in the exact spot. Once there, he pushed back slightly. "You like to be scratched behind the ears, Jasper? How about if I get the other side, too?" He reached across and scratched behind the other ear. After scratching Jasper a while longer, he slipped his pistol harness over the saddle horn and fastened the rifle boot to the saddle. While he was doing that, Ezra had been tying on his saddlebags.

When they finished, Floyd looked around at his brothers. They were just finishing tying on their gear. Ezra called to Liza, "You about ready, honey?"

She nodded and left the mule she was working with to walk forward.

Ezra turned to Floyd. "She's going with you."

Floyd jerked back, eyes wide in astonishment. "Ezra, as much as we like Liza, she doesn't need to be riding out of here with us. You never know when Johnson and his gang might be waiting to ambush us. Anyway, I know where the caves are."

## 12

E zra shook his head. "I've been all over that with Liza, and it's done no good. She's even taking the baby with her."

"Of course I am," Liza said, hands on her hips. She had been walking forward to get to her mule, Queeny, when she stopped after overhearing the conversation. "Look, you two, you can't go showing up at that cave without someone Keri and Reuben know. Those horses need to be brought in, unsaddled, and taken care of, and, Ezra, you know my back has bothered me since the baby was born. There's no way I can unsaddle those three horses, and the boys are too small. No, you need to do it. And the past few days I've gone to that cave several times. I can do it again. One more time will make no difference. Now let's get moving. Daylight's coming fast." She gave a sharp nod of her head, spun around, skirt whipping out, and continued to Queeny.

"See," said Ezra, with a shrug. "I've tried to talk her out of it, but there's no changing her mind. Feel free if you think you can do anything."

Floyd watched Liza swing her leg over the saddle as she mounted Queeny. "She's got Benjamin with her?"

"She sure does. You think I can feed him? She's got a harness she made, which fits under her coat. He slips right into it, hanging against her chest. He's warm as toast under there, but like I said, if you think you can change her mind, have at it."

Liza turned in the saddle and said, "You boys coming with me?"

Floyd looked back at his brothers, who both stood with their hands in the air, palms up, looking their question at him. He just shook his head and swung into Jasper's saddle.

Ezra laid his hand on Floyd's leg. "All these mules have been trained soft-like. Treat them that way. They like you, and they'll do anything you ask of them. I'll see you when you get back."

Floyd extended his hand to his friend and said, "I reckon I won't be coming back, Ezra. My folks had a talk with me this morning and said it was time I was getting back to my wife and boy. It's been good seeing you. You've got yourself a fine family." He stopped and looked around the barn. "I'm proud for you and all you've done and what you're doing. You take good care of yourself, and don't worry about your mules. They'll be well taken care of. On the way back, Nathan will meet us at the crossroads with my horses, and bring back your animals."

"Well, I'll be danged," Ezra said, realizing Floyd was saying goodbye. He slid his hat to the back of his head before taking Floyd's hand. He looked down at the ground and shook his head, again saying softly, "I'll be danged. I was lookin' forward to us maybe goin' squirrel huntin'. I for sure wasn't expecting this. I'm right sorry for taking you away from your folks."

Floyd could see the hurt and surprise on his friend's face. Ezra had never been much at hiding his feelings. "Nothing to worry about, Ezra. You're doing a fine thing here, and we're all proud to help. We'll make that squirrel hunt on my next trip back." He gave his friend's hand one last shake. "*Adios.*"

Ezra stepped back, looked at Floyd for a moment more, turned, and jogged to the doors at the opposite end of the barn that opened onto the pasture. Floyd watched Ezra pat Liza on her leg as she led the procession out of the barn and across the pasture to the tree line.

A faint line of daylight extended across the tops of the trees to the east. *Good*, Floyd thought, *we got out just in time.*

The only way the slave-catchers would spot anyone at this time of morning was if they were outlined on a ridge, and that wouldn't be happening here. Entering the trees, Floyd looked back and saw his friend sliding the big door closed. Just before it closed, backlit by the light inside the barn, he could see Ezra lift his arm in a final salute. He sat stoically in the saddle, not willing to give away their position even in this dim light, and whispered softly to his friend, "So long, Ezra."

Within moments the barn, house, and any semblance of civilization was lost behind them. He turned his attention to the trail ahead. The sadness Floyd felt gradually fell away. This wasn't the Rockies, but it was still a wild part of Tennessee. It felt good to be back in the woods.

Floyd's eyes adjusted quickly to the near darkness. He could dimly see the trail they were following. But this was the trail, as a boy, he had followed many times, and he knew exactly where it was taking them.

A faint smile slid across his face as he watched Liza's back sway from side to side with Queeny's gait. It was hard to believe the woman ahead of him was the same flighty girl he had grown up with. Now a young woman with four sons, the wife of his best friend. He shook his head, thinking, *She's become quite a woman, taking care of a family, and rescuing another. Hard to tell what a person is made of, man or woman, until their mettle is tested.*

Light from the east increased slowly, illuminating the trail ahead. It was a well-used game trail, narrow, cutting through a forest of hardwoods interspersed by thick stands of pine. The early morning light was welcomed by the cheerful whistle of bobwhite quail and the mournful call of the dove. He caught a flash of movement. A redheaded woodpecker lit above his head on the tall pine and began hammering.

After riding for no more than thirty minutes, they left the trail and splashed through a clear, fast stream. Floyd watched Liza disappear behind a screen of tall tulip poplar. He knew the cave opening was just behind the poplars. By the time he had ridden to the back side of the trees, Liza had dismounted, and he caught a glimpse of her disappearing into the small opening of the cave. He had always liked this cave's hidden location and roominess inside. Although, it was a good thing they were in a mass of timber. Otherwise the taller poplars might easily give away its position.

He stepped from the back of Jasper and waited until Owen and Matt rode up with the remaining mules. As they were dismounting, Liza stepped out of the cave entrance with two companions. The three were speaking in low tones. The young man carried a carpet bag and a tow sack. The brothers ground hitched the mules and stepped forward to meet the strangers.

Liza, speaking softly, said, "I want you to meet Reuben and Keri Foster."

The two newcomers, eyes wide, looked askance at Floyd's dress as he stepped forward. The early morning had been cold, so he wore his heavy buffalo coat, and his long legs sticking out beneath it were adorned in fringed buckskin trousers and tall Shoshone moccasins.

He grinned at the two of them and said, "Howdy, I'm Floyd Logan." He nodded at his two brothers standing next to him. "These fellas are my brothers. They aren't much to look at, but they'll do in a pinch. The old one here is Matt, and the other is Owen."

All three shook hands with the couple, and Matt spoke up. "What my *baby* brother means to say is we're pleased to meet you, and we'll take good care of you all the way to Friendsville."

Floyd's and Matt's comments seemed to relax the couple.

Owen, who had always been reserved around strangers, at least until he got to know them, said, "Hello," and added to Keri, "ma'am."

The young woman smiled at the three of them and said, "My gracious, your mama must have fed you men well."

Matt grinned back at her. "She surely did, though my baby brother here obviously missed out on a few meals, since he ended up being the runt of the family."

Floyd made a fist and shot a short left jab into his brother's upper arm. It rocked him, but he remained rooted where he stood, still grinning but rubbing his arm. "Only in height, old man, only in height."

Growing serious, Floyd said, indicating the sack and bag, "Is this all you have with you?"

"Yes, sir. These are all of the earthly belongings we brought from Alabama."

"Alright, we'd best get you loaded up and on our way. Liza, would you show Reuben and Keri which mules they should ride?"

Liza led the two over to Nibbles and Zipper. Owen went with them, and while Liza was introducing them to their mules, Owen adjusted the stirrups.

Floyd said to Matt, "Like we planned, I'll take the lead out of here until we get to the road. If you don't mind remaining with them, I'll ride north toward town, and Owen can head down the road in the opposite direction. We'll just ride far enough to ensure it's clear, then come back and cross everyone."

Matt nodded and said, "Today we'll be traveling through both timbered and open country. There's also a mite more farmland now than when you were here last. We'll need to skirt that carefully. There's some folks around who'd turn in their own mothers for the reward, but if we stay clear, we'll be fine. I don't think there'll be any problems with the water crossings, just a couple of small creeks until we get to Collins Creek. Hopefully it won't be bad, either."

Floyd, pensive for a moment, gazed out through the timber. "It still doesn't seem like ten years."

Matt clasped his brother's shoulder and grinned. "Tell my bones that. Just remember, brother, we're with you all the way." He turned and headed back for his mule.

Reuben and Keri had mounted their mules and waited patiently. Owen, who was bringing up the rear, had walked back to his mule, Theo, and was waiting for Floyd's signal. Floyd stepped to Jasper and scratched his neck, waiting as Liza walked up.

She gave Floyd a faint smile, and with an almost imperceptible sideways nod toward the couple, she said, "I think they are really scared. I've had quite a bit of time with them, and they've talked freely. You'll find out a lot about them on this trip if they relax. Both are exceptional people, and he is from New York." Then she looked up at Floyd's face. "I heard you tell Ezra you'll be leaving for the mountains after Friendsville. I'm so sorry that this is taking you away from the time you had planned with your family and Ezra. He talks about you all the time."

In the daylight, Floyd could make out a few tiny wrinkles at the corners of her eyes, and she looked very tired. "Days when I'm fairly relaxed, hunting or scouting or maybe fishing, I think about Ezra and the good times we had. He's a good friend, and I think he's loved you since before he chased you with that frog, you screaming through the schoolyard." Now his face broke into a wide grin. "Although, I also remember coming over to your house, not long after that happened, and seeing you helping your mother dress out a mess of bullfrogs."

With that, her melancholy smile also turned to a grin. "I liked him, too. When I talked to Mama about him, she'd always tell me that he would follow you anywhere. 'Don't tie your star to him, my dear,' she'd say. I always knew better."

With that, Floyd glanced through the trees toward the east and looked back at Liza. "He was caught a long time ago, and I'm thinking he could never find a better woman. Now, Liza, we got to be heading out."

She stood on tiptoe, her arms around his neck, and gave him a big hug. "You've always been a good friend to both of us. Take care, Floyd Logan, and stay safe in your mountains." She kissed him on the cheek and stepped back.

He tipped his hat to her, grasped the saddle horn, and swung into the saddle. After surveying the forest one last time before starting east, he bumped Jasper in the flanks. They were off, Floyd in the lead, followed by Matt, Reuben and Keri, with Owen bringing up the rear and leading the two pack mules. The sun climbed upward, occasionally breaking through the trees, sending early morning light with little warmth.

The column slowly began its eastward trek. *I'm sure thankful,* Floyd thought, *we have an abundance of cover here. We'll have to be careful crossing the road, but unless those slave-chasers have somehow heard about this trip, there should be no problem.*

They reached the road within the hour. Floyd pulled Jasper to a stop while holding up his right hand. The column halted. Matt continued until he was next to Floyd. Owen rode forward, leading the pack mules. He stopped beside Reuben, and Floyd watched him talking in low tones, then handing the pack mules' reins to Reuben.

When Owen was near, Floyd asked him, "Can he handle those mules?"

Short-spoken as usual, Owen said, "Says he can."

Floyd nodded. "You go right. I'll go left. We need to make sure it's clear for the crossing. As soon as you're comfortable, come on back and let Matt know. When we're both satisfied, we'll head across. This should be the most exposed crossing we'll have today."

The two brothers walked their mules up to the edge of the

trees, checked in both directions, and rode out. Before Floyd made his turn north, he watched Owen for a moment, then bumped his mule into a trot. He had ridden about a half mile when the road straightened and he could see for at least five hundred yards. He pulled Jasper to a halt and sat listening for a count of ten. Nothing. He turned the mule and raced back to the column.

Owen was pulling up as he got there. "All clear back down my way."

Floyd nodded. "Me too," he said, turning toward the trees.

He was gratified, even knowing where everyone was, he could not make them out in the trees. He waved, and moments later, Reuben and Keri rode out, followed by Matt with the pack mules. The crossing was uneventful, and Floyd signaled for them to continue. After following them to the opposite tree line, he pulled up among the thick trees, tied Jasper, and ran back to the road, picking up a broken limb as he went.

*I'm sure glad,* he thought as he wiped out the tracks, *the road has dried out. Otherwise, seven mules crossing at one point would have left an obvious trail in the mud. This won't fool a decent tracker, like a Blackfoot, but the crossing won't be obvious.* After he finished, he ran back to Jasper, tossed the limb in the brush, mounted, and after a last look to ensure it was still clear, followed his companions.

For the rest of the day they continued east, crossing several creeks, through timber and pasture. They'd been lucky so far. They had seen no one. With the sun lowering, Floyd called a halt at his predetermined camp spot. He'd traveled through these woods many times as a boy and camped along the way on several occasions.

Reuben and Keri immediately pitched in, unsaddling their mounts. After Floyd had removed the tack from Jasper and hobbled him, he moved over to the two pack mules, Cookie and Flint. He remembered what Ezra had told him about these two. They had been named by Sam and Bull. Sam had given Cookie his name after the young mule colt stole a cookie from Sam's hand without getting a finger. Bull, more of a common sense kind of boy, had named the mule Flint because of his dark gray color.

The packs were moved near the campfire bed. Owen started the fire, and Keri went through the packs. She quickly pulled out the items she needed and went to work.

As soon as they pulled up, the sound of hickory nut cuttings raining down on the forest floor could be heard. The brothers looked at each other and grinned. Floyd said, "Matt, I see you brought your bow. Can you still hit anything with it?"

Matt chuckled. "Don't know, but I plan to find out." He untied the bow and quiver from the back of Flint. "If you boys think you can manage to take care of these mules without me, I'll go get us some supper." He slipped off, disappearing into the thicket.

Reuben walked over to Floyd. "Mr. Logan, may I ask where your brother is going with that bow?"

"We're not formal around here, Reuben. You just call me and my brothers by our first names, but to answer your question, he's going after a mess of squirrel."

"Does he have previous knowledge of this area and possible squirrel locations?"

"Doesn't need it," Floyd said as he continued giving the two pack mules a quick grass rubdown. "You hear that sound? It sounds like it's raining back in the trees? That's a passel of squirrels in a hickory nut tree. By now, most of the nuts are on the ground, but the squirrel will go down on the ground, pick up the nut, and go back up the tree to eat it. What you're hearing are the pieces of the nuts falling through the limbs and onto the ground, which is covered with dry leaves. That sound is a dead giveaway."

"So Matt is good with the bow?"

"Well, Reuben, you ever hear of William Tell?"

"Why, yes, it's a classic."

"If Matt had been around during William Tell's time, he'd been teaching that old boy how to shoot."

Owen, who was getting the fire started, looked up from his task and said, "That's for sure the truth. I never saw anyone who could shoot that good." He thought for a second, then continued, "With the bow, that is. Reuben, that fella you're talking to is about the best shot with a rifle or pistol I think I've ever seen."

While Owen was busy starting the fire, Keri had taken utensils and supplies from the packs and was engaged in the preparation of supper. Using a heavy stick, she separated the fire into two parts. Floyd looked around, quickly found three sturdy limbs and cut them to length, building a temporary but efficient support from which to hang a pot. He laid them near the fire, waiting until the flame lowered to erect it.

He had just finished when he heard leaves crunching. Picking up his rifle, he silently faded into the forest.

## 13

M oments later Matt stepped out, carrying four large red fox squirrels. He looked around and asked, "Where'd Floyd go?"

"Right here," Floyd said, appearing back in the glade. "Looks like you got us some supper."

Matt nodded. "You should've seen that tree, a regular first national squirrel bank. I'm surprised there's any hickory nuts left. Why don't you come on over here and help me get these cleaned so we can eat."

Later, the three brothers relaxed around the fire, supper completed, listening to Rueben and Keri share their story. Reuben was saying, "I grew up in New York, never realizing how fortunate I was. My father owns a large restaurant in the city. It is frequented by a most influential clientele. I had met and knew slaves, and when I was younger, I heard my parents talk about it with others, but I was never greatly impacted. I went to a private school, grew up, and read for the law."

Rueben poked at the fire with a stick, pushing a hot coal that had rolled out back inside the circle. "I received my certificate, while all the time thinking about Keri." He took her hand, and she raised her head from his shoulder.

"My life," Keri began, "has been much different from Reuben's. I was born into slavery in Alabama. I barely remember my daddy. We were sold, my mama and I, shortly after I turned five. You see, my mama has always been a lady's maid and worked hard to improve herself. Fortunately, the folks who bought us were good people."

Keri paused, looked up into her husband's face, smiled, and continued her story. "We had a good life. The Howards, the folks who bought us, took real fine care of us, and everybody else they owned. In fact, from the time I was five years old until the day they died, I was happy.

"They had a daughter my age, Sissy, and we grew up together. Their library was filled with books, and they would loan them to Mama. Mrs. Howard helped teach me to read, and she read to me and Sissy when we were growing up. It was nice. Mama and I went on trips with them."

She paused and sighed. "That's how Reuben and I met. The Howards would travel to New York on occasion to see family, and when they did, they took us. They had heard about this restaurant that catered to Blacks. It was called Foster's and had become the talk of the town with lots of well-to-do white folks frequenting it. So they took us there, and that's where I met Reuben."

Floyd stretched, yawned, and grinned sheepishly across the fire. "Sorry. It's been a long day for all of us. That's a mighty interesting story, and I want to hear the rest of it, as I'm sure all of us do, but I reckon we need to get to sleep."

Keri's eyes grew large in the firelight. "Oh, I'm so sorry. I didn't realize . . ."

Floyd rose from where he had been sitting, and said, "No, ma'am, it's me who's sorry. I meant no offense. It's just that we have an early start in the morning, and, if you wouldn't mind, I'm sure we all want to hear the rest of the story. Tomorrow night?"

He could see her, in the dimming firelight, relax.

Reuben said, "Thank you, we'd be glad to share the rest of our story with you at the appropriate time, and I want to thank all of you for what you're doing."

"No thanks necessary," Matt said, and started straightening his blankets. "Floyd, how do you want to handle this watch tonight?"

"I reckon we're lucky to have four men. That'll give all of us a good night's sleep. I'll take first watch, then Reuben, Owen, and you. Figure a couple of hours apiece, and we'll be on our way nice and early, if that works for everyone."

They all nodded their agreement. Floyd laid a couple of logs across the fire and eased over to where the mules were. Jasper and Zipper, Rueben's mule, watched him until he settled down under a sweetgum tree, leaning back against the trunk. Through the leafless limbs, he could see the mass of stars twinkling like jewels in the dark sky. Keeping an eye on the mules, he knew they were the best lookouts a man could have, and with his ears tuned to the sounds of the forest, his mind drifted back to the mountains.

In his mind's eye, he could see Leotie laughing as she walked through the valley, green grass waist high on her. Thistles waved their purple heads throughout the grass. Blue-and-white columbine, combined with purple elephant flowers and yellow dandelion, dressed the cold crystal stream with color. She moved with animal grace, hardly making a dent in the grass she passed over.

He blinked, and the picture changed to stark and white, with deep snow piled up against the teepee. His view suddenly switched to the inside of the teepee. Leotie and Mika were huddled over a tiny fire. They both looked pale and drawn. The muscles in Floyd's jaws stood out like ropes, his teeth clenched together. *I've got to get back,* he thought. *But even if I left right now this minute, it might be too late.* He and Jeb had set aside huge portions of buffalo, elk, and venison for the starving time. It came in severe winters, near the end of the coldest months when all of the game was gone from the mountains or impossible to reach due to deep snow. That time was fast approaching.

Floyd, his anguish like a deep knife driving deep into his heart, pulled himself from the torture at hearing Reuben getting up. He watched as the man stood and looked around, finally spotting him under the sweetgum. Floyd stood and walked over to him. "All clear. Nothing's happening except the mules eating, and I don't expect much else. Be sure to wake Owen when it's time."

Reuben leaned closer to Floyd and said softly, "You let me sleep a long time."

Floyd shrugged. "You two needed the rest. I was wide awake." He turned and walked away to his bedroll.

THE SECOND DAY of their journey had been uneventful. They crossed the Collins River on the ferry with no problem. Fortunately, there had been no one around other than old Mr. Simmons, who was still operating the ferry. Floyd remembered thinking him old long before he left for the mountains. All the old man could talk about was the Logans, the middle Tennessee Logans, the flatland Logans, and the Cumberland Logans. Floyd shook his head thinking about it. It was a good thing he didn't know about the rest of the Logans.

They had made it to just south of Sparta. *We're making pretty good time,* Floyd thought. He'd just finished supper and was leaning back, relaxing. *If the weather holds, and we keep this pace up, we'll be in Friendsville by late Saturday, and by Sunday, I can be on my way back to Leotie.*

They had made camp a little early to give everyone and the

mules a good rest. The terrain would start getting rougher later tomorrow or the next day, and it would be tough from then on. He turned to Keri and Reuben. "Why don't y'all tell us more of your story."

Keri glanced up at Reuben, who said, "Go ahead. Finish your part."

She smiled and began. "Well, if you're sure that we're not boring you."

Owen, surprising everyone, for that day he had said no more than ten words, spoke up. "You go right ahead, Mrs. Foster. I was a bit upset with Floyd when he stopped you last night. I wanted to hear the whole thing. I'd be much obliged if you'd tell us."

She smiled at Owen and said, "please call me Keri, Owen, and I would be happy to tell you the rest of the story." She giggled softly and said, "Of course, I might let Reuben tell part of it," and patted her husband on the leg.

Almost to herself, she said, "Now where do I begin?"

Owen must've heard her, because he immediately said, "You were in the restaurant."

She smiled at him and said, "Thank you. We were in the restaurant, and I was astounded. There were white people sitting at tables right next to black people. I had never seen that before except when Mama and I went to Europe with the Howards, but never had I seen it in Alabama. So, anyway, we had no more than been seated, when this handsome young man walks up and hands us all a menu. Yes, Mama and I were sitting *with* the Howards." Here, her voice was in awe.

"I was so nervous. Sissy noticed it and slapped me on the arm. She leaned over and said, 'Would you stop fidgeting? You're gonna make me nervous.' It seemed like only seconds, and that handsome young man was back with the wine, and speaking in such perfect diction. I assumed, for quite some time, that all young black men of New York City spoke as he did. But I could not take my eyes from him, and every time I looked at him, I caught him looking at me. Somehow he found out where we were staying and sent me a note. But he was very proper and sent it to Mama."

It was Matt who spoke up this time, with a knowing look. "So what did your *mama* think of that?"

Her mind obviously traveling back to that time, Keri smiled to herself, then said, "Well, I must say, she did like him, and the note, she thought, was quite considerate, which she liked. But she was *not* pleased about the suggestion from Reuben. In fact, she was not pleased at all. I couldn't understand it. He was only asking if he, accompanied by his sister, could take me to the park."

At this point, Reuben laughed out loud. "I did not receive an answer for three days. So what could I do but assume that there would be no answer? I couldn't leave it at that. This most beautiful girl had come into my life, and I couldn't let her leave without at least talking to her. So I took it upon myself to personally see her mother and convince her of my sincerity. Which I did."

"Which he did," Keri joined in, "with his older sister in tow. I was quite surprised, as was my mama, but she did invite them in and gave each a piece of cake and a glass of milk while we sat in the kitchen and he pled his case. I knew right then he should be a lawyer, because he did so well at convincing my mama. She said yes, and we went to the park with his sister that very afternoon."

With the last statement, she clapped her hands on her lap. "And that is all there will be for now. I am very tired and sleepy tonight."

Floyd stretched his long arms and yawned. "Thank you, ma'am. I know there's a lot more, and maybe over the next couple of days we can talk you into sharing it with us."

She smiled up at Floyd. "I would be glad to. Good night, Floyd." She stood, arranged her and Reuben's blankets, crawled between them, and was fast asleep.

Matt, watching the interchange, said softly to his brother, "The sleep of a righteous person."

"Yep," Floyd said, "she is quite a lady." He looked around at the four men. "The same rotation for tonight?"

Everyone nodded, and Matt said, "You're spoiling me."

Floyd grinned at his brother. "Old men need their rest."

Matt had already slipped between his blankets, and only a muffled reply could be heard. "I'm sleeping. You go play watchman."

THE NIGHT HAD BEEN cool but not cold, and the weather continued to warm. Floyd thought, *I sure hope this weather holds. It would make the trip back to the mountains so much easier.* But this was winter, and he knew his luck wouldn't hold, and only hoped it would last until reaching Friendsville.

So far, no trouble. They'd had no human contact other than Mr. Simmons at the previous crossing. But in a short time they would be nearing Calfkiller River, and that meant taking another ferry. At the ferries there was always a chance of trouble with other folks. Not everyone in Tennessee felt the way the Logans did about slavery, though eastern Tennessee was much more against slavery than the rest of the state.

The river wasn't far now. They had camped fairly near so they would have the opportunity to cross early, providing them with almost a full day to put distance between themselves and the crossing, should it be necessary. The last couple of miles would be along a well-used trail that ran to the ferry. Floyd was riding point when the timber started to thin. He held up a hand to stop the column, turned, and motioned to Matt. When his brother had joined him, Floyd said, "You know the trail up ahead can be well used."

Matt said, "What's your plan?"

"Don't have much of one. I figured we've got to cross here, so we'll just ride up like we own the place. How does that sound to you?"

"If that's the only way, and I agree it is, then I'd say we best get with it, but have your guns handy."

Floyd removed his hat and combed his hair back with his hand. "I reckon. How about telling Reuben and Keri there might be people around, and they need to act like slaves. There'll be no problem with Keri, but Reuben doesn't take to kowtowing very easily. Can't say as how I blame him. It isn't an easy thing, but he'd best get his acting face on."

Matt nodded his agreement, turned his mule, Badger, around and headed back to the couple. Floyd shifted in his saddle to watch. Reuben didn't seem too well pleased with the idea. Floyd watched the interchange, thinking, *If he's going to make it back to New York City, he'd best learn to follow directions no matter how difficult they are.* Matt waved and rode on to alert Owen. Floyd waved back and led the procession out of the trees.

They made a left turn onto the double-track trail, putting the rising sun on the right shoulder. Wrinkles across Floyd's brow emphasized his concern for being in the open. Life-preserving habit, developed from long years dodging Indians in the mountains, kept his deep blue eyes scouring the trail for movement.

A short distance ahead, the trail turned left and then swung hard back to the right, disappearing behind the thick brush and trees and forming a point. Out of this point of trees stepped a doe with two fawns. Once in the middle of the trail, she froze, as if a statue, the fawns following suit. Floyd watched with more than a passing interest. The three deer were not watching them, but looking toward the hidden portion of the trail. She watched for only an instant, flicked her tail, as a warning to the fawns, and dashed into the far timber with the fawns close behind.

Just prior to riding out of the timber, Floyd, as Matt had suggested, had checked his weapons. Now he turned and signaled the others. Matt and Owen had also watched the deer and waved back in readiness. They continued toward the point. Nearing, Floyd heard voices and laughter. It was accompanied by the sounds of at least one wagon. He knew, just around the bend, another trail joined this one. Sure enough, as he rounded the trees, five men rode ahead of them, toward the ferry. Two of those men sat side by side in a wagon, which appeared to be loaded, covered with a tarpaulin.

The group of men were laughing loudly and passing a bottle around. Floyd noted that the pace of the men with the wagon was about the same as theirs. Their destination had to also be the ferry. *Well,* Floyd thought, *fortunately there won't be room enough for all of us on the ferry, so they'll be gone by the time we get across, hopefully.* He had no desire to deal with loudmouths who were drinking this early in the morning, with Reuben and Keri along.

They rode a good half mile before the strangers spotted them. One of those on the wagon had turned to a horseman, who was holding the bottle, and began to yell and wave for the liquor. But as he turned, he spotted Floyd and the others. At the sight, he stared for a minute, then said something to the man who was driving the horses. When the driver turned around to look, so did the three riders. As one of the riders turned in the saddle, he wobbled from side to side, quickly grasped the saddle horn, and managed to stay in the saddle. All five of the strangers stared at Floyd for a few moments, then turned back forward, and, from what one of them must've said, burst out laughing.

Floyd hoped the morning would go smoothly, with no problems from the strangers, but he had a bad feeling about the group. Continuing on, in a short time the ferry landing came into view. Unfortunately, for he had been hoping the ferry would be there to load the drunks before his group arrived, it was on the other side of the river, slowly making its way back.

The arrival of the men ahead, now at the river landing, would have been humorous if Floyd hadn't been concerned about

Reuben and Keri. Once they arrived at the riverbank, the rider who had swayed in the saddle attempted to dismount. He reached the ground, but not on both feet. As his right leg swung across his horse's back, he lost his grip on the saddle horn and collapsed backwards. Fortunately, the driver of the wagon quickly stretched out and grabbed the bridle of the drunk's horse. Otherwise, the man very well may have been killed. For as he was falling, his left boot slipped through the stirrup, trapping the booted foot. If the horse had taken off, the man would've either been drowned or kicked to death by the animal.

# 14
---

As it turned out, evidently the only thing that was hurt was his pride. One of the other riders removed the man's boot, pushed his foot back through the stirrup, and helped him to his feet. By this time, not only was the ferry nearing, but Floyd and his group were closing on the landing. The fallen man, now back on his feet, staggered over to the wagon and yanked out the driving whip. He began to viciously beat his totally innocent horse. One of the other men, who had dismounted, said something to the man with the whip, but for his reward he had the same whip brandished at him. Then the drunk turned back to his horse and resumed the beating.

Floyd pulled his rifle from the scabbard and walked Jasper toward the abuser. The other men had stepped aside and were watching, their responses to the armed man riding into their group slowed by their alcohol consumption. Ignoring them, Floyd turned Jasper slightly so that he was in reach of the man. As he lifted the rifle, holding it with his right hand around the grip, the man with the whip must have sensed or heard Jasper. He turned, whip drawn back. Floyd, adding little impetus other than the weight of the rifle, allowed the barrel to fall, striking the man, whose surprised face was turned up toward him. The man's forehead, cushioned slightly by the brim of his hat, took the full brunt of the blow from the barrel of the ten-pound rifle.

As the man was falling, Floyd yanked the five-foot wooden driving whip from his hand. He deftly grasped one end with the hand holding the rifle, and the other with his left hand, and snapped the cane stick, throwing the two pieces on top of the collapsed man's chest. "I can't abide harsh treatment," Floyd said, "toward man or beast from any man."

The action had happened so quickly that none of the men reacted. Now, the driver, who was still holding the bridle of the chestnut gelding that was being beaten, glared up at Floyd. "That was my best driving whip," the man said.

Floyd pointed the muzzle of the rifle at the unconscious man and said, "Reckon that gentleman, flat on his back, owes you a new one."

Now, the one man who remained mounted reached for his rifle.

"That would be a really bad mistake, mister." Floyd heard Matt's cold voice over the sound of a cocking hammer. Floyd smiled to himself. It was nice to have his brothers along, for he knew they had his back.

The mounted man released his rifle, allowing it to slide back into the scabbard.

Floyd also slid his rifle into its scabbard and dismounted, ground hitching Jasper. The driver still held the bridle of the chestnut gelding beaten by the man on the ground. He watched Floyd approach and released the bridle when Floyd grasped it.

The man who had dismounted, to remove his partner's foot from the stirrup, spoke up. "You ain't a-gonna steal that horse, now are you?"

Floyd, rubbing the injured animal's neck and humming to him, continued rubbing and turned cold blue eyes on the speaker. "I'm no horse thief, mister."

The riverman, really a boy, had docked the ferry and stood well out of line of any possible shots while the altercation took place. Now he spoke up. "Which group of you gents are taking this here ferry first?"

Floyd spoke up before anyone else could. "That would be us. Can your raft handle seven mules and five people?"

"Whoa there, feller," the wagon driver said. "We was here first."

"That you were, *feller*," Floyd replied. "But you forfeited that option when your friend went for his rifle. Now here's what we're going to do. First, we'll take all your guns and leave them on the ferry. That way you'll have them back when the ferry comes back across to get you. Plus, we don't have to worry about being sitting ducks in the middle of the river."

The driver looked askance at Floyd while the man sitting next to him on the wagon seat leaned slightly forward, obviously reaching for a weapon.

Owen had eased up in line with Matt, except on the opposite side of the wagon, where they could cover everyone. Owen brought his rifle's hammer to full cock, the harsh clicks reverberating along the bank, and said, "Mister, if you come up with anything other than a bottle, you'll be a dead man."

The passenger's body momentarily froze in position, then slowly eased erect, hands empty.

The chestnut, with Floyd's hands and soft humming, had calmed, eyes no longer wide with fear. Floyd now reached back and pulled the prone man's rifle from the scabbard just as he began to awaken.

"Hey," the man said, in a drunken slur, "whatcha doing there?" Rolling halfway over, he placed both hands on the ground beside himself and started to push up.

Floyd placed his foot on the man's chest, shoved him back down, and said, "Stay down." He bent over and checked the man for any additional weapons. Finding none, he said, "Get up."

Once he was on his feet, Floyd hit one of his arms. "Hold your arms out with your fingers spread, and don't try anything. You have two rifles pointed straight at your heart."

The drunk man's expression was complete confusion, but he did what he was told, and Floyd laid the rifle across his extended arms. Then he turned to the other dismounted man. "Hand me your rifle and also the pistol from your saddle, carefully."

The man's face was sullen, yet he pulled his rifle from the scabbard, then his pistol, and handed them to Floyd. Floyd also laid this rifle across the drunk's arms and hung the pistol from a finger.

He went around to each of the remaining men, collecting weapons. When he finished, the drunk was carrying five rifles, and two pistols hung from the fingers of each hand.

"This is heavy," the drunk said, looking around at his friends.

"Follow me," Floyd said, turning toward the barge.

"What's your name?" the drunk asked.

"Floyd Logan, what's yours?" Floyd said, not slowing his stride.

Staggering after him, the drunk replied, "King, but everyone calls me Jolly."

Jolly didn't reflect his name at the moment. He had a line of blood running from his forehead to each side of his face and down his cheeks. "You're the one who hit me, aren't you?"

Floyd said to the boy, "Where do you want these?"

The boy pointed to a horizontal locker on one side of the ferry. "Just stick 'em in there."

Floyd motioned the drunk over to him, took the handguns, firing each into the water before putting it inside the locker and followed suit with the rifles. When he finished, he turned and strode to the wagon driver, the drunk following.

As soon as he got there, the driver said, "You had no call to do that."

Before speaking to the driver, Floyd said to Matt, "Why don't you get everyone loaded."

Matt nodded, held his position with his rifle trained on the group, and motioned to Owen and the others. Owen, rifle ready, led Reuben and Keri onto the ferry.

Once they were on, Floyd said to the driver, "I have every right to, mister. The last thing I'm looking for is a slug in my back. Now tell me how much you want for this chestnut gelding."

Immediately, the driver said, "He ain't for sale."

"Sure he is. Just give me a price, and make it high."

"Jolly ain't gonna like this," the man said, but Floyd could tell he was thinking. After a bit, he said, "A hunerd dollars, not a penny less." When Floyd nodded, the man continued. "In gold."

His friends had been listening, and now both of them chuckled. The driver grinned at them, nodding his head in satisfaction, and said to them, "Not bad," as if he felt sure neither Floyd nor his friends were carrying gold.

Floyd said to Matt, "Throw a rope around the gelding." He pointed at the man on the ground. "You, get the tack off that animal, gently." Reaching into his possibles bag, he fumbled around inside it for a moment and brought out a handful of ten-dollar gold eagle coins. He counted out ten eagles, dropping the rest back in the bag, and put the ten into the extended hand of the astonished driver. "Bill of sale."

"What?" the dumbfounded man said as he sat staring at the gold coins in his hand.

"I need a bill of sale from the owner," Floyd said, enunciating each word slowly and clearly.

"But I ain't got nothing to write on, and it wouldn't do no good anyway. None of us can write a lick."

Matt, having dropped a loop over the gelding, sidled his horse next to Floyd. He reached into his coat pocket and pulled out a small notebook and a stubby pencil. "Floyd, you want me to write out a bill of sale?"

Floyd nodded. "I'd appreciate that, Matt."

When he finished, Matt said, "I'd have the owner leave his mark, and there's a place where the witnesses can leave theirs. You probably ought to have them all witness."

Floyd took the note and said to the driver, "Who's the owner?"

The driver thumbed in the direction of Jolly, who had followed Floyd and was standing next to him, eyes glued on the gold in the driver's hand.

Floyd scooped the coins from the driver's hand, noting the surprise and sadness across the driver's face with the loss of the coins, and held them out to Jolly. Without an instant's hesitation, Jolly's hands shot out, forming a cup. "Is the chestnut your horse?" Floyd asked.

The man was dumbstruck by the gold. All he could do was nod his head rapidly.

"All right then, before you get this gold, you have to sign a bill of sale. Is that agreeable to you?"

Again, the only response was Jolly's head bobbing up and down.

Floyd gave the pencil to Jolly and held the paper on the side of the wagon where he could make his mark. With his tongue sticking out one corner of his mouth, Jolly gripped the pencil in a death grip and slowly made an X. Then he looked up at Floyd expectantly.

"First," Floyd said, "your partners here need to make their mark as witnesses."

Jolly immediately growled to his companions, "Get over here, and make your mark."

They all hurried to form a line. Each one recited his name, which Floyd wrote on the paper, and then each man made his mark. As soon as the last one finished, Jolly, who appeared to be sobering, thrust out his hand and said, "Gimme my gold." Once he had it, he looked up at Floyd. "You shouldn't oughta hit me like that. That was hurtful. I ain't likely to forget it."

Matt had led the chestnut and Floyd's horse onto the ferry, where all the animals were loaded, and everyone waited. Ignoring the now more sober drunk, Floyd turned and strode to the ferry, nodding at the boy.

As the ferry pulled away from the bank, Jolly said, his voice threatening, "I said I ain't likely to forget it."

Floyd stared at him, saying not a word.

As they were unloading on the opposite bank, the yell of Jolly floated across the river. "I ain't likely to forget it!"

They mounted the mules and, with Floyd leading the chestnut and Matt alongside, started down the trail. Matt looked at his brother, whose face was gradually changing from the flint-hard, unforgiving stare, to the brother that he was used to. He grinned at Floyd and said, "Brother, I think he ain't likely to forget it." At that, the three brothers burst out laughing.

Matt looked at Floyd again. "Little brother, you've changed a lot since last I saw you. I've seen that look on other men. You were ready to kill him, or at least deal him some pretty severe damage. You've taken control of that temper you had as a boy, but it's turned into something cold and dangerous. You'd best keep a handle on it and let it out only when you need it."

They continued riding as the morning warmed. Floyd chewed on what Matt had said, thinking, *Maybe I don't have as much control as I think I have. But, then again, I don't think I was really going to kill him. Although I wouldn't have minded thumping him a bit.*

They rode for a while, and Floyd said to Matt, "I really can't stand to see someone or something being abused. Maybe it wasn't a good idea to hit that old boy with my rifle barrel, though it seemed to work pretty well. Probably should have just taken the whip away from him and given him a few stripes, but I hear what you're saying, brother. I'll keep it in mind."

"You are sudden, Floyd. That happened almighty quick." Changing the subject, Matt said, "So what's your plan for this chestnut? He doesn't look nearly like a hundred-dollar horse."

Floyd sat quiet as Jasper circled a boulder in the trail, Matt riding around the other side. When there were back together, he said, "I really don't have a plan. I just wanted to get him away from those folks. I guess we can give him to the first farmer who comes along. A working life on a farm will be a lot better than what he had to put up with."

Matt shook his head. "That's a lot of money for a plow horse."

HE RELAXED, his back against the saddle, feet extended to the fire. While everyone else was getting settled, he reflected on the past few days. Except for the run-in with Jolly and his bunch two days ago, this trip had been the way he liked it, uneventful.

It was hard to believe that this was the first day of the new year, 1841. He shook his head, *How time flies. It's been over ten years since I left home.* He smiled to himself, running his hand along the knife scar on his left jaw, and thought, *But they've been exciting years with, I will admit, some very harrowing moments. Tomorrow morning, we'll be crossing the Tennessee River, then on to Friendsville, say goodbye to the Fosters, and I'll be on my way to Leotie.*

Owen's voice pulled him out of his reverie. "I'm thinking those folks you gave that chestnut to are still thanking their lucky stars."

"I'd say," Keri added, her dark eyes glistening in the firelight, "it's more like they are thanking God for their blessings." She turned to Floyd. "That was really nice, rescuing that horse and then giving it to the family."

The compliment succeeded in embarrassing him. He gave a curt nod and cleared his throat.

Owen glanced at his brother and said quickly, "Yes, ma'am. I imagine you're correct. They were mighty happy to have that horse."

"Yes," Reuben said, "they certainly were, and I admire the

husband. He politely, but firmly, asked for a bill of sale—a smart and honest man."

"Yep," Matt joined in, "they didn't have much, but insisted on providing us a meal before we moved on, and I have to say, some mighty fine cornbread and black-eyed peas. It had sure slipped my mind that today was the beginning of the year. But I hope that meal didn't cut too deeply into those folks' larder."

Floyd still feeling self-conscious from Keri's remark, readjusted himself against his saddle, and gave a belated reply. "Reckon I just don't care for overbearing people, and I can't stand for animals to be treated mean. Anyway, they looked as if a horse would be exceptionally handy. Their old mule looked pretty tired, and the son and that chestnut took right to each other." Floyd stretched his long arms and changed the subject, saying, "Now, Miss Keri, we didn't get a chance to hear more of your story, and tonight will be our last opportunity, if you feel you could oblige us."

Owen had been lying back, his head resting on his saddle. He leaned forward, drew his knees up, wrapped his arms around his legs, and, clasping his hands, said, "Yes, ma'am, we'd sure like to hear the rest of it."

Keri looked around the fire at the three brothers, leaned softly against her husband, and began her story. "I think I ended with our first chaperoned outing to the park. After that, we saw each other quite often for the next month, and I knew I was smitten. However, it broke my heart, because I also knew that it would be impossible for us to be together. He was free, and I was a slave. He lived in New York City, and I lived in Huntsville, Alabama. It was heartbreaking."

"There were obstacles," Reuben said, "but my father says that obstacles are placed before us to give us the opportunity to grow and overcome them."

Matt was nodding in agreement. "Sounds like your pa is a mighty smart man."

Keri smiled up at her husband and said, "Yes, he is very wise. So we left for home, in Huntsville, after a very short month. Reuben and I, thanks to Mrs. Howard, were able to correspond. This went on for well over three years. During that time Reuben became a lawyer and, with the assistance of his father, wrote the Howards requesting the opportunity for his father to purchase my and my mother's freedom. He also wrote that along with the money for the purchase, he would send money for our transportation to New York.

"They were such good people, the Howards. They, along with Sissy, one evening invited us into the sitting room for a discussion. Mama and I were beside ourselves with happiness when they told us their decision. She knew I was deeply in love with Reuben." With the last comment, Keri reached across her chest to grasp and squeeze Reuben's hand draped across her shoulder.

She continued, "They asked Mama and me if this was what we wanted. We assured them, as much as we loved them, this was something we both longed for. Mr. Howard said he would contact his attorney, draw up the papers, and have them sent to Reuben. We were so happy. The next few days Mama and I talked about what we would do in New York City and what it would be like for me to be married to Reuben."

Keri grew silent. A lone tear drifted down her cheek, and a soft low sob escaped.

## 15

"Ma'am," Floyd said, "if these memories are too painful, you sure don't have to continue."

Reuben, his arm around her, squeezed her to him.

She shook her head. "Sorry, but I would like to continue."

Floyd nodded and said, "Then please do, ma'am."

After a long sigh, Keri began again. "Unfortunately, the happiness soon ended. Before Mr. Howard could get to his attorney, he became deathly ill, quickly followed by Mrs. Howard and Sissy. Mama and I were kept busy taking care of them, until Mama got sick. It was terrible. All of them were throwing up terribly and had absolutely no control over their bowels. The doctor pronounced it was cholera.

"Mr. Howard lost weight so very quickly. You could actually see him growing thinner, and he died on the second day. Then poor, sweet Sissy passed. It was all so horrible. Mrs. Howard lasted the longest of all. She had to watch her husband, her lovely daughter, and her friend, Mama, for they truly had become friends, die. Before she passed, she held my hand and told me how sorry she was that they had been unable to set me free. Those were her last words. I was left alone."

Silence reigned around the fire. Floyd watched the fire's reflections in the girl's sad eyes. It was getting late, and though he would love to hear the end of the story, he wasn't sure Keri was up to telling it. She had already been offered the opportunity to stop, and had elected to continue. For a young man, he understood the importance of patience and continued to relax against his saddle, allowing the girl time to compose herself. All of the Logans waited.

Finally, she lifted the handkerchief she had held crushed in her hands and dabbed at each eye. When she was finished, she gazed around the fire and said, "Thank you. It is getting late, and I'll try to make this last part short.

"Mr. Howard had a brother who also lived in Huntsville, not as nice as him. He immediately put the house, animals, and the slaves who worked there up for sale. Though the sale frightened me, I was more afraid he would take me into his home, but his wife would not allow it. We, there were only three others, the carriage man, the gardener, and the cook, were auctioned that week. It was a terrible experience, but for the sake of keeping the story short, I'll skip that part. The lady who bought me wanted me as a maid. I was so relieved my purchaser was a woman. She was from Athens.

"How wrong I was to be relieved. The first thing she did when we got to her home was to take me to my quarters, make me lie across the bed, and she beat me with a leather strap. She told me the beating was to impress upon me that she was the owner and I the slave. She continued to give me a beating on the first of every month thereafter."

Keri looked at her clenched hands in her lap, relaxed them, and exercised her fingers for a moment before beginning again. "Those were the longest and worst eight months of my life,

Mama gone and having to work for that demanding, wretched woman. Then one morning I was at the farmers' market. I heard the most beautiful voice I've ever heard. It was Reuben." She relaxed, the tension appearing to flow from her as she laid her head on her husband's shoulder.

"Yes," Reuben said, "I hadn't received a letter from her for months. So I tossed a few things in a bag and, with my parents' blessings and cautions, left for Alabama. As a black man, it was very difficult for me to track her, but after locating and talking to the gardener, he told me who had bought Keri. I spoke to several leaders in the black community of Athens and was informed it would be impossible for me to purchase Keri's freedom from that woman. So I turned to the only avenue remaining, the Underground Railroad. And that, gentlemen, brings us to this campfire and your kindness and protection, for which we are deeply indebted. Thank you for listening to our story."

Floyd picked up his rifle and stood. "As usual, I'll take first watch." He turned to Reuben and Keri. "We're just happy that we were in the right place to help you, at the right time."

Matt chimed in, "And it isn't over yet. This venture won't be successful until we hand you two off to the Quakers in Friendsville tomorrow so you can continue your journey home."

"WHAT DO YOU THINK?" Floyd asked his brother Matt.

They had left their party and their mules about a couple of miles back, this side of Muddy Creek. On foot, they had soundlessly moved through the forest. The strong south wind worked both in their favor and against them. It helped cover up what little sound they were making, but in turn hid any sound from others who might be near. Now, they were lying beneath an old sweetgum tree, watching the ferry operating between the east and west bank of the Tennessee River.

"I think we're in big trouble," Matt said, looking up at the blue sky through the whipping and barren limbs of the sweetgum tree. "This is the hottest January I can remember. We'll have a storm to deal with before we get back home."

Floyd had taken out his small telescope and was examining the far landing. "No, Matt. I'm asking what you think about the possibility of those slave-chasers being around here."

His brother followed the ferry with his gaze as it was thrashed by the wind blowing up the river. The winding river had straightened, and for a short distance flowed almost due south. This allowed the full strength of the wind to blow straight along the river and severely buffet the travelers on the ferry.

"Well, brother, I *have* been thinking about that. The little altercation you had with Jolly could have brought some attention to us, and I don't think Jolly is the type to forgive and forget. If those slave-chasers managed to run into them, and that's a big if, I'm sure they'll hear about Reuben and Keri."

Floyd took the glass from his eye and handed it to Matt. "Yeah, I've been thinking on that. It may not have been the smartest move in the world, but if I had it to do over again, I wouldn't change a thing."

"You were right. If you hadn't acted, I would have." Matt turned his head and grinned at his brother. "Probably not with quite as much force as you used." Matt took the glass and began watching the landing on the opposite side of the river.

The two men stayed in position for another hour. Finally, Floyd said, "I think, since we can't see it very well from here, I'll edge over to the landing on this side of the river and see if there's anything suspicious going on there. If you're all right with it, I'd like you to wait here. I'll be back shortly."

Floyd was thankful for the wind as he moved through the leaves and brush, allowing him to move faster without fear of anyone hearing him. Twenty minutes later, he was lying in the brush on the low bluff overlooking the ferry's landing. As soon as the landing came into view, he spotted the chasers, but now the size of their group was enhanced. Along with Rufus Johnson and Felix Barnam, he spotted Jolly and the man who had been driving the wagon. But there was no Leroy Tatum in sight.

"I was afraid of that," Floyd said softly to himself, his voice immediately lost in the wind. "While we had to stay away from traveled roads, they didn't, and beat us here. Plus they had the luck of running into Jolly." He shook his head in disgust, taking a moment to work through it.

Then he realized there was no Tatum. Of the three chasers, he had struck Floyd as the most dangerous. Not that Johnson and Barnam weren't dangerous, but Floyd had seen the sly, mean streak in Tatum. If he had to shoot any of the three, that man would receive the first load. The fact that he wasn't in sight caused the little hairs on the back of Floyd's neck to start tingling. Those little hairs had saved his life more than once.

From his position, he had a good look of the ramp, landing and gin crane. The crane held the rope that extended across the river, secured to the ferry, which provided the ferry a stable track, crossing the river, as long as the current wasn't too fast. As he continued to examine the far tree line on the other side of the road, he found the thick brush and trees gave him a shallow view of the trees surrounding the landing, especially across the road nearest the river.

*Where would I position myself if I wanted to cover the landing and the approach?* Slowly moving his head, he followed the road's approach to the landing. It faded from his vision quickly, drifting to his right, north. Looking back, and now wishing that he had brought his glass, he began examining the area he would most likely set up in.

Most of the opposite side of the approach to the landing was open about twenty feet from the road, with low brush. Because of the bluff bank on his side, on the north side of the road, the side he was on, there had been little trimming except up to the road edge of the steep bank, which was only two or three feet from the road.

Finally, he picked out a likely spot he might use, set back quite a ways from the road, under a growth of several pin oak trees. Each had low limbs that either drooped all the way to or near the ground, and though it was January, they still retained their dull red leaves. Those trees would give a sniper an excellent rest for his rifle while providing concealment.

He waited and watched.

He hadn't moved for almost an hour. The ferry, during this time, had made three roundtrips. The voices of the travelers drifted up to Floyd, though he couldn't make out what they were saying.

Johnson and Barnam, along with Jolly and his driver, talked to everyone who came through the landing heading east. There had been several wagons, and Johnson made it a point to check the bed of each one before allowing them to board the ferry.

Floyd continued to watch the pin oaks. From one of them drooped a lower limb that rested on the ground before turning back up. It too was still covered with leaves. He started concentrating on that one limb, knowing that if Tatum was lying behind the leafy limb, he would be almost impossible to see.

His eyes moved from leaf to leaf. Examining each, he concentrated more with his peripheral vision, knowing if there was something out of place, his side vision might have a better chance of picking it up than a direct stare.

Ten minutes of intense searching paid off. Behind a pattern of leaves, a piece of smooth gray cloth leaped out at him. Tatum was behind the low limb. Floyd remembered the man being left-handed, so his right side *should* be facing the tree and Floyd. The sun was now well past its zenith. He knew what he had to do, but was concerned about the hour. He also hoped Matt would not lose patience and come this way in an effort to find him.

Knowing Matt's actions were out of his control, Floyd, one last time, marked the tree where Tatum was hiding. He slowly crawled backwards, careful to shake no bush with his movement. The last thing he wanted to do was give away his position and alert Tatum. Once deep into the woods, he stood and began running west. He would cross the road out of sight of the landing and Tatum.

Nearing the opening, and before stepping out from the concealment of the trees, he listened. There was no sound of people, horses, or wagons. He stepped from the trees, quickly looked both ways, and dashed across the road into the trees and underbrush on the far side. When he was again deep in the trees, he turned south and ran for about a half mile. He estimated that would put him far enough past Tatum to prevent alerting him until it was too late for the lurking chaser. Starting a slow turn to the east, he slowed to a walk. He trusted, implicitly, his internal compass and judgment of distance. It had guided him with unerring accuracy over the years, and today was not the day to begin doubting it.

Now, deliberately, he slipped through the woods, cautiously placing foot in front of foot, allowing his weight to gradually be transferred from one to the other. In so doing, he was able to move over the dry leaves and tiny brittle limbs that littered the ground. His early years of hunting and traveling in the Tennessee woods, plus the ten years spent dodging hostile Indians, had taught him the skills he used now. Plus, the wind, and the commotion it was causing in the trees, covered any slip or mistake he might make. The only thing he was even slightly concerned about was Tatum's skills.

When he was directly south of Tatum, he stopped for a moment, searched, and listened as best he could, then turned and headed north directly toward where he knew Tatum was lying. If Tatum was a seasoned and experienced woodsman, he just might smell Floyd, since the wind was blowing from Floyd to

Tatum. At other times, when the wind had been right for him, Floyd had smelled both Indians and white men. He knew the sense of smell was powerful and had alerted him to a foe's presence, saving his hair, on several occasions. Fortunately, it was blowing hard enough that the odds were that any smells would be shredded quickly.

His eyes constantly searched as, in a crouch now, he slipped forward. Finally, he could make out the pin oaks ahead. He stopped behind a sycamore, waited only for a moment, and eased his head around the tree until one eye was exposed. Sure enough, there sat Tatum. He was no longer prone beside the log, but sitting up smoking a cigarette. His rifle lay parallel to the oak limb in front of him.

Floyd eased back behind the trunk of the sycamore and shook his head. *Smoking*, he thought. *He must be pretty confident.*

Slowly, he eased out from behind the tree and began, ever so slowly, approaching the man who had been waiting to ambush and murder them. Closer and closer, one soft step at a time. Gradually the distance narrowed. Fifteen feet, lowering a foot and lifting the other. Again. Again.

Now he was only six feet behind his adversary. Tatum continued to smoke without a care in the world.

Floyd slipped within three feet of his quarry. Easing the barrel of his short .54-caliber, custom-made Ryland rifle forward, he eared back while simultaneously pressing the cold muzzle to Tatum's neck, just below his skull.

Floyd Logan had spent ten years in the mountains hunting with, and fighting against, Indians. He knew them well. He also knew mountain men and their reactions. Under no circumstances would Floyd ever allow the muzzle of his rifle to get within range of a swing or kick from his quarry. But today his overconfidence led him down the wrong path. He was unprepared for Tatum.

The man, in one smooth motion, flashed a hand around behind his head, grabbed the barrel of Floyd's rifle, and used the resistance as a lever to assist him in spinning and leaping to his feet. He held the barrel of Floyd's Ryland in an iron grip and, while he made the turn, twisted, almost wrenching it from Floyd's grasp.

In a smooth motion, the barrel locked in his left hand, his right was pulling an Arkansas toothpick with a long, glistening blade from the scabbard at his waist. At the same time he let out a yell to alert his companions, who were now talking at the ferry landing. At any other time, they would've quickly been across the low knoll and into the trees, ruining Floyd's plans.

Fortunately for Floyd, who was now busily repairing his youthful lapse of judgment, the noise of the wind and limbs blowing and the waves splashing on the river drowned out Tatum's call, leaving Tatum to fend for himself.

Floyd instantly realized his error. He clenched his rifle and pushed hard against Tatum's grip. The muzzle was pointed directly into Tatum's belly, but the last thing Floyd wanted to do was kill him, so he made sure his finger stayed clear of the trigger. Tatum staggered back from the force of the muzzle driving into his belly, and while he was trying to recover his balance, Floyd reversed the force and gave a powerful yank on the rifle, wrenching the weapon from the chaser's hand. In the process, the front sight ripped a wide, deep gash through Tatum's palm, instantly pouring blood. Tatum ignored it and leaped for Floyd.

Unfortunately for Tatum, Floyd was well past his surprise and ready for his opponent's move. He had recovered the rifle to a defensive position, his right hand holding it by the small of the stock and his left hand at the forearm. Seeing Tatum's move developing and the approaching knife blade, Floyd took a half step forward, twisting slightly to his right. The blade, which was driven straight for his heart, caught on the receiver of the rifle and was knocked up and to Floyd's right. The sixteen-inch blade missed all vital organs, slicing through the buckskin shirt and long johns, finding Floyd's right bicep.

Tatum was successful in drawing blood, but his evil grin at seeing the blood lasted only a moment. Floyd unleashed the coiled strength waiting in his right shoulder and arm, driving the butt of the rifle into Tatum's belly. The blow lifted the man completely off the ground, rotating him in the air as he was thrown back. His face and forehead slammed against the trunk of a silver maple. As he collapsed to the ground, unconscious, both hands and face dragged down the shaggy, vine-covered tree trunk.

Floyd watched Tatum for a moment, then checked his shoulder. Blood was dripping down his arm to his hand, but when he pulled the sliced clothing open, he could see that it was a shallow wound. It could wait until he had Tatum tied and gagged. Looking down at the man, he silently admired the speed with which his opponent had responded. The chaser had certainly caught him off guard. Floyd bent to roll Tatum over and glanced at the maple's blood-streaked trunk. A slow grin of recognition broke out on his face as he examined the trunk. With a chuckle, he carefully pulled the unconscious man farther away from the tree and rolled him over on his face.

Pulling his knife, he sliced several strings from his buckskin shirt, tying Tatum's wrists behind him. He cut a strip of the man's shirt and, using it for a gag, carefully covered his mouth, making sure he didn't touch Tatum's face, and tied the knot behind his head. Next, he dragged Tatum back to the big limb where he had been, pulled the man's knife belt off, and tied it around his ankles. Then he rolled him so that his back was to the limb, and using another piece of the man's shirt, he tied first his hands and then his legs to the tree limb. Standing up, he examined his work, nodded, and picked up Tatum's knife. He first examined it and thought, *I'm sure glad he didn't get this thing into me. That's a nasty-looking weapon.* He threw it deep into the woods and picked up the man's rifle.

Though the man was unkempt and dirty, his rifle was the complete opposite. It was a well-cared-for weapon, clean with the faint smell of oil. The stock was smooth, showing a dull glow from many hours of rubbing. As he admired the rifle, he glanced toward Tatum, to see the prone man staring at him, eyes wide. Floyd knelt by him and said, "If I don't do something to your rifle, you will kill me with it."

The man shook his head vigorously, unintelligible grunts coming from his mouth. Floyd carefully slipped the gag from the man's mouth. "Don't break it, Logan. I bought that rifle when I left home, and I've had it all these years. It's a good rifle."

Floyd's face turned hard as stone. He knew the kind of man Tatum was, and what he'd do to Reuben and Keri if he caught them. "A good rifle you've used to kill innocent men." He jerked the gag back over the man's face. "If you want it, swim for it." He slipped to the edge of the river and dropped it into the swirling water. Even in the current of the river, the rifle wouldn't be taken far. If Tatum really wanted it back, it would take some time and diving, but he might find it.

Ignoring the grunts and glaring that came from him, Floyd put Tatum from his mind and checked the sun's position, noting it had drifted much lower. He had to be getting back to Matt and back to Owen, Reuben, and Keri. He was sure they were all worrying. He looked again at Tatum, who, eyes wide, was still staring. Floyd turned and started running west.

He knew there was a small pond just a short distance past the road. Upon reaching the pond, he searched around the edges and found what he was looking for, jewelweed. Ma had taught him about the healing properties of many herbs and plants. He knew jewelweed could cure poison ivy. This time of year, the leaves were dead, but with the water, they might still be effective. It was at least worth a try. He scraped up a handful, moved to the water's edge, and crushed them between his hands. Floyd rubbed them all over his hands and wrists, dampened his hands with water, and continued to rub. He made three trips between the leaves and the water, repeating the crushing, rubbing, and washing process. Finally satisfied, he dried his hands on his trousers and resumed his run.

# 16

Floyd raced through the timber, caring little about noise. The wind had picked up even more, and there was no chance of his being heard. In hardly any time at all, he was back with Matt, whom he found sitting comfortably against a fallen log.

Matt, upon his arrival, stood. "You were gone for quite a while. I was starting to debate if I should come and bail you out."

"Sorry. I ran into a small situation that took a little more time than I thought it might."

At Matt's raised eyebrows, Floyd responded, "The slave-chasers are at the landing. Jolly has joined them, and the fella who was driving the wagon is also with him."

"I'm sure," Matt said, "it didn't take you that long to work out who was there. What else was going on?"

"Yeah, you're right. Tatum, the chaser I was most concerned about, wasn't anywhere to be seen around the landing. So, after a little examining, I spotted him across the trail, set up for an ambush. That's what took so long. I had to stay out of sight of the people at the landing while I circled around behind Tatum."

Matt spotted the slice in Floyd's buckskin shirt and the blood around it. "I see you didn't get away scot-free. You all right?"

"I'm fine. We need to get back to the others. I'd like to make the landing well before dusk. If it starts getting dark and Tatum isn't back, the others will go looking for him. For now, they're satisfied he's hiding in the trees, waiting to ambush us."

Matt picked up his rifle, and said, "Let's go."

The brothers ran easily through the woods. They paused only briefly to check the road before crossing it and continued to run. *This feels good,* Floyd thought as he stretched out his legs. *I haven't had the opportunity to run like this since before I left the mountains.* The thought of the mountains brought a quick tightening to his throat. *I wish I knew how Leotie and Mika are doing.*

The two arrived at the dry camp quickly, but time was becoming critical. Shadows were starting to march out from the base of the trees as the sun drifted lower in the sky.

The first person who spoke was Keri. "You're hurt. What happened to you?" She turned to the sack lying beside her saddle. "I need to fix that."

Floyd shook his head. "No time. We need to get moving, now." To emphasize his words, he laid down his rifle and began saddling Jasper.

Everyone picked up on the urgency in his voice and went to work, all except Keri. She continued to search through the sack. Reuben, who had begun saddling his mule, Zipper, stopped, and in a sharp voice, said, "Keri! We need to follow Floyd's orders."

Surprised at the shortness of his tone, she stopped, looked first at him and then at Floyd, who gave her a slight nod. She closed her sack, hefted it and the saddle blanket in one hand, the saddle in the other, and headed for her mule, Nibbles. Saddles and packs were quickly loaded, and they were on their way.

Before joining the road, Floyd stopped the column and gathered everyone, taking a few precious minutes to explain the situation. After he had finished, he said, "I do have an idea. Most of the folks in Blount County are against slavery. In fact, there's a hefty population of Quakers." Addressing Reuben and Keri, he said, "You do know it's Quakers we are taking you to."

They both acknowledged with a nod.

Floyd continued. "Keeping that in mind, I think we can take care of the chasers and Jolly and his partner at the same time." He looked at his brother Owen. "I'm thinking you and I pull off just before we get in sight of the ferry landing. With this wind, they'll never hear us. We'll ride through the trees and set up a little ambush of our own.

"Matt, you and Reuben can collect their guns after they know we have the drop on them. The river is close enough, and it'll make a great place to bury them, just the guns. We tie 'em, pull 'em up into the trees, and leave them with Tatum for a long, cold night."

As soon as Floyd stopped, Reuben spoke up. "When they get loose, won't they just follow us?"

Floyd smiled. "Got a plan for that, too. As soon as we drop you off, we'll head back to Limerick, but use the ferry north of this one. So everyone will see us riding north with you. I'm thinking there'll be a couple of the Quakers to take your place. A little dirt on their face and hands, and without a close inspection, this late, nobody will know. By the time we turn west, it'll be dark. People will think nothing of three men and a few mules traveling on a January night, except they're happy it's not them. By the time the chasers figure it out, you'll either be well hidden or on your way north."

"Got it," Reuben said.

Floyd looked at his brothers. "Does this make sense to you two?"

Both Owen and Matt nodded. Matt said, "Makes good sense to me. Now let's put this plan in action."

Floyd turned Jasper and headed out with everyone following him. They rode a short distance down the road, and Floyd pulled

Jasper to the side, motioning to Owen. Without a word, the two brothers trotted their mules into the timber.

They rode as fast as they dared, to get to the spot Floyd had in mind. Once there, Floyd stopped Jasper and stepped down. Owen followed suit. They tied the mules and eased forward through the trees until they could make out the ferry landing. Floyd's apprehension disappeared when he saw Tatum was still missing from the group. Getting set up, they waited.

It wasn't long before Matt, leading the pack mules, followed by Reuben and Keri, rounded the bend. Immediately the group of waiting men started checking their weapons, and, though they couldn't be heard, their agitation was obvious. A faint peal of laughter reached Floyd and Owen.

Floyd leaned close to his brother. "We don't want to shoot anyone if we can help it. The chasers have the law on their side even though they're in the wrong. I might toss a warning shot should it look necessary, but I prefer not to do it in case someone down there might have an itchy finger."

"Got it," Owen said.

Floyd watched Matt stop his mule. Jolly and the driver had Matt covered, while Johnson and Barnam marched back to Reuben and Keri, also pointing their rifles at the two. He saw Matt nod his head toward the hillside. With that movement all four sets of eyes turned toward his position. He and Owen stepped from the trees and waved. Floyd watched Johnson turn toward the big limb Tatum was tied behind, and wait. When nothing happened, Johnson took his hat from his head and waved it toward the trees. He turned, looked left and right, as if he expected Tatum to be somewhere else, but received no response.

Matt said something, and Jolly shook his head so hard, even from this distance, it looked like it would fly off. Matt said something else and pointed at Floyd. Everyone looked up while Floyd and Owen slowly brought their rifles to their shoulders.

Floyd knew this might bring one or more shots, but they had

to chance it, for the sun was about to go down. But instead of rifles raised, the men stood like statues while Reuben collected their rifles, knives, and pistols. He marched to the bank with his load, tossing everything into the river.

At that point the two brothers lowered the rifles, and Floyd said, "Why don't you get the mules, Owen."

Owen returned quickly with the mules. They mounted, rode a short distance to where the bank was sloping, and descended. As they approached, Floyd, his rifle resting across his legs, watched as Matt and Reuben tied the men's hands. He could see Johnson was mad, but Jolly's face was so red it looked as if he might explode. By the time Floyd and Owen made it to the group, Matt was finishing tying the four men's hands.

"Come on," Matt said, "it looks as if the ferry has made it to the other side, and he'll be starting back soon. We need to get these four hidden in the trees before they get here." Matt continued, speaking to the prisoners, "Get up the hill by the limb that's lying on the ground."

Jolly's face had now turned from brilliant red to a ghostly white. "You fellers ain't gonna kill us, are you?"

In a low, threatening voice, Johnson said to Jolly, "Shut up! They ain't gonna kill us. If they wanted to, they'd already done it."

They reached the limb and moved around the end, halting when they spotted Tatum still tied to it and gagged.

Floyd glanced across the river and jumped down from Jasper. "We've got to get these guys tied and be quick about it. The ferry is pulling away from the other side, but, mind my word, don't touch Tatum."

Matt motioned to the ground with his rifle. "Lie down." The four men did as they were ordered, stretching out on the rocky ground. Their legs were quickly tied.

Standing up, Owen asked, "We gonna gag 'em?"

"Nope," Floyd said. "They can yell to their hearts' content, and no one will hear them in this wind."

"Floyd Logan." It was Johnson calling him. "I'll catch those two slaves, and they'll regret running. And I'll tell you something else. I'm gonna find you, Logan. And when I find you, I'll kill you."

Floyd looked at the big man prone on the ground and shook his head. "Johnson, I'm headed for the Rocky Mountains. You want me, you'll have to come and get me. I'll be waiting for you, but let me give you a word to the wise. Don't mess with any Logans around here. This country's full of them, and they're all family. You hurt anyone around here, and you won't live the day out. *Adios.*"

Floyd turned back to Jasper, mounted, and headed for the landing, Matt and Owen following. The last he heard from Jolly was him screaming something about them freezing to death, while Johnson could faintly be heard cussing out Jolly. Before they reached the landing, they could hear nothing from the hill.

The men's horses were tied to the rail of the ferry landing. Floyd dismounted Jasper and untied them, wrapping the reins around their saddle horns. They began grazing on the grass they hadn't been able to reach from the landing.

After the horses were released, Floyd stood watching the approaching ferry and thought, *The light's growing dim. But we should still have enough time to get Reuben and Keri into Friendsville, and us out while there's still enough light for people to see us.*

The ferry arrived, banged against the landing, then continuously rocked in the waves. They rapidly loaded everyone and led the mules on board. The ferryman, and his assistant, looked around, shrugged, and pushed off. He and his assistant strained at the rope as they pulled the ferry across the river. Floyd, from past experience, knew this trip usually only took about ten minutes. But today, in the crosswind, it would take longer, maybe twice as long, because of the wind and the waves.

He looked at Matt and Owen, who were each holding two mules. Matt shrugged and looked up at the sky as if he was looking to heaven. Floyd grinned, nodded, and turned to check Reuben and Keri. Reuben was holding their mules, and Keri smiled back at him. Floyd patted Jasper on the neck, leaned forward, and said into one of the mules big ears, "She's calmer than any of us." Jasper, anything but calm, stared at him from a big dark eye. Floyd continued to pat and rub the frightened animal, in hopes of keeping him from trying to jump from the barge.

They gradually pulled past a southern point of land that blocked much of the ferocity of the wind and waves. The rivermen kept pulling on the rope, but became visibly relaxed. Floyd leaned close to the ferryman and said, "When's your last run?"

"Don't know where those other fellers are. I was supposed to pick them up on the last run, which this is. I don't know where they might be. They've been around the landing almost all day."

Floyd said, "Those fellas told me to tell you they were going to hang around on that side tonight. They'd see you in the morning."

The man shook his head. "This is promising to be some mighty bad weather. I sure wouldn't want to be out tonight."

"Yes siree," Floyd said, "I surely agree with you." He looked around, seeing the landing growing close. "How much we owe you?"

"A nickel apiece for horse or man or mule. That'll be sixty-five cents."

Floyd counted out the sixty-five cents, dropping it in the man's hand. "Much obliged. We'll see you on the way back."

The man nodded and, with his helper, began tying the ferry securely to the bank. Floyd and his party mounted and headed out. They passed several people, who looked up, smiled, and waved.

Reaching the Quaker church, the group dismounted, and Floyd trotted up to the door and knocked. There was no answer.

He was about to look for another entrance when a lady stepped from around one corner of the building.

Smiling at him, she said, "May I help thee, friend?" She wore a full-length dress, with a collared neckline, and cuffs tight around her wrists.

Floyd jerked his hat off and said, "Yes, ma'am. I sure hope you can. There's supposed to be someone here at this church who is expecting these folks." He pointed his hat at Reuben and Keri, who stood beside their mules.

"Please wait here, friend," she said, turned, and disappeared around the corner of the building.

She was gone only a minute or two before she reappeared with a man at her side. He wasted no time. "I am Brother Lambert, friend. Will thou bring the couple and follow me."

"You bet I will. Give us just a minute while they say their goodbyes."

"Please hurry, friend. They must be seen as little as possible here."

Floyd spun and jogged back to Reuben and Keri. "Come on, quickly. We've got to get you off the street."

"Oh," Keri gasped. She turned and threw her arms around the neck of her mule, Nibbles. "You have been so good to me." She gave the mule one last squeeze, turned and hugged first Matt and then Owen. "Thank you so much. You will never know just how much this means to us." Her tears ran quietly down her cheeks.

Owen pulled his hat from his head. "Miss Keri, it was a pleasure."

Matt did the same and said, "Ma'am, I'm glad we had the opportunity to help you. I hope you have a most prosperous life."

Keri stepped back and picked up her sack. Reuben extended his hand, first to Owen and then to Matt. Even the New York City attorney was choked up. He said simply, "Thank you."

Both Owen and Matt nodded, and Matt said, "Good luck to you both."

"We must hurry," Floyd said, then to his brothers, "I won't be long." He grabbed the sack from Keri while Reuben picked up his carpet bag. The three of them walked quickly to the waiting couple at the corner of the church.

"Come, friends," the man said. He led them around the side of the building, through some trees, and to an adjacent house. Stepping inside, he turned to Reuben and Keri. "You will be safe here."

Inside the house was warm and inviting, plus it felt good to be out of the wind. "We still need some help," Floyd said. "We've delayed slave-catchers across the river, but they will probably be here in the morning. We need two people to take the place of Reuben and Keri while we ride north of town to throw them off the path. It's getting dark. If they're about the same size and wearing their coats and hats, I don't think anyone will be able to tell any difference."

The man called to the front of the house. "David, Nancy, come here."

Two youths came from the front room. They were unable to take their eyes from the big scarred mountain man wearing buckskin and moccasins. "Yes, Papa?" they said in unison.

The man said to Floyd, Reuben, and Keri, "This is our son, David, and our daughter, Nancy." He placed his hand on the woman's arm, continuing, "My wife, Sister Lambert. I believe that my son and daughter are close enough to the same size. They will do fine."

Reuben and Keri had slipped from their coats and now handed them to the youth. Keri, with some shame, said, "Thank you. I am so sorry they are filthy. We have traveled a great distance."

"Thou need not worry," Mrs. Lambert said, having helped Keri remove her coat. "They will be fine."

After the coats and hats were on, Floyd gave them a cursory

look. "If you've got some charcoal handy, you might darken your hands and faces."

The two young people turned and ran into the front room. They were gone only a short time and were back, followed by the soft laughter of children. Nancy was still busy rubbing the charcoal across her forehead.

Reuben and Keri, upon seeing them, couldn't help but laugh.

Keri said, "I'm sorry, but you do look funny. Thank you for doing this."

Reuben, a wide grin on his face, said, "You two will do very well."

"Good," Floyd said. "We've got to be going."

Keri quickly grasped Floyd's left hand in both of hers and gazed up at the face of the scarred man. "Oh, Floyd, I want to thank you so much. Liza told us about your family. I know it was a huge sacrifice for you to help us. I so hope you find your family well when you get back to those mountains."

Reuben had grasped Floyd's right hand and was shaking it. "I cannot find words to describe my gratitude. If you ever need an attorney, I will be at your service. Thank you."

Floyd had never taken recognition or praise very well. Now was no different. Gruffly, he said, "It's been a real pleasure meeting both of you. Hopefully the rest of your trip will be as smooth as a fawn's back." He looked at Brother and Sister Lambert. "We'd best be going."

"Thank you, friend. May the Lord be with you and keep you safe in your journey."

## 17

F loyd opened the door and stepped out into the fading light, David and Nancy on his heels. Arriving at the mules, quick introductions were made, and everyone was soon mounted, headed slowly north out of town, passing many people waving and nodding at them.

Matt rode up next to Floyd. "They taken care of?"

"Yep, they're in good hands. I'm thinking they'll have no trouble making it home now, with us leaving enough sign to convince Johnson and his bunch we headed north with them."

"What about the youngsters? How far they going to go with us?"

"Not far. Brother Lambert mentioned their uncle runs the ferry north of town. That should work out well."

As they rode by the general store, four men stood beside the door, talking. They stopped for a moment to watch the procession, then went back to their discussion.

"This is good," Floyd said, once well past the store. "I think we've had enough people see us that it will fool Johnson."

They continued through town, passing several other people, while darkness slowly enveloped them. After leaving the last houses behind, Floyd pulled Jasper over and stopped. When David approached, he bumped Jasper to move out alongside the boy. "How far is your uncle's place?"

"Up the road about another mile, it forks. The right fork heads north, and the left is the road to Sparta and Nashville. Only another couple of miles after it forks."

"You think your uncle will be up to take us across tonight?"

Nancy, who was riding on the other side of her brother, spoke up. "Oh yes, he will be most happy to help once he is told what thou hast done."

It wasn't too dark for Floyd to see the frown cast from David to his sister. "I was about to say that," the boy said.

"But thou didn't, did thou?"

"Well," Floyd said, interrupting the brewing argument, "I'm much obliged for the help you two are giving us. I think your disguises have fooled quite a few people. I figure we have seen the last of the slave-chasers." With that he bumped Jasper and moved back into the lead with Matt.

They continued in silence, taking the left turn when they reached the fork. After completing the turn, Matt said, "These mules are tired. They had a long five days and need some rest."

Floyd nodded in acknowledgment. "Yep, they've done a yeoman's job. You remember that big cave, west of the river?"

"I do. Pa liked to use it whenever we were traveling to see relatives."

"That's the one. There's water, and there used to be good grass for the mules. Course, it'll be dry, but it should still be good, and I'm thinking the weather is going to be changing here real soon. That might be a good place to hole up."

Matt looked up at the star-studded sky, high thin clouds beginning to obscure the stars in the northwest, and said, "You're right. I was watching it close while we were at the church, and you can feel the wind has dropped some, and it's starting to swing to the west. As far as the mules, they haven't started balking yet, so we oughta be fine."

Ahead, lights from a house came into view.

"That's my uncle's place up ahead," David called.

Floyd, without turning, gave a wave, and they continued. Reaching the house, both David and Nancy leaped from their mules and raced toward the door. David beat his sister by no more than a couple of steps, disappearing into the house with her on his heels. Owen gathered up the reins of their mules, and they all waited.

Shortly, a tall slim man with a torch, followed by the two siblings, came walking from the house. Reaching them, he said, "Understand you fellas need a ride across the river?"

"Yes, sir. We sure do," Floyd said. "David, I want to thank you and Nancy for helping us and the Fosters. Like I told you earlier, I think we've fooled several people, and I'm sure that'll be a big help. You tell your pa I'm much obliged."

David, smiling up with his blackened face, said, "Pa always says, 'If you're not helping people, you don't deserve to be here.'"

"Your pa is a good man, and those are mighty fine words."

"We'd best get moving," the riverman said. Following up first to his nephew, "Why don't you give me a hand," and then to Nancy, "Tell 'em we'll be right back." Walking past Floyd, he said, "The ferry's right this way."

Floyd and his brothers tipped their hats to Nancy as they rode by. Once there, Floyd jumped down, while Matt and Owen held the mules, and helped David and the man untie and position the ferry. With three of them working, they had it ready quickly. As soon as it was lined up and stable, the other two brothers led the mules onto the ferry. The man nodded to David, and he cast off the ropes. He turned, grasped the guide rope, and started pulling.

Floyd stayed with his brothers at first, assisting with the mules. However, with the wind dying down and the waves no longer breaking over the side of the ferry, the mules stood calm and relaxed. After watching them for a few more minutes, Floyd said, "Looks like the mules are fine. How about if I give you a hand?"

Both David and the man were pulling the rope now. "I'd be obliged, Mr. . .?"

Floyd grabbed the rope behind David, began pulling, and said, "Floyd Logan, and those are my brothers Matt and Owen." They nodded to the man.

"Howdy, my name's Frank Lambert."

Floyd continued to pull, the ferry picking up speed after he joined in. "If I was to be asked, Frank, I'd have to say you don't sound like your brother."

"Well, my brother and I are alike in many ways. I'm just not a member of the church, not his church. It's a long story. Let's just say my wife didn't like changing her religion. She has a mind of her own."

"Didn't mean to pry," Floyd said, "but I noticed you didn't talk the same."

"Used to, just got out of practice. Now let me ask you something. You boys the Limerick Logans?"

"That we are," Floyd said as the ferry grounded against the landing. He straightened, stretched his back, and took the reins of Jasper and Queeny from Owen and led them off the ferry. Once off, he handed the reins back and returned to Frank and David. "How much we owe you?"

"Normally, it'd be fifty cents. But I don't charge men when they're doing what you fellas are doing. Anyway, I've never seen you. I just imagine you must have taken the other fork in the road, and that's what I'll tell anyone who asks."

"I appreciate that, but I'd not ask any man to run this river, on a night like this, for free."

"Son, I understand what you're saying, but you ain't asking, I'm giving. Let me receive a blessing for helping you. On the other hand, you *can* do me a favor. Tell your pa I said howdy, and it's been a while."

Floyd extended his hand. "Thanks, Frank. I'll sure tell him." After shaking Frank's hand, he shook David's and mounted Jasper. The three men and seven mules rode west, along the darkened trail.

Matt, riding behind him with two of the mules, called, "You think you can remember where we leave this trail, or do you need some help?"

Floyd, turning in the saddle to respond, noticed it had grown even darker, for he could barely make out the outline of his brother. Foregoing his comment, he checked the sky again. From their current position to where the western horizon should be, no stars could be seen, and now there were lower clouds moving fast from the northwest. He turned back to Matt, whom he could faintly see looking up at the sky. "Matt, we may get wet before we get to that cave."

"Possibly, but if I'm remembering right, it's no more than five miles from the river. These ole long ears may have some steam left. Why don't we pick up the pace."

They urged the mules into a trot, held it for about a mile, and brought them back to a fast walk for another mile. The wind had died completely out, but the clouds overhead were moving faster. Approaching the area Floyd remembered, he slowed Jasper and began looking for the prominent shelf of rocks that marked the turnoff.

They were almost on top of it when they picked it out, a darker shadow in the dark night. They turned off the trail as a blast of frigid wind struck. Beneath the trees, with no light from the few remaining stars, it was almost pitch black. Floyd could barely make out the slope of the ridge to his near right. He gave Jasper his head, allowing the mule to set his own pace through the forest. He took a quick glance back to make sure that everyone was still with him. He couldn't see past Matt. His brother must've realized his concern, for he checked Owen's position, turned back, and signaled Floyd to keep going.

Relieved, he allowed Jasper to continue, knowing that even at this slow pace, the cave shouldn't be more than fifteen minutes away. The base of the ridge he was following had begun to steepen. He dismounted and moved closer to the base so he could feel along the sloping rock wall with his hand.

He could hear thunder rumbling in the distance. Even as far away as it must be, each flash, though blocked by the ridge, lightened the sky enough he could see forward. He kept moving. Fortunately, the ridgeline was blocking much of the wind, and he gave thanks that this cave was on the south side of the ridge. Had it been on the other side, the wind would have been blowing directly into it.

Floyd knew this trail was wide enough for a wagon, so he was not deeply concerned about falling off a ledge in the darkness. His pa had used the cave many times when he was traveling in the wagon. The lightning grew brighter, the thunder louder, and the mules crankier.

In the last flash, the cave blossomed ahead, no more than thirty feet. At that same moment a deluge of water poured from the sky. When the lightning flashed, Floyd noted the open ground between him and the cave and began running with Jasper. Matt and Owen, who had remained mounted, urged their mules forward. The animals and men ran for the shelter. Reaching the entrance, Floyd ran into it, leading Jasper. Though the ridgeline had provided protection, both of them were already soaked. The rain was deafening, making it impossible to hear anything or anyone else.

Floyd led Jasper to one side of the cave, leaving room for his brothers and the other mules. He opened his possibles bag and pulled out a small oilskin pouch. After untying two buckskin strings securing it closed, he pulled out a dry lucifer. He was standing next to the south interior wall. He rolled the oilskin pouch tight and struck the lucifer against the wall. Light flared in the cave.

*This is it,* Floyd thought as he looked around the cavern.

There were a lot of caves in this country, and he could see why Pa had picked this one. The entrance was wide and high, allowing space for horses and even the wagon. Before the match went out, Floyd could see that after about fifteen feet, it started tapering down until at the back, it was no more than seven or eight feet high and fifteen or so feet wide. He remembered, as a boy, when they had stopped here. He wanted to go exploring the back of the cave. Ma had told him not to, because you never knew what kind of beast could be waiting in the shadows, or where a pit might be. He hadn't listened, and it was only Pa's protection, for he understood Floyd's need to explore, that kept him from getting a very sore bottom.

Matt yelled over the din of the rain, "Let's get this gear off these animals and get them rubbed down." He had already begun unsaddling Badger.

Floyd chastised himself for not thinking first of Jasper, and began unsaddling him. Though the darkness was thick, he finished quickly and moved the gear to the side of the cave. With the heavy rain falling, He felt no concern any of the mules would wander from the cave. So he moved slowly, in the dark, feeling with his feet for the firepit. Unfortunately, he found the stacked wood before he found the pit, crashing across the wood. "I'm all right," he called. "I just had some firewood jump up and attack me."

He heard Owen's laughter over the rain. After locating the firewood in such an effective manner, he began looking for and found starter material. From there he crawled forward, feeling for the pit. Finding it, Floyd put in some of the starter, pulled out another lucifer and struck it. It flamed and quickly lit the dry starter. Once lit, he stacked a few small twigs across the tiny blaze and waited. He didn't have to wait long. The twigs caught rapidly, and soon he laid several larger limbs across the fire.

"Now that's one of the most welcome sights I've seen today," Owen said.

Matt chimed in, "I'll second that."

Floyd reached for the stacked wood, picked up two split logs, and added them to the fire. The flames licked at the wood, tasting the fibers and liking them. Soon, the fire blazed, sending warmth and light throughout the cave.

The contrast between the inside and the outside of the cave was almost overpowering. Inside was dry and growing warmer. Outside, the roar of the rain, falling in sheets, driven by a fierce frigid wind, battled to overcome the comfort enjoyed by men and animals. Shadows from the flames danced across the walls and ceiling, as if they were lonely souls of the past condemned to the cave and celebrating human contact.

Floyd stood from the fire, examining their shelter. "I've got to say I'm mighty beholden to whoever last stayed here. That's a fine stack of wood. It should last us until this rain lets up, and we can get more cut."

Owen, busy wiping down his mule, Theo, said, "I'm beholden to Pa for showing us this place. I'd sure hate to be out in that rain right now."

Matt laughed and then shouted, "Yes, sir. I can't think of anything much more miserable than being soaked in that cold rain and wind, with no hope of getting warm or dry anytime in the near future."

The brothers continued to unsaddle and unpack the mules. They had stopped trying to talk over the din of the rain, which now had gotten even heavier. Water poured over the lip of the cave, hammering and washing deep ruts before disappearing into the darkness. Floyd stopped what he was doing, pulled a bucket out of the supplies, eased close to one of the cascades, and slipped the bucket under the pouring water. He then went back to taking care of the mules.

In a short time the bucket filled and began running over. He retrieved the bucket, and, starting with Jasper, he started watering the mules. When his brothers saw what he was doing, they took turns watering the animals.

Owen had always been the best cook of the boys. He now pulled out the utensils he needed, a big slab of bacon, and the sack with the remaining biscuits Ma had donated.

Before long, the smell of frying bacon filled the cave. Matt and Floyd finished with the mules, arranged saddles, bedding, and blankets, and settled down with Owen around the fire.

"Owen," Floyd said, "that bacon smells better than the finest meal you could find in Nashville."

"Yep," Matt said. "It surely does. Of course, any meal I don't have to cook is a mighty fine meal."

When the eating began, the talking ended. While they were eating, the rain ceased. It happened so suddenly, not only did the men look outside the cave and into the darkness, but several of the mules, who were still facing the fire, turned their heads to look out. Now, instead of the roaring rain, all that could be heard was the moan of the wind through the trees and boulders, and the drip, drip, drip, of water falling from the cave lip, rocks, and trees.

Floyd shook his head. "My ears are still ringing. That was some of the hardest, loudest rain I've seen in a long time. I'm guessing there could have been some cyclones in that, somewhere."

"Could be," Matt said, "but they weren't here, and I'm mighty glad of that." He yawned and stretched. "I'm thinking we should hobble these mules now that the rain has stopped. Once that's done, I'm sacking out. These bones are getting too old for this kind of travel."

Floyd and Owen laughed as they stood and joined Matt, hobbling the animals.

Once finished, they slipped under their bedding, stretching their tired bodies.

After a few moments, Owen said, "Floyd, are you asleep?"

"Considering it, but not yet. Why?"

# 18

---

"When we were tying up that bunch at the landing, you made a comment about staying away from Tatum. That's stuck with me. He looked like he was well tied, and I guess one of us might have gone over and checked his bindings, but that was just kinda curious."

Floyd chuckled. "I'm guessing those boys are having a rough night, especially if they haven't gotten untied yet.

"I was in a hurry, but that wasn't it. When Tatum had that little scuffle with me, he kinda fell back against a tree, unconscious. What made matters worse for him was he had turned as he was falling and hit facing the tree. As if that wasn't bad enough, he slid down the trunk, his hands and face dragging against the bark. And guess what was growing up the side of that tree?"

Both of the brothers started laughing, and Matt said, "You have got to be kidding."

"Yes siree, poison ivy. It was all over that tree. He was all but wallowing in it. So, not only did it get on his face and hands, but all over the front of his clothes. By the time he figures out what he got into, he, and any of the other fellas who release him, will probably have it all over themselves."

"Floyd," Owen said, "that's about the best bedtime story I've heard in a long time. You were mighty lucky not to get any on you."

"I was luckier than you think. You remember how Ma used to rub us down with jewelweed when we got into it?"

A couple of acknowledging grunts came from his brothers.

"I went straight to a pond and found some. Of course, this time of year it's dead and dried, but I didn't have anything to lose. I crushed a bunch of it and, using the pond water, rubbed it all over me. Either it worked, or I was purely lucky."

"Lucky, little brother," Owen said, "you were always lucky."

Floyd continued to chuckle until his mind drifted back to the mountains and Leotie. As cold as it was here, he knew it was much colder where she was. The past few days, with all of the activity, had kept the worry chased from his mind. Still, it occasionally slipped back to gnaw at him, and in the cave, firelight casting the dancing figures on the walls, it came back with a vengeance.

He knew she would be out in the snow and cold, moving from teepee to teepee, tending the sick, delivering babies. Leotie always put others before herself. Now that evil word *smallpox* slipped back into trouble his mind.

While he had been at the last rendezvous, he and Jeb had learned smallpox was infecting the northern tribes. The word was, it had been brought in by eastern traders, and the Blackfoot, up around the Missouri River, were being decimated. He prayed it would stay up north.

His mind labored over his concerns until finally drifting off into a troubled sleep.

~

LATE MORNING, the following Tuesday, found them nearing the turnoff to Limerick and Short Mountain. The three brothers rode side by side, with Floyd in the middle and the remaining mules following in train.

Matt said, "Floyd, it's been real good seeing you. Other than the constant fear of being shot, drowned, or thrown in jail, I'd say this has been a fine trip."

Owen said, "Yep, it sure has. Though, I'm not sure my heart can take this kind of excitement more than about once every ten years."

Floyd laughed. "I understand your thinking, Owen. If I pick up a scar every time I come home, I think ten years is more than often enough."

Laughter broke out again from the brothers. After it had quieted down, Matt said, "All kidding aside, it's been good to have you home, and you couldn't have timed it better. I know Ma and Pa were really happy to see you and enjoyed your being home for a while. I'll tell you something else, too. I think if Wallace and Callum could figure out how, they'd hide in your saddlebags and go to the mountains with you."

"Those are fine boys you got there, Matt," Floyd said. "Maybe, one of these days, I'll get to show them and all of you the mountains."

They rode a distance in silence. The sky had cleared except for a thin layer of high clouds, which were doing their best to withhold what little warmth the January sun provided.

Owen spoke up. "I'm thinking about going west, myself."

Surprised, both Matt and Floyd turned in the saddle to look at Owen, and Floyd said, "You're joshing me."

"Not at all," Owen said, watching ahead, more musing than answering his brothers directly. "My farm adjoins Matt's. I might sell it to him. I found I don't have a great interest in farming, and I certainly don't have a desire to see the mountains. I'm really inter-ested in going to Texas and maybe starting a ranch. I have some money saved, and whatever Matt feels like paying me for the property should set me right up."

Matt looked aghast, and Floyd was nodding his head. "Makes sense. There's a lot of opportunity there now, what with them being an independent republic. It's wide open. Of course, they're having a lot of Indian trouble. If you go where you can set up a good-size ranch, you'll be right in the middle of Comanche and Kiowa trouble. When are you planning on doing this?"

Owen contemplated the question for a time. "Soon. Not today, but soon. I've been thinking about it for quite a while."

Matt leaned forward and looked around Floyd at Owen. "You've never said anything about this to me."

Owen nodded. "You're right, but after Sue and the baby died, I've kinda lost interest in the farm, and everywhere reminds me of her. Course, it's taken quite a while to get past losing her, but I'm getting there. It'll be a lot easier if I'm not reminded of her everywhere I go." He thought about it and gave an emphatic nod. "Yep, I'm going."

"Have you said anything to Ma and Pa?" Matt asked.

"Not yet, but I will. And, Matt, don't say anything to anyone about this." Now it was Owen's turn to look past Floyd at Matt. "Not until I tell the rest of the family!"

Matt nodded. "I hear you, brother. I'll say nothing, not even to Rebecca, until you give me the go-ahead. By the way, I'll buy your land anytime you're ready to sell. That's choice property, good for horse pasture and farming."

The three brothers rode on in silence, each deep in his own thoughts, and each dreading their parting. The soft pad of the mules' hooves, on the dirt road, marked the passage of their time together.

Finally, Matt broke the silence. "Floyd, you planning on traveling straight through to the mountains?"

"No, I'm not. I'll be stopping in Nashville to meet a fella there. I met him in Independence this last time through. He was in a mite of trouble, and I helped him out. Haven't any idea what he wants, but he asked me to stop by. So that's what I'll do. Then I need to drop these horses off in Dyersburg, where I catch the riverboat. I'll leave the boat in St. Louis and head on over to Independence by stage. Probably spend a day or so there, pick up my animals and supplies, and head on out for the mountains."

"I reckon," Owen said, "it'll take a little more than just talking about it."

"Yep, two to three months. Two if everything goes well, and three, well, let's just say I'm not planning on three."

A small village showed up ahead, just two or three houses. Off to the left side of the road, unable to yet be identified, a man, his hat pulled over his face, lay resting against a large oak tree. Three horses cropped grass nearby, saddles and packs on the ground next to the man. Even as they were watching him, he reached up, lifted the hat just high enough from his face to see down the road, looked for a moment, then stood and waved the hat before putting it back on his head.

"Looks like Nathan beat us here," Owen said.

Even as Owen spoke, Nathan began saddling the horses. By the time they arrived, he had finished saddling two and was positioning the packs on the third. Finished, he slapped the bay on the rump and walked over to them.

"Glad to see you all made it back in one piece. Did the Fosters make it okay?"

"So are we," Floyd said as they all shook hands. "They did. We had a couple of little bumps in the road, but everything turned out well."

"Good. Ma and Pa will be real glad to hear those folks made it safely. You heading west now?"

"I am, Nathan. As it stands, I could be as late as March getting back home. I'm still hoping they're all fine."

"Sorry you didn't get to town. Everyone was asking about you. Mr. Webley asked me to tell you howdy and wish you well."

"Mr. Webley . . . Nathan, I'm mighty glad you reminded me of him." Floyd walked over to the bay packhorse and opened one of the packs, shoving his arm deep inside. He felt around for a moment, then pulled out three elk-hide bags. With the heavy bags in hand, he walked back over to Nathan. Once there he dropped two of the bags to the ground and opened the remaining one. "Hold out your hand."

Nathan held out his big hand, and Floyd started counting out gold eagles. He stopped at ten and said, "Nathan, if you don't mind, next time you're by Mr. Webley's store, give him this. He gave me that pistol when he had absolutely no thought of being paid for it. You tell him his pistol saved my life several times, and don't let him buck up at the amount. He took a chance on a kid who, I suspect, he never expected to return. This is interest. Tell him I'm much obliged." He pulled the drawstrings tight on the still full bag, turned, and tossed it to Owen.

Owen caught it, hefted it for a moment, and said, "What's this, Floyd?"

Without answering, Floyd bent and picked up the other two bags, handing them to Matt, for which he received a frown. "All right, I know you all have questions. Matt, that first bag is for Ma and Pa. The second bag is to be divided up among the kids."

All three of his brothers took deep breaths to speak, and Floyd, anticipating the arguments, held up both hands. "Now listen, let me explain. I'm not much of a drinker, and I've been successful trapping over these years, so I saved up some money. I'm sure all of you remember Hugh Brennan, the man who took me west. I worked for him for a while, and he offered to help me invest my money, which he has. I've done quite well. I've got everything I need or want in those mountains, and the money he's invested for me just keeps growing. So don't tell me you can't take it. You're my family, and I want you to have it.

"Owen, I think that'll come in handy for you. In fact, this"—

he indicated the three bags—"might be an aid to all of you. Do with your portion as you see fit. That's all I've got to say."

Matt was first to speak. "Floyd, I don't know what to say, but thank you, brother. This will help all of us, and most importantly, it will chase away a lot of the worry for our folks. But I'm concerned about you. You still have a long way to go. I hope there's enough to get you back home."

Floyd grinned at his brother. "Don't worry about me. I still have a couple more of these in my bags. I'll be fine."

Owen spoke up next. "If I ever had any doubt as to what I'm going to do, my mind is made up now. Thanks, Floyd."

Nathan extended his hand again, and Floyd felt the strong, gratifying pressure of his brother's hand. "Thank you, Floyd."

Floyd looked at each of the men standing in front of him. These were his brothers. He might never see them again. "Well, boys, I'd best be on my way. Tell Ma and Pa I'm real sorry I didn't spend as much time as I had planned with them. It don't change the fact that I love them a bunch, and tell Martha and Jennifer I'm sorry, but I have to get back. Be sure to tell Ezra it was good seeing him, and we'll make that squirrel hunt yet, and all of his mules were great, and Jasper is a mighty fine animal."

He looked at them once more, shook their hands, swung onto the back of the sorrel, and said, "*Adios.*" With the bay's lead dallied around his saddle horn, Floyd headed west.

STARS EMERGED in the darkening sky as Floyd rode through the streets of Nashville. The past two days had ticked by slowly. His desire to race the thousand miles back to Leotie battled with his common sense.

Fortunately, for him and the horses, good sense had won out. Reaching the livery, he stopped at the watering troughs in front and dismounted. After allowing the horses time to drink, he led them into the stable. Floyd could hear someone mucking out one of the stalls in the back of the barn. Once inside, he dropped the horses' reins, returned to the door, and rolled it shut.

At the sound of the rollers grinding over the guide, the man working in the stall stopped what he was doing and stepped out where he could see. Upon spotting Floyd and the horses, he leaned his shovel against the side wall of the stall and walked forward. "Need to leave your horses?" the man said, his voice cracking halfway through the sentence.

Floyd examined the young man. *It might be stretching it*, he thought, *to call him a man. He looks like an overgrown boy. He definitely has the size of a man, but that's about all.*

"Hiya, mister," the man said, grinning and rubbing his dirty hands on his manure-covered trousers, "my name's Bobby Sutton. Whatcha need?" extending his still dirty hand to Floyd. Floyd grinned back, taking the extended hand and giving it a good shake.

"Floyd Logan, Bobby. I need to put these horses up for at least tonight, maybe longer."

"Why, yes, sir, I can sure do that." Eagerly, and still grinning, Bobby continued, "I just finished cleaning out the stalls and put fresh straw in each one, and I'll give them a good rubdown and some corn besides the hay I just put in there, and I'll bring them some fresh water, too. Is that all right with you?"

Floyd found himself liking this young man immediately. Bobby was tall, with a broad, innocent face, clear blue eyes, and blond hair hanging to his shoulders. "That would be perfect, Bobby," Floyd said. "I'll be staying the night either at the Broadway Hotel or the Nashville Inn, should you need to find me. How much do I owe you?"

Bobby shook his head. "Oh, no, sir, you don't owe me nothin'. You can pay my uncle Fletcher when you leave. He owns this stable. If you just stay the night, I can tell you it won't be much at all. My uncle don't charge no more than twenty-five cents a night.

Course, it will be an extra nickel apiece for the corn. He says corn is expensive. But you don't need to pay until you leave. You headed west?"

"I am, Bobby, all the way back to the Rocky Mountains." Floyd patted the packs on the sorrel. Do you think my supplies and gear will be fine here? I'd be mighty upset if anything went missing."

Bobby responded, nodding enthusiastically, "Yes, sir. Nothin' ever gits stolen from my uncle. Folks around here respect him almighty strong."

Floyd nodded, turning his back to Bobby as he dug through one of the packs on the bay. Finally when he retrieved what he was looking for, he slipped the items into his saddlebags, fastened them, and turned back to Bobby. "In that case, if you have a place to store the packs from this horse, I'd appreciate you doing that. Also, just hang up those two horse pistols, and I'll get them when I leave."

"Yes, sir, Mr. Floyd. I'll be sure to do that. You have a nice night."

"You too, Bobby," Floyd said, slid his rifle from the scabbard, and stepped out into the cold night.

It was only a short walk to the Broadway Hotel, and he enjoyed stretching his legs. Stepping through the etched-glass double doors, he walked straight to the desk. The clerk, who sat behind the reception desk, rose, straightened his vest, and watched him approaching.

"May I help you, sir?"

"You sure can," Floyd said. "I need a room and to know the number of my friend's room."

"May I ask his name, sir?" the desk clerk asked while laying the sign-in ledger in front of Floyd.

Floyd turned the ledger slightly, signed in, and spun it back around for the desk clerk while stating, "Mr. Ransom Gates."

The clerk looked up from the ledger and said, "Yes, sir. Mr.

Gates is here. He stays with us quite often. Do you have business with him?"

"You might say that. What room is he in?"

"You'll find him just down the hall from you. He turned, examined the cubbyholes for a specific key, selected it, and handed it to Floyd. "You will be in room number two ten, Mr. Logan. You will find Mr. Gates in two eighteen. Do you have any bags, sir?" As he spoke, the desk clerk stood on tiptoe, placed his hands on his desk, and looked over the counter so he could see the floor.

"Nope, just these." Floyd held up his rifle and saddlebags.

Lifting the saddlebags, Floyd's left arm came above the counter and near the clerk's face. He jerked back while grabbing a white handkerchief from his vest pocket. Holding it up to his nose, and then realizing his reaction to a hotel guest, he performed an obvious fake sneeze and sheepishly looked back up at Floyd.

"I am so sorry, sir. Please forgive my rudeness."

"Don't you worry. I'm thinking I must be a little ripe. What's the chances of getting a bath around here?"

Relieved, the clerk replied, "Oh, yes, sir. I'll have a tub and water brought up to your room immediately."

"Much obliged," Floyd said. He started toward the stairs, stopped, and turned back to the clerk. "Forgot to ask. What do I owe you?"

"Oh, no, sir. You are a friend of Mr. Gates. We can take care of the room charges when you leave."

"Thanks," Floyd replied, turning back to the stairs. Up the stairs and to his room was only a short distance. He glanced down the lamp-lit hall, thought only for a moment about knocking on Ransom Gates's door, discarded it for a bath first, and opened his door.

## 19

A typical hotel room, larger than most and a little plusher, but still a hotel room. One thing he did like, in addition to the stiff-back chair at the dresser, was a large, soft armchair with a rectangular cushioned stool at its foot.

He had no sooner laid his rifle across the bed and dropped his saddlebags into the big chair than a knock came at the door. "Service, sir, with your tub and bathwater."

In two long steps he was across the room and had opened the door. Two young men, each with one hand gripping the opposite end of a tub and the other hand holding a wooden bucket containing steaming hot water, stood at the door. "Your bath, sir."

Floyd stepped back, pulled the door wide, and allowed the young men entry into his room. They moved quickly to an open area near the armoire and set the tub on the floor. After removing the two large towels with bar soap from the tub and placing them on the bed, they poured in the hot water. The shorter man said, "Mr. Logan, we will be right back with more water."

Stepping quickly from the room, they disappeared through the door. Within minutes they were back, each carrying two more buckets of hot water. After repeating this action once more, the shorter man said to Floyd, "Mr. Logan, I am James"—and indicating his companion—"and this is Philip. If you need anything else this evening, please ask for us."

Floyd fished out two twenty-cent pieces, extending one to each man. James's and Phillip's faces lit up. James, who evidently was the spokesman for the two, said, "Why, thank you, sir. Oh, the man to ask for, should you need anything during the day, is Randolph. He will be more than happy to assist you." With this last comment, James ushered Philip rapidly from the room, grasped the door handle as he was leaving, and smiling, said, "Good night, sir," and pulled the door shut.

Floyd walked to the straight-backed chair, picked it up and slid the top against the door latch, effectively blocking his door. Then he turned to his saddlebags, pulled out some clean long johns and a clean heavy wool shirt, laid them on the bed, and quickly stripped. He tested the water with a toe. Not quite hot enough to parboil, but plenty hot to wash away miles of dirt and relax tired muscles.

He scrubbed himself with the rough soap bar until his skin turned red. With the bucket James had left, he dipped and poured soapy water over his head and his dirt-caked, shoulder-length hair. Floyd had never been much of a wearer of beards, a carryover from his mother's dislike, and now, as he washed his face, the ten-day-old growth irritated him.

The cooling water chased him from the tub. He grabbed a towel from the bed, stood, and quickly dried the remaining drops from his body. In the dresser mirror, Floyd examined the cut he had received from Tatum. It was healing nicely. Then, he pulled his razor from his bag, lathered the shaving brush, and went to work clearing the growth from his face. Once finished, he paused to looked at the scars he had accumulated in the last ten years of his short twenty-seven years on this earth.

He momentarily considered each scar. However, he didn't think about the pain or danger or fear. Each carried him to the location of the incident and the wonderful land he had been fortunate to see with his own eyes.

First, his mind saw the Neosho River and Post Office Oak. Without thinking, his left hand reached for his cheek and followed the thin scar that ran from cheekbone to jaw, while his mind saw the waving ocean of grass extending as far as the eye could see. Next, he touched the pouty scars on his left bicep, where the Comanche arrow had pierced his arm, and saw the majesty of the Cimarron. The green of the tall cottonwoods along the river punctuated the reds and yellows of the broken and rocky land. Again, his hand drifted across the streak of white that ran through his dark brown hair. Though the huge bear was there, he saw the shimmering quaking aspen, heard the gurgling of the stream, and smelled the fresh pines of his beloved mountains.

Floyd's growling stomach snapped him from his reverie. Still looking in the mirror, he said, "You've got a long way to go, son," and wondered if he was talking about this thousand-mile journey remaining before him, or, maybe, being a little prophetic.

Quickly pulling on his faded long johns, he couldn't help but notice his elbows protruded from the red wool. *I need some new long johns. In fact,* he thought, *I need a whole batch of clothes.* After he had finished shaving, he slipped the clean but worn woollen shirt on over his long johns and finished getting dressed. He removed a pistol from its holster, checked it, slipped it back in the holster, and swung the belt around his waist. After buckling the belt, he positioned it so the pistol was handy and moved his knife to where it rode comfortably.

Stepping back to his saddlebags, he removed the two elk-hide bags of coins and looked around the room. Floyd knew an accomplished thief could find them no matter where they were hidden, but he wanted to make the man earn his money. There was a hook on one end of the armoire. He picked up his shirt and long johns, and before he hung them on the hook, he hung one bag of coins, then covered them with the clothes. *If he wants to dig through those stinking things,* Floyd thought, *then I guess he'll find it.* He dropped the other bag in his pocket and opened the door to leave the room. He was met by James, with Philip in tow.

"How was your bath, Mr. Logan?" James said.

"Mighty fine. Feel like a new man."

"I am glad, sir. Shall we take the tub and the other things?"

"You certainly can, and thanks so much," Floyd said, reaching into his pocket.

James held his hand up. "Oh, no, sir. We have been more than adequately compensated. You have a good night."

"Thank you, James. Good night to you both." With that he strode down the hall to room two eighteen. Stepping up to the door, Floyd knocked twice and was surprised to see it immediately open.

"Floyd Logan, it is a pleasure to see you. Please come in," Ransom said while shutting the door. He grasped Floyd's hand and shook it enthusiastically. "I was wondering if you would make it before I left, and I am so glad you did. All is well with your family?"

"They are all doing very well," Floyd said. "I can honestly say that I'm glad I made this trip. Our time together was very special."

Once inside, Floyd examined Ransom's room. It was much larger than his. Of course, it had the bed, dresser, dresser chair, padded footrest and the big chair. But it also had a large table and a desk with a desk chair. However, it wasn't the additional furniture that caught Floyd's attention. It was what was resting on top of the table. Most of the space was taken up with weapons. Superb weapons, of a type he had never seen before. He walked directly to the table, and without taking his eyes from the weapons, asked, "You mind?"

"Of course not. I laid these weapons out for you to see. What do you think?"

In awe, Floyd picked up the nearest handgun, examining it

closely. Minutes passed while he inspected and handled the first one he picked up. "What do you call this?"

"That," Ransom said, "is the Colt Paterson number five revolver."

Floyd examined the muzzle and the empty chambers of the revolver. "Thirty-six caliber?"

"Yes. Thirty-six caliber and five shots. You load it once and shoot five times before needing to reload again."

Floyd turned and stared at Ransom, then shaking his head, whispered, "Five times. That would be a real surprise to some folks out west."

Ransom laughed heartily. "Believe me, Floyd, that's a real surprise to folks back east."

Floyd chuckled at Ransom's comment. "I reckon." He continued to examine the revolver, finally laying it down to pick up one of the rifles. He turned it so he could see the chambers and counted, "One, two, three," continuing until he reached eight. "This looks like about forty-four."

"Yes, sir, forty-four caliber and a twenty-eight-inch barrel. What you're holding, Floyd, is a Colt Second Model Ring Rifle. I'm sure you've already noticed, the rifle you're holding doesn't have an exposed hammer. To cock the hammer and rotate the cylinder, you pull the ring, located in front of the trigger guard, to the rear. Once it's cocked, it fires like any other rifle. So if you were equipped with this rifle and two of these revolvers, you would have the firepower of eighteen men carrying muzzle loaders. Can you imagine what that might do to an Indian attack?"

Floyd laid the rifle down and turned to Ransom. "These are mighty nice weapons, but I'm betting they're mighty expensive."

Ransom sat on the edge of the bed and indicated the easy chair for Floyd. He waited until Floyd relaxed in the chair, and said, "Compared to today's weapons, yes, they are, but I'm sure you can see the potential firepower they provide for anyone who owns them." Floyd started to speak, and Ransom held up a hand.

"Floyd, you saved my life. The owner of this company, Samuel Colt, is a friend of mine and also my boss. We've known each other since we were kids, and he is a great inventor. I saw what he did with these revolvers, and I implored him to allow me to be a salesman for him.

"When I returned to New Jersey and told him about what you did and how you prevented my death, he said that a mountain man like you needs this kind of protection."

Floyd had been relaxing in the soft chair, but now sat forward to object to what he felt he knew was coming. Ransom grinned and again raised his hand. "This is a gift, Floyd, for the way you fearlessly stepped in and drove those men from me. Mr. Colt wants you to pick out any two revolvers and any rifle. They are yours, with his and my deep gratitude." With that, Ransom nodded to Floyd.

"I can talk now?"

"Yes, as much as you want."

"First, I'm amazed at such an offer. These look like exceptional weapons any man would be proud to have. I was definitely considering turning this down, because frankly, Ransom, those men may have just been robbing you and not planning on killing you. But turning down a gift from an Indian can get you in bad trouble, and I've learned a lot from those folks. So, simply put, I accept, and you can tell Mr. Colt that I am mighty pleased to have his weapons. I'm sure, over the years, they will save my life many times." He leaned forward and extended his hand to Ransom.

They shook hands, and Ransom said, "You had me worried, Floyd. I thought I might have to fight you to get you to take them."

This time, Floyd grinned at him. "I'll tell you a secret. You would've won hands down."

"Now I wish I had. Then I could say I whipped the famous mountain man Floyd Logan."

At that, they both laughed, and Ransom said, "We can go out

tomorrow, and I'll show you the workings of them and give you a chance to shoot them."

FLOYD POPPED the reins and clucked to the dun mare, guiding the horse west on the main street. "I reckon you have a favorite spot."

"Yes, I certainly do," Ransom said. "Continue straight. As soon as we're out of town, which won't take long, there is a perfect place. A small open knoll with a few handy trees." He pulled his heavy coat tighter. "My, it is quite chilly this morning."

Floyd yawned and then grinned at his friend. "Not as bad as it was the night we met in Independence."

"No, that was a miserable night, in more ways than one." After passing the last town building, they crossed a low hill passing through a wide pasture. As they began to climb the next slope, Ransom pointed to his left. In the faint early morning light, Floyd could see the knoll that Ransom had mentioned earlier. "See? Turn left up ahead, and follow the tracks."

Floyd followed the clear-cut buggy tracks. They continued around the knoll until the main road from town could no longer be seen.

"Here," Ransom said, "this will do just fine."

Floyd pulled the mare to a stop near a small tree, looped the reins around the brake handle, and stepped from the buckboard. He walked to the mare and secured the lead from the halter to the tree.

"You're from around here, Floyd. Is it always cloudy in Nashville?" Ransom asked while he was busy loading one of the Colt Paterson revolvers.

"In January, it's like this most all the time, cloudy and cold. But we're about to warm up, aren't we?"

"Yes, we certainly are. Grab your pistol and we'll start something which will really get your blood pumping." He held up the

Paterson and looked at it for a moment. Pointing with the barrel of the revolver, Ransom said, "See the rocky area there, about thirty feet?"

Floyd nodded.

"You pick a rock and fire at it, reload and fire again. Do that five times. I will fire five times with my revolver, and we will see by how much time I beat you."

Floyd looked at his friend. "You're mighty confident."

Ransom's face broke into a wide smile. "Oh, yes, I am extremely confident. Are you ready?" At Floyd's nod, he said, "Fire!"

Floyd held one of his .54-caliber US Harpers Ferry Model 1805 single-shot pistols, which his friend Oliver Ryland had converted to caplock, in each hand. At Ransom's call, he raised first one and fired, and then the other. Ransom's fifth shot fired as Floyd was lowering his second weapon. Floyd stared at the smoking Paterson Colt in disbelief.

"You fired all five in not much more time than what it took me to fire two."

Ransom, grinning at the consternation on his friend's face, said, "Yes, I did, and I can get it reloaded before you can reload one of your pistols."

Floyd watched closely as Ransom walked back to the wagon, and from the large trunk, he removed the walnut box that had contained the Paterson. Inside were several tools and accessories needed for reloading or disassembly.

Floyd, who knew he was very quick on the reload, grinned at the thought of this competition. He knew how fast he was, and he only had one barrel to load. Ransom had five. Neither Ma nor Pa could abide gambling, and he had been taught to feel the same way. *But it really isn't gambling if I know my own ability.* After that quick thought, he said, "Ransom, I think you've gone too far. I'll bet you a quarter eagle that I can beat you. But let's just be sure about what you're saying. You're telling me I only need to load one pistol, and you'll be loading all five of those chambers. Is that right?"

Ransom's grin had not changed. "That is exactly right, Floyd. I will be firing this weapon before you can get yours loaded and capped. And I feel so strongly about accomplishing that, though I hate to take your money, I will accept your bet, but only to provide you with more incentive to beat me." If anything, his grin widened.

Floyd looked again into the box with all the paraphernalia. He then pulled his powder horn around to his front and opened up his possibles bag containing his ball starter, and said, "Whenever you're ready."

"Go!" Ransom said.

Both men began working rapidly and efficiently. Ransom pushed the barrel wedge through to the screw stop and yanked the barrel from the Paterson, while at the same time thumbing the hammer back to half cock. He pulled a loaded cylinder from his pocket and, using the same hand, grasped the fired cylinder and removed it from the arbor. Next, he positioned the loaded cylinder in place on the arbor, lining up the key to the cylinder, slipped the barrel on, pushed the wedge back through, locking the barrel, indexed the cylinder, lifted the revolver, and fired, one, two, three, four, five times.

Floyd was bringing his pistol up to fire when Ransom fired his first shot. He watched Ransom fire the five shots, shook his head again while pulling a quarter eagle from his pocket, and flipped it to Ransom. "That's impressive. I knew you wouldn't be able to load all five of those barrels before I could load one, but I sure didn't expect you to pull out an extra cylinder all capped and loaded. That provides tremendous firepower."

"More than that," Ransom said. "If you have more than one revolver, just think how each additional weapon would multiply your firepower. Then, add in the revolving rifle—"

"And a man could stop," Floyd said, "an attack from any number of men."

Ransom became all business and said, "Yes. Now, we need to get you trained and practicing on your Paterson revolvers and your rifle. I've showed you all the good points, but there are some quirks with these weapons you need to learn."

## 20

The early morning had passed quickly. When both Floyd and Ransom were satisfied with the mountain man's skill both using, disassembling, and reassembling the weapons, they had headed back into town. Once back, Floyd purchased six additional handguns and another rifle, which had set him back a pretty penny. Though each rifle and pistol came with single bullet molds, Ransom had molds that could cast four round balls at one time. Floyd bought several of those, plus a large supply of precast balls. Additional lead and powder was not needed, for he had plenty in his supplies. However, he purchased several pounds of beeswax for the revolvers. Ransom had suggested a mixture of beeswax and animal tallow of some type, he used beef, to be spread lightly over the round ball in the chamber.

After saying goodbye to Ransom and thanking him profusely, Floyd wasted little time. He also purchased needed clothing.While in the general store, he purchased several things for Leotie and Mika. Finished, he checked out from the hotel and, with the help of Randolph from the hotel, carried all of his gear to the livery.

Once there, he gave Randolph four gold dollars, thanking him and asking him to give James and Philip each a dollar. Randolph thanked him profusely and hurried back to the hotel.

Now, back at the livery, it was time to load the new gear into the pack bags. While with Ransom, Floyd had loaded four of the eight handguns, two would be saddle guns and he'd carry the other two, and one of the revolving rifles. The four extra revolvers and rifle he had purchased were for Jeb. He felt sure his friend would be glad to get them.

"Howdy."

Floyd rose from his repacking and looked around. He could see the resemblance in the older man approaching him and the boy he had met last night. The man had the same wide shoulders, broad face, and ready smile.

"You must be Floyd Logan. Bobby told me about you. I'm Fletcher Sutton. Most folks call me Fletch." He approached with his right hand extended.

Floyd took the hand and said, "How are you? Yes, I'm Logan."

"Good. I've been wanting to speak to you about an important matter."

Feeling a slight apprehension, Floyd said, "Is that right?"

"Yes, this could benefit both of us. Would you have time to come to my office?"

Floyd could feel the time pressure. He wanted to get on the road today, soon. His valley was a long way off.

Fletch must have sensed Floyd's concern. He said, "Please hear me out. It won't take but a few minutes, and if you can't help, that's fine, too."

Never a man who could easily turn down someone's honest plea for help, Floyd regretted his exasperated look and said, "Sure. Lead the way."

The two moved quickly toward the small office and entered. Fletch, while sliding behind his desk, waved at a straight-backed, cane-bottomed chair, and said, "Have a seat."

Once they were seated, Fletch said, "Let me explain. I have a sister in Independence. Bobby said you were headed that way."

Floyd nodded.

"She is older than me and is in failing health. We need to get someone out there who cares about her and could help her travel back to Nashville. Bobby not only can do that, but would like to. When she lived here, she was very kind to him. She loves him very much." The man paused.

Floyd thought, *I don't have to be a genius to see where this trail is headed. I'm not at all excited to be taking care of that young fella all the way to Independence, even if he is easygoing.*

Fletch heaved a big sigh, looked out the window that overlooked the main street, watched two horsemen ride by, looked back to Floyd, and continued. "Here's my problem. Bobby's folks were killed in a freak accident twelve years ago. Judith, my sister in Independence, her name is Judith Kingsley, took Bobby in. She took care of him for several years. About six years ago, her husband got a wild idea of starting a business in Independence, so she had to move. It absolutely broke her heart, and Bobby's.

"Raymond, Judith's husband, started a dry goods store, and, I've got to say, it was mighty successful. What with all the folks headed west, he had a booming business. He and Judith were doin' fine, right up to a little over a year ago. Judith wrote us the story.

"Raymond had just received a big shipment from St. Louis and was working late. Because of the shipment, he had forgotten to go to the bank to make his daily deposit. Wouldn't you know it, he was robbed. The bandits took all of his money and several of the guns that were on display, plus a load of powder and lead. But, may they all burn in Hell, they went and killed Raymond, him that wouldn't hurt a flea. What made it even worse was that Judith was at the store helping him. Thank the Lord they didn't kill her, but poor Raymond died in Judith's arms. It was just a sad, sad thing.

"Anyway, sorry I've gotten a little long-winded. Judith's health began failing shortly after the robbery. She kept the store open as long as she could but finally had to sell it. She got a fair price for it, and she's in good shape financially, but she needs help for the long trip back."

Floyd readjusted in the uncomfortable chair and glanced out the window. *I'm sure sorry for this boy and his aunt,* Floyd thought, *but I have a family I need to get home to. How much will taking care of Bobby delay me getting back to Leotie?*

"Mr. Logan, I've—"

"Call me Floyd."

"Floyd, I've got to tell you, Bobby is a little slow. Ann, my wife, doesn't like to talk about it, but you need to know. His ma had a difficult time in delivery." Fletch shook his head. "It took a long time, but he finally came out okay, everybody thought, and seemed fine. But when it came time for walkin', he didn't, not until much later. The same with talkin', and as he got older, we could see things must've been jumbled upstairs. Now don't get me wrong, he's a good boy, and you won't find a harder worker. He's a handsome boy, too, what with that blond hair, blue eyes, and almost constant smile. It just breaks your heart."

Fletch turned away again, cleared his throat, coughed, and, withdrawing a dirty rag from his desk, blew his nose. Turning back, he cleared his throat again. "Yes, sir, he's always happy, and you'll never hear him utter a cross word. If anything, he's too nice. I've tried to teach him about people and how some will take advantage if a person ain't careful, and how a few are just plain mean, but it's never taken. I don't think it's in him to think bad of people."

Floyd pulled out his watch, opened it, pointedly checked the time, and slipped it back into his pocket. "Fletch, is there any other way to get him to Independence?"

The man behind the desk shook his head in resignation. "I've tried to think of some other way that might work. He's good enough if he has an adult with him, but he couldn't make that kind of a trip by himself. We've asked other folks who are headed that way, but have had no takers. Frankly, Floyd, you're our last hope."

Floyd examined the man who was asking so much of him. *He looks honest,* Floyd thought. *If he has any other motive, I can't tell, and I sure can't leave that poor woman in Independence in a lurch.*

"Also, Floyd, I'd be glad to pay you."

Floyd instantly held up his hand, shaking his head emphatically. "No, sir. I'd not take advantage of someone's difficulty to make money. Should I decide to help, it will cost you nothing other than the necessary supplies for Bobby."

"Let me address that right now," said Fletch. "I see you've rented horses from Javitts', in Dyersburg. It looks like you have quite a bit of gear for your only packhorse. If you decide to do this, I'll provide mounts for Bobby and his supplies. He won't have a lot, so you will have room on his packhorse to store part of your gear. Leave his horses at Javitts', and when Bobby and Judith come back, he can pick up the horses. I think that will simplify things for everyone."

Floyd thought over the proposal and liked it. "That will help, Fletch. But time is passing, and I need to leave right away. I can't wait until you folks get Bobby's supplies and cold-weather clothing. I need to be on my way."

"I thought you might say that, and on the hope that you would take Bobby along with you, we have him already packed. I have the horses ready, and all I need to do is load them up. You two can be on your way."

Floyd stood. "Well then, you'd best get Bobby and we'll head out."

Fletch stood, walked around the desk, and grasped Floyd's hand, shaking it like he was trying to get a pump primed. "Thank you, Floyd. Thank you so much. You have no idea how much this means to everyone. We have been so worried about Judith, and now you have become the solution."

Floyd finally regained his hand, and turning, said, "Glad I can help. It'll be a long trip. I just hope Bobby is up for it."

Starting toward the packs and horses, Fletch said, "Oh, he will be. You'll be amazed at how much help he is, and I promise you, he will be no trouble." Fletch jogged around the office to several wide lockers. He opened one and slid out two packs while Floyd continued to his. Fletch arrived with the two he was carrying and set them close to Floyd's. "Those are Bobby's. They're already packed. Feel free to add whatever you need to." He wiggled one and continued, "Be careful with this one. Ann slipped some goodies in here for the two of you. Also, this pack contains most of the foodstuff. Now, if you'll excuse me, I've got to run over to the house to get Bobby." With his last remark, Fletch darted across the busy street, disappearing around a corner.

The first thing Floyd did before putting anything into Bobby's packs was to check their contents. Sure enough, finding the food in the pack Fletch had indicated, he added several pieces of Bobby's clothing from the other pack. The clothing was soft and would do no damage to the food supplies. First, he put the lead he was carrying in the pack containing the food and clothing, sliding it all the way to the bottom. Then he moved the extra pistols and powder into the remaining pack. He checked the weight as he went along. His goal was to have all four packs evenly loaded by weight, with none having sharp edges protruding that would rub on the animals. Finished, he straight-ened up and again tried the new Patersons in his old holsters.

They weren't a perfect fit. They were tight around the cylin-ders, and the barrels were too long. He had cut off the ends of the holsters, which allowed each barrel to protrude about an inch. Now that he was finished with the packs, he took the two saddle holsters to a chopping block he had seen in the barn. After checking the edge on the ax, he laid the holster on the block, picked up the ax with one hand, and chopped the end from the holster. Then he repeated the action with the other holster. *They'll do,* he thought. *They're not the prettiest things, but they'll get the job done until I can get some new ones made.* Finished, he tossed the holsters and belt over his shoulder, picked up his tack, and headed for the sorrel.

He had finished saddling both horses and turned to look out the door for Fletch and Bobby just as they walked in, accompanied by a woman near the age of Fletch. Bobby was consumed with excitement.

"Hi, Mr. Floyd," Bobby said as he came dashing up. He didn't stop until he reached Floyd and threw his arms around him, giving him a big hug. "It's good to see you. I'm really happy we're going to Independence together. This will be so much fun." He jumped up and down a couple of times, clapping.

The woman with him said, "Calm down, Bobby. Don't get too excited. You don't want to upset your new friend."

"This is my wife, Ann, and, honey, this is Floyd Logan."

"Yes, Auntie Ann," Bobby shouted. "This is Mr. Floyd Logan, and he's taking me to Auntie Judith's, and she loves me, and I love her, and she's coming back to live here."

Fletch said, with a severe tone of voice, "Bobby, relax. What have we said about interrupting grown-ups?"

Immediately the smile on Bobby's face disappeared, and he stared at the ground. Crestfallen, he finally said, "I'm sorry, Uncle Fletch. I'm sorry, Auntie Ann. I'm sorry, Mr. Floyd."

*What have I gotten myself into?* Floyd thought. *I hope he isn't going to be like this all the way to Independence.*

As if he were reading Floyd's mind, Fletch said to Floyd, "Don't worry, Floyd. He only gets like this when he's excited. If that happens, you just tell him to relax. It may take a couple of reminders, but he'll calm down." Then pointing at the two additional packs, he asked, "Are these ready?"

Floyd nodded. "They are, and so am I. I only need to get the pack saddle on the bay, hang the packs, and we'll be headed out."

Fletch turned to Bobby and said, "Son, why don't you go saddle your horse and get these packs on your packhorse."

"Yes, sir, I'll get that done." Bobby turned and raced to a stall at the end of the barn.

Ann said to Floyd, "Mr. Logan, thank you so much for taking Bobby with you. Judith will be so thankful, and believe me, please, he will be a big help to you and not a hindrance."

Floyd touched his hat. "You folks are quite welcome. I'm sure that we will get along just fine." He looked at Fletch. "Two things, one I feel sure I know the answer to, but I need to ask. Can Bobby shoot?"

"He is one heck of a shot, both with a rifle and pistol. And I'll tell you something else, he loves to shoot. If you have time, let him shoot occasionally, and he'll do anything for you."

"That brings me to my next question, which I'm sure the answer is no, but I still need to find out. Has he ever shot a man?"

"No, Mr. Logan, he has never shot another human being," Ann Sutton said stiffly, "nor has he shot an animal. I just don't know if he could ever do either."

Floyd listened, nodded, and turned to Fletcher Sutton. "Fletch, we're going to be traveling for almost a month. Bobby could be placed in a situation where he will need to shoot someone, so if he had to, do you think he could?"

Fletcher shook his head. "Floyd, I just don't know. Maybe, if there was a strong enough reason. But I couldn't guarantee it."

After listening, Floyd nodded. "Thank you, ma'am, and you too, Fletch. I needed to know what he might do. Believe me, it's my goal to get both of us to Independence without either of us having to fire a shot. However, there's a lot of bad guys out there who are looking for something free, and they don't mind taking it from innocent people. Sorry for the straight talk, but you need to know what Bobby is headed into."

Ann Sutton nodded. "Thank you, Mr. Logan. I certainly have my concerns about sending him west, but we have no other choice. I believe you will take good care of our nephew. Your family is well known and has a very good reputation."

Bobby walked up at the end of the conversation, leading his two horses. "I'm all set, Mr.

Floyd. Are you ready?"

Floyd looked Bobby over, heavy wool coat, wool shirt, red long johns peeking through at the throat, thick wool mittens, a solid set of boots, and a good hat. He was definitely ready. Having completed his loading, Floyd checked the packs and saddles one last time and swung onto the sorrel's back.

"Reckon I am as ready as I'll ever be." The warmth of the sun flooding in through the open livery stable door felt good on his face.

As they were about to leave, Fletch said, "Oh, one more thing." He pulled a small leather bag from his coat pocket and held it out to Floyd. "Take this. There's about two hundred dollars there. What you don't need, give to Judith. That'll help them get back."

As he reached for the bag, Floyd's peripheral vision caught movement on the boardwalk across the street and in front of the saloon. Two unkempt, rough-looking characters watched as Fletch handed the money bag to him. The instant they saw it, one turned and said something to the other. Floyd gazed at the two of them, marking them in his memory. Then thinking, *Nothing we can do about it now*, he said, "I'll make sure she gets it, and I'll keep a close eye on Bobby."

Ann and Fletcher stepped back. Floyd tipped his hat to Ann and trotted the sorrel from the stable, leading the bay.

"Bye Auntie Ann. Bye Uncle Fletcher," Bobby said as he rode past them, following the bay.

Floyd turned in his saddle, ostensibly to watch Bobby and the Suttons, but primarily to keep an eye on the two characters who had seemed so interested in the money bag. He saw them make quick turns and hurry into the saloon. *Probably where they've been all day with their partners,* Floyd thought. *Those two will be making trouble. I can feel it in my bones. It would be a lot easier to handle them if I were by myself.* He laughed softly. *Yeah, and I wouldn't be near as cold if it were summer.*

He looked back again, and Bobby was still waving. Floyd lifted his hand in a single wave and called, "Let's go, Bobby." His eyes fell to the holstered Patersons across his saddle, and he felt the comforting weight of the two on his hips. Those two across the street would be coming along, and soon, with the goal of making the money bag, and anything else of value, their own. Knowing their type ran in packs, they'd be bringing more with them. "I've got a surprise for you boys," he said, only loud enough for him and the sorrel to hear. "Yes siree, you will get a surprise that you can't even imagine." He slowed to let Bobby ride up next to him, and looked at the boy. His face was wreathed in excitement. "Are you ready for this trip, Bobby?"

The boy turned his face toward Floyd. Even in the cold, his excitement couldn't be dampened. "Yes, sir. This is about the most exciting thing I've ever done."

Floyd smiled back at him and said, "I'm thinkin' you're right. It might even be a most exciting trip for both of us."

## 21

O nce clear of Nashville, the two riders, one looking much older than his age and the other much younger, bumped their horses up to a trot. Floyd had asked Bobby if he had ever been to Charlotte. For most people the answer would've been short, anywhere from a one-word answer to a short sentence. But not so for Bobby, for he had been to Charlotte and, Floyd thought, he wanted to share every detail. So he talked, and talked, and talked.

He talked about his uncle Fletcher bringing him to Charlotte. He talked about the penny bag of candy his uncle bought for him. He talked about the deer they saw coming back from Charlotte. And most of all, he talked about the people.

When it came to people, Bobby had excellent recall. While he talked, Floyd looked. He noted the terrain ahead and the road behind, especially the road behind. He was determined to know if they were being followed. The past few days had been dry. That meant dust rose in thick clouds as the four horses trotted west. The wind had slowed appreciably, and it was now only a faint breeze, strong enough to gently lift the dust kicked up by the horses.

Dust was what Floyd was looking for, and after they had covered about ten miles, sure enough, there it was. Faint, only a tint on the gray, cloud-covered sky. Occasionally, the sun would break through, and it felt great on Floyd's cold body, but it didn't last long. The breaks in the clouds soon disappeared, and the cold gray returned. But the dust remained, never drawing closer, nor disappearing, but always back there.

Eventually Bobby quieted down, riding in silence. Floyd enjoyed the quiet. He had hoped to spend the night in Charlotte, but now with thieves dogging their trail, he felt it would be better if he quickly remedied the situation.

"Bobby, has Fletch explained to you about bad people?"

"Oh, yes. He's told me many times there are bad people in the world. I believe him, I've just never met any. Have you, Mr. Floyd?"

"I have, Bobby. I have known some very bad people. Do you know how to protect yourself from bad people?"

"Yes, I do. Uncle Fletch has always told me that if I am dealing with a bad person, I just need to leave or call him."

"That's good advice, Bobby. Today we have bad people following us."

Bobby spun around in his saddle and stared behind them. "I don't see anyone, Mr. Floyd. Why is it I can't see anyone, if they're back there?"

"You can't see them yet, but, trust me, they are following us. Do you know why they are following us?"

Bobby shook his head.

"I'll tell you. Do you remember, we were leaving, and your uncle gave me a bag of money to give to your aunt Judith?"

"Of course I do, Mr. Floyd. I'm not stupid."

"You definitely are not stupid, Bobby. The reason I ask is those men behind us are thieves, and they want to take your aunt Judith's money."

"No! That's not nice. You're not going to let them, are you, Mr. Floyd?"

Floyd had slowed the horses to a walk, and he occasionally checked behind them to see if the dust was getting any closer. It did for a short time, then held its distance. The thieves had closed the distance until they realized Floyd and Bobby had reduced their horses' speed to a walk. They then had also slowed to match their speed to Floyd's.

"No, Bobby, we're not. We are going to give them a big surprise."

"Oh, I like surprises."

"I'm thinkin' *they* might not like this surprise."

The two continued to ride while Floyd searched for the right spot. They were in hilly, rocky country, and he felt sure the perfect place would show up soon. He checked the sun, which was drifting lower. It would be time soon.

Sure enough, off to the right, maybe three hundred yards across a pasture with patches of oak, jutted a rocky point with a small stream running beneath it. "Bobby, I think we've found the right place."

"Where?" Bobby asked.

"Just follow me, and we need to be quiet from here on."

"All right, I'll be quiet." The two rode across the broken land, circling around the scattered trees. When they arrived at the base of the point, Floyd turned the sorrel to ensure he could see the road clearly from here, and he could.

"Jump down, Bobby. We need to water all the horses and unload and hobble the packhorses quickly. I'll get a fire built. Do you have another coat and hat in your pack?"

Grinning, Bobby said, "I sure do. Auntie Ann packed my old ones. They're a little small for me, but I can still wear them."

"Good. Remove our packs from the horses, and bring the packs over here where I'm building the fire. Get your extra hat, coat, and a blanket out of your pack. Lay the blanket there, next to the fire, along with your hat and coat. Then hobble the two packhorses, and tie the reins of our riding horses to the trees with slipknots. I'll get the fire going and take care of everything else."

Floyd went to work, assuming Bobby would follow his directions. Fletch had said Bobby was a good worker. Now he would find out. He gathered up leaves, brush, kindling, and larger limbs. Once he had the spot cleared, he laid out the materials, pulled out a lucifer, and lit the kindling. It caught and the fire grew rapidly. As soon as Floyd felt sure of the fire, he turned to Bobby's coat from where the boy had placed it. Buttoning it first, he started pulling grass and stuffing the body, then the arms. He laid out some larger rocks, leaned the coat against the rocks, and set the hat on top of the coat. Then he tossed the blanket across the bottom of the coat and over the ground and stepped back to examine his handiwork.

It wouldn't fool a close examination, but he was betting these guys would shoot long before they got close enough to identify the dummies. Bobby had stacked the packs against the steep slope behind and to the side of the dummies. Floyd opened his, the one containing his buffalo coat, and pulled it out along with another slouch hat and another blanket. In only a few minutes, he had built another figure to his satisfaction.

Floyd turned to Bobby, who was standing watching in amazement. "Grab your horse and come with me," Floyd snapped as he grabbed the sorrel's reins. With Bobby right behind him, they trotted across a small stream and around the point. Reaching the opposite slope, he tied the sorrel. Bobby copied his action. Then Floyd pulled out his Ryland and Paterson ring rifle, along with his two saddle weapons. He stuck one in his belt and handed the other to Bobby. "Come on."

They climbed the slope until just below the ridgeline. "Take your hat off, Bobby. We're going to crawl to the top of this ridge. When we get up there, I'm just going to ease up above the ridge far enough to see over it. After I've looked, I'll motion you up. Keep that muzzle away from me. You understand all that?"

"I sure do, Mr. Floyd."

"Good, once we're there, I'll show you how to work that revolver."

In the dim light, Floyd could see Bobby grin. "Oh, no, sir, you don't need to. Mr. Ransom let me shoot one. It's fun."

Floyd grinned back, thinking, *This is gonna be fun.* "That's good. When I tell you to shoot, shoot until it's empty. But don't try to hit anyone. Just shoot over them."

Bobby, still grinning, said, "We're just going to scare them? Is that right?"

"You're just going to scare them. I might hurt them just a little bit. Now, wait here."

He crawled up to the top of the ridge, their fake figures and fire directly below them. Darkness was coming on quickly. Only a few minutes more, and it would be too dark for his telescope. He pulled it out of his possibles bag, quickly removed it from its leather case, extended it, and checked their back trail. Sure enough, four riders had just topped the last hill before dropping into this valley. Upon topping the hill, they pulled their horses to a stop and sat watching the fire in the distance.

He could tell they were in animated conversation, probably arguing. He turned and motioned Bobby to join him. Turning back, he watched the thieves make up their mind and start their horses straight toward the fire. He could also see them pull their rifles from the scabbards. *All right, boys*, he thought, *it's up to you. With all the law that's come to this country, I'd prefer not to have to shoot anyone, but if you shoot those dummies, all bets may be off.*

Floyd pulled the spare Paterson from his waistband and laid it over in front of Bobby. "When you get through shooting that first one, pick up the second one and empty it."

He almost missed the return whisper, it was so soft. "Oh, boy. I get to shoot two."

The riders kept slowly riding forward toward the fire. Finally, Floyd had to close and put the glass back in its case and the possibles bag. It was just too dark to use it. But now he could hear the horses walking closer. He slipped the rifle to his shoulder and pulled the ring back, cocking the weapon. He heard Bobby cock the revolver.

Finally the horses stopped. The clouds had broken, and stars were twinkling through the breaks. A coyote barked in the distance and was answered by the long, mournful howl of a red wolf. Suddenly, the night was split by the blast of four rifle shots, followed by the bark of two pistols.

"That was your first and last mistake, boys," Floyd said, in an even conversational tone.

Immediately, low, rapid talking and the rattle of ramrods could be heard. Floyd whispered, "Now, Bobby!"

The night was again rent by the overpowering sound of gunfire. Only, this time it didn't stop. It was almost a continuous roar. Bobby's revolver emptied. He laid it down and picked up the other. His firing continued.

Floyd fired five rounds from the Colt Ring rifle. Then he stopped and took in Bobby's pure joy firing the second Paterson. The young man was firing and laughing. The muzzle was pointed at about a forty-five-degree angle. The only thing he might hit was a passing cloud, and he was having such fun.

When the thieves had shot the dummies, if there had been enough light, Floyd would've shot them, for their intentions were to kill Floyd and Bobby. There was no way of telling how many other travelers they had killed and robbed, or would in the future. His earlier thoughts of delay and problems with the law disappeared. But it was dark, and he didn't want to take the chance of hitting the horses, so he fired well over their heads.

Though his ears were ringing from the blasts, he could hear the thieves racing across the uneven land. *Riding like that, at night, they're gonna take a fall,* he thought. The thought had only begun to form when he heard horses fall and men yell.

The moon was just starting to brighten the eastern sky. He reloaded the handguns with the extra cylinders he had bought from Ransom. He was slower than Ransom, but knew that with practice and time he would grow faster. When he was finished, he shoved one of the Patersons behind his waistband and handed the other one to Bobby, and he took the time to reload his revolving rifle.

While he was reloading, he could hear the thieves talking in low tones, not too far across the pasture. After listening for several seconds, he made a decision. "Bobby, we can prevent this from happening to other innocent travelers. Would you like that?"

In the firelight reflected from below, Floyd could see Bobby's wide eyes staring at him. Slowly the boy nodded. "I'd like that, Mr. Floyd."

"Good. You stay here, and don't go down to the fire. I'll only be gone for a little while, but if something happens to me, get on your horse and go home. You can get home from here, right?"

"Oh, yes. I know all this country real well."

"That's good, Bobby. You're a good man." With that, Floyd gave Bobby's shoulder a squeeze and disappeared into the darkness.

He could hear the men arguing in the distance. *They have to be drunk,* he thought. *No one would be stupid enough to hang around this close after trying to shoot up a camp.* He continued to slip through the darkness even as the yellow moon slowly showed itself above the horizon.

As he neared, Floyd could make out three figures standing together, looking down at the fourth, who from his vantage point, was only a shadow on the ground. He eased closer, his trained feet testing each step before receiving the full weight of his body. Years of living daily with his life at risk had made him into a quiet deadly fighting machine. Now all of his trained senses were engaged as he slipped closer and closer.

"Now listen to me." A gruff voice came from one of the men standing. "I'm telling you, we need to ride back up there and kill those fellers right now."

He was answered by a thin but insistent, whiny voice. "Bodean, there must be ten or twelve folks up there. You heard all that shooting. We're liable to get ourselves kilt. Anyways, we need to get Cletus to a doc. He's hurt bad."

In the moonlight, Floyd could see the one who must be Bodean pointing a finger at the man who had just spoken.

"You listen to me, Earl Mutton, I'm the boss here, and what I say goes. I'm tellin' you, there ain't ten people up there. I don't know what they've got, but they's only two, and in the dark we can slip back up there and kill 'em."

The man on the ground, speaking through pain, said, "Bodean, you got to get me to a doctor. I know my arm's broke, and it's hurtin' something fierce."

"Shut up, Cletus. We've got to take care of those fellers first, or we'll all be going to prison. You want 'em to find out what we've done?"

The sky had cleared, giving the glow of the rising full moon rule over the night's darkness. Floyd stood in a small patch of scrub oak no more than twenty feet from the thieves. He could see each of the men clearly, even as one stumbled his way to his horse. At the correct angle, he could make out the features of their faces in the brightening moonlight.

The one staggering turned back to his horse and said, "I need another dri—"

The sound of Floyd thumbing back the hammer on the Colt Paterson he had drawn from his waistband froze the would-be robbers in their place. The only other sound heard in the moonlit pasture was the pain-filled moan from Cletus.

Floyd, his voice as cold as the northwest breeze tickling the back of his neck, said, "You boys drop your guns and stand easy. I can see you clearly in the moonlight. One false move, and I'll kill you where you stand."

He could see all three men's heads twisting and turning, straining to spot him, but he knew, standing in the dark shadows of the trees, they'd never so much as see a hint of his outline. "I said drop those guns, now!"

The outlaw who had been going for a drink spun toward Floyd's voice while bringing his rifle to his shoulder. Floyd shot him where he stood. The man, in a slurred, gurgling voice, said, "Bodean." His rifle fell from his hands, and he dropped to his knees. He held that position for a few seconds, then fell forward, his face making a sickening thud as it struck the rocky ground.

The man called Bodean ran to the fallen man's side and dropped to his knees. Rolling him over, he called, "Jimmy Ray," but received no response.

Floyd knew the man was dead, because he knew where the .36-caliber round ball had been aimed.

Bodean quickly realized the outlaw he was kneeling alongside was dead. His head whipped around, first left, then right, frantically searching in the pale light. It stopped, his eyes focused on Jimmy Ray's rifle. He lunged for it.

"Don't do it," Floyd said.

But, for whatever reason, Bodean ignored Floyd's warning, his fingers finding the cold metal.

Earl, in his high, nasal voice, whined out, "He'll kill you, Bodean!"

"Don't make me shoot you, Bodean," Floyd said. "Leave the rifle alone."

The outlaw, as he brought the rifle up, said, "You killed my brother. I'm gonna kill you."

Floyd waited, taking careful aim, as the man called Bodean, from his kneeling position, brought the rifle toward his shoulder. When the butt of the rifle reached Bodean's shoulder, Floyd fired.

The round ball, much like the previous one, traveled straight and true, striking him in the chest. It broke through the ribs, carrying bone fragments with it, and tore through his heart.

Bodean collapsed over his brother, pulling the rifle's trigger as he fell. He had twisted to his left, and in falling, had swung the muzzle toward Earl, who cried, "Don't shoot me, Bodean!" The rifle's blast was quickly followed by a squeal, a fall, thrashing on the ground, and screaming. "Oh my, oh my, you've killed me. Bodean, you've killed me."

Floyd, ignoring Earl, said, "Cletus, if that's your name, if you have a gun, you'd best get rid of it."

"I ain't got no gun, mister. And if I did, I couldn't use it. My right arm is broken something fierce."

Meanwhile, Earl was still rolling on the ground, saying over and over, "I'm dying, oh Lordy, I'm dying."

## 22

Floyd stepped from the trees, comfortable in knowing though he had fired twice, he still had two shots left in his Paterson. "I'm coming out, boys. It would be in your best interest if you don't make any sudden moves." Revolver ready, he walked over to the one with the broken arm, pulled the man's pistol from his waist, and picked up his rifle, moving it out of reach.

Next, he walked over to the man holding his head and moaning about dying. He laid his rifle carefully on the ground and pulled Earl's hand away from his head. Blood streamed down the side of his face, but it wasn't fatal. The ball had only cut through his scalp, creasing and leaving him a wound he could lie about for many years.

Floyd picked up his ring rifle, stood, and raising his voice, called, "Bobby."

From across the pasture, he heard the young man's answering call. "Yes, sir."

"Everything's all right. Take the horses back to the fire and hobble them."

"Yes, sir," floated back to him. He then kicked Earl's foot and said, "Get up."

The moment Floyd had released Earl's hand, it had flown back to his head wound. He whined, "I'm dying, mister. If I move my hand, I'll bleed to death."

Floyd, in a cold, threatening voice, said, "If I slap you upside your head with the butt of this rifle, you'll bleed more. Now get up."

Muttering, the man called Earl struggled to his feet, trying to keep at least one hand on his head wound at all times.

"Lead the horses," Floyd said, "to the dead men. Then load and tie each man on his horse. Be quick but careful about it. I can see well enough in this moonlight that I'll know if you pick up a gun. If I even think you've gone for a gun, I'll shoot."

"Oh, no, sir, I ain't goin' for no gun. That's for danged sure. But I don't know if I can lift these boys across their saddles. They're mighty big."

Earl struggled, but managed to load first Bodean and then Jimmy Ray on their horses, accompanied with much complaining. Floyd silently watched the man. Once the bodies were across their saddles, he had Earl tie them in place with lengths cut from one of their ropes. He pulled on each of the bodies. They both remained tight to their saddles.

"Now," Floyd said to Earl, "go help your partner up. We're walking back to the fire."

Earl helped Cletus to his feet. The man moaned through gritted teeth. Once he was up, he said to Floyd, "I'm busted up pretty bad."

"I'll take a look at it," Floyd said, "when we get back to the fire. Earl, you lead three of the horses, and I'll lead this one." He picked up the reins to one of the horses that had a body on it, and waited until Earl and Cletus led out. He followed them to the fire.

Bobby had been busy. He had hobbled the two riding horses, gathered enough firewood for the night, and had coffee brewing.

He was standing, Colt hanging by his side, when they walked into the firelight.

"You can put your weapon up, Bobby. We won't be needing it."

Earl eyed the revolver. "Is that one of them crazy things that lets you shoot so many times?"

"Sit over there," Floyd said, pointing to a spot with his rifle. He looked at the man with the broken arm. "Your name's Cletus, right?"

Cletus nodded through the pain.

"Come over here by the fire, and let me take a look at that arm." Floyd turned. Gripping his rifle around the receiver with his left hand, he pointed it at Earl. "Stay there. Don't try anything, and I might let you have a cup of coffee." He turned back and carefully removed Cletus's coat. The man broke into a cold sweat from the pain as the sleeve slid past his bicep. Taking him by the good arm, Floyd helped him sit on the log Bobby had pulled up. Then, facing the broken arm, he straddled the log.

Taking his knife from its scabbard, he ripped the man's shirt and long johns from wrist to shoulder, exposing the broken limb. Floyd puzzled over it for a few minutes. The upper arm was a grisly mess. Halfway between the shoulder and elbow, Cletus had a jagged, stark white bone glistening in the firelight where it protruding from his bicep. The man gripped his arm by the wrist in an effort to prevent it from moving. "This is bad," Floyd said. "You need to see a doctor, soon."

Floyd glanced over at Bobby, who was busy not looking at the broken arm or the bone protruding from the skin. "Bobby, you think you're up to riding on into Charlotte tonight?"

"Sure, Mr. Floyd. I feel fine. We've got some hand pies Auntie Ann made for us. We can drink this coffee now and eat those pies in the saddle."

"Good thinking, Bobby. Let's do that."

"Mr. Floyd? Did you see what they did to our coats?"

Floyd had been busy with the prisoners and hadn't even

noticed the remains of the coats. Now he looked from the prisoners to the punctured coats, in particular his buffalo coat. They both had been holed significantly. *We'd be dead right now if we had been wearing them*, he thought. Pointedly he looked at the broken arm of Cletus and the bloody head of Earl and the two full saddles, then said, "You boys paid a mighty big price for the opportunity to shoot our coats full of holes."

"Yeah," Cletus grunted out, "Bodean said it would be easy money, especially with the Sutton boy. I'm guessing, knowing what he knows now, he would've rode right on by."

Floyd shook his head. "You know Bobby Sutton, and you'd still kill him?"

Earl whined, "It were just business, mister. If you're through taking care of Cletus, could you see to my head?"

Floyd was almost eleven years older than when he had first headed west. He had learned much. From his several mentors he had developed the ability to maintain a cool head, not letting his anger take control of his body. But here, listening to this sniveling killer, he was having great difficulty holding the anger in. The thought that these men would think of taking the lives of two people who had done them no harm, even one a boy they knew, and call it business, filled him with a deep burning rage. He sat staring at Earl, every fiber of his body yearning to shut the man's whining mouth permanently.

Slowly, reason exerted control, although he did stand and walk toward Earl. Bobby had given the man a cup of coffee, saying in the process, "Here you go, Mr. Mutton. This'll warm you up."

Earl accepted the coffee, but kept his eyes riveted on Floyd. As the big man closed the distance, Earl stuttered out, "I-I-I ain't meant nothing, mister. If it ain't been for Bodean forcin' me to come along, I wouldn't of done it. Don't hurt me. I'm not a strong man. I—"

Floyd continued, passed Earl, and reaching the horses, began saddling and loading the packhorses. "Bobby, we need to get loaded and on our way."

"Yes, sir, Mr. Floyd. Can we shoot some more?"

"Yep, we'll shoot some more, but not tonight. We need to dump this trash so we can be on our way." Floyd quickly loaded the animals and, walking back to Cletus, picked up several short, strong limbs. Reaching Cletus, he again sat on the log, facing the man's broken arm.

"Bobby, I'm gonna need your help here."

Bobby walked over from the fire, squatting next to Cletus, gazing at the bone protruding from the bandit's arm. "That looks mighty bad, Mr. Darby. We had a horse with a broken leg like that, and Uncle Fletcher had to shoot it." Bobby looked up at Floyd. "We're not going to have to shoot Mr. Darby, are we, Mr. Floyd?"

Floyd gave Cletus a humorless grin and said, "Not right now, Bobby, but we haven't gotten them to the sheriff in Charlotte yet." He picked up a small stick and handed it to Cletus. "You might want to bite on this. What I'm about to do is going to hurt like sin."

Cletus said nothing but stared at Floyd as he bit down on the stick. Floyd grasped the injured man's arm, which had been hanging limp. As soon as his hand touched the man's elbow, Cletus let out a moan, and the stick crunched in his mouth. Immediately, Floyd positioned the forearm perpendicular to Cletus's upper arm and pulled down from the elbow. The jagged end of the protruding bone disappeared beneath the man's skin. In the cold night air, sweat poured from his face.

"Quick, Bobby, take this forearm and hold it steady." Floyd could see the man turning deathly pale, and knew he had only seconds before Cletus passed out. He felt the upper arm and could feel the bone had slipped back together. Cletus was no longer moaning. His eyes rolled back, and he started to collapse backward from the log. Floyd caught him, still gripping the man's upper arm to hold the bone in place.

"Keep his arm steady, Bobby. I'm going to lay him down while we finish." Carefully, he allowed Cletus to slip back off the log and onto the ground. "Lay his forearm across his belly, and hold it there." Floyd went to work. He sliced the sleeves from the man's shirt and long johns. After feeling for the break again, he pulled on the elbow slightly and, when he was satisfied, laid two of the sticks he had picked up along the upper arm, tying them firmly in place with the sleeves he had cut. Next, using two more limbs, he made splints for the forearm. When completed, he stopped and surveyed his work. Satisfied, he bound the man's arm to his body and started to spread his coat across the unconscious Cletus when his eyes opened.

"How are you doing?" Floyd asked.

"Arm's hurting like the blazes. You done?"

"Pretty much. You're going to have to ride, though. Think you can do it?"

"Guess I have to, right?"

"If you want to keep that arm. The sooner a doctor sees it, the better chance you have."

Cletus nodded. "Then get me on a horse and I'll ride."

Floyd looked over at Earl, who was just finishing his third cup of coffee. "Get on your horse, Mutton."

"Don't know if I can ride, Mr. Logan. Not with this head wound."

Floyd stared at the man who had been calmly drinking coffee while his partner was suffering intense pain. "Mutton, you'll either ride, or I'll hang you from the nearest strong limb." Seeing the miscreant's eyes widen with fear, Floyd turned back to Bobby. "Why don't you put out the fire while I get Cletus and Mutton in the saddle.

"Mutton, get over here and help me with Cletus."

The man stood, starting toward Floyd and Cletus, still

drinking from his coffee cup. "Toss the rest of the coffee on the fire, and give the cup to Bobby," Floyd said.

"But I ain't finished."

Floyd stared at the man, who immediately tossed the coffee onto the fire and the cup to Bobby, who caught it. "Gently," Floyd said. Once up, Floyd guided Cletus to his horse and, steadying him as he put his foot in the stirrup, pushed him up and into his saddle. Then he turned to Mutton and said, "Get on your horse." Once he was settled on his horse, Floyd handed him the reins of the two horses carrying the bodies. Taking a rope from one of the saddles, he made a loop and tossed it over Mutton's head, allowing it to settle on the man's shoulders.

"You ain't gonna make me ride like this, are you?" Mutton asked. "A man could choke to death should his horse spook."

"Shut up, Earl," Cletus said. "You ain't got no idea how tired I am of hearing you run your mouth."

Hobbles removed and packed, Floyd and Bobby mounted and, following the thieves, rode toward Charlotte. The night was cold, a light breeze nipped their cheeks, but the moon gave them plenty of light to see the road and the two men ahead.

"You know where the Charlotte sheriff lives?"

"Yes, sir," Bobby said. "He's a good friend of Uncle Fletcher. Why, anytime he's in Nashville, he comes by."

"That's good to know, Bobby. I'm glad you're with me, because we're going to be waking him up. Having you here should make him a bit more sociable."

"He's a friendly man, Mr. Floyd. I like him."

The remainder of the ride was in silence, broken only by the occasional moan or gasp from Cletus. Floyd's mind drifted west, his concerns for Leotie coming to the forefront. *She'll be sleeping now,* Floyd thought. *I imagine it's been a cold, hard day, what with her taking care of the health of the whole village. Hopefully she's doing fine.*

With his mind on the valley, and his eyes continuously

watching the two thieves ahead, the miles fell away under the plodding hooves of the horses. In the early morning hours, the sparse lights of Charlotte came into view.

They rode straight through the small town. Floyd noted the darkened sheriff's office as they passed. Bobby guided them onto a short side street holding only three houses. After pulling up in front of the last house on the right, Bobby jumped from his horse. Looping the reins around a hitching post, he opened a gate, being sure to pull it closed, and dashed up on the wide covered porch. Reaching the front door, he pounded on it three times. Soon, there was a lamp moving through the house.

The lamp halted at the front door, and a gruff voice called, "Who is it, and what do you need?"

"Howdy, Sheriff Nixon. This is Bobby Sutton, and we need your help."

The door jerked open, and by the lamplight, Floyd could make out the sheen of the pistol jammed in the sheriff's waistband. He was a large older man sporting a thick, drooping mustache that, much like his hair, had gone to white.

Holding the lamp high so the light might make it to the horses and men in front of his house, he said, "Bobby, what in blue blazes has you out on a cold night like this?"

"Sheriff Nixon, Bodean Akers and Jimmy Ray Akers and Earl Mutton and Cletus Darby shot our coats and tore them all up."

The sheriff reached behind the door facing, brought out his hat, and slapped it on. Wearing long johns with no shirt, his galluses hanging from dark trousers, the sheriff held the lamp high and stepped onto the porch. "Is that you, Fletch?"

"No, Sheriff, it isn't. I'm Floyd Logan, of the Limerick Logans, and I've got a man here who needs to see a doctor bad."

"All right, Logan," the sheriff began and stopped. "Are those bodies on them horses?"

"They sure are, Sheriff," Earl Mutton said. "This here Logan and that innocent-looking Bobby Sutton done ambushed us and kilt Bodean and—" Mutton's sentence was cut off in a strangling gasp when Floyd yanked the noose tight around the man's neck.

The sheriff was off the porch in two long strides, Bobby rushing to keep up with him. He hardly broke stride to jerk the gate open and was quickly to Bodean Akers's horse. He grabbed a handful of the man's hair and lifted the head high enough to see the man's features. Unceremoniously, he dropped the head and moved to the other body, repeating the process and exposing Jimmy Ray's face.

After confirming the identity of the dead men, the sheriff held the light up so that he could see Floyd's face. "You look like a Logan. You have any evidence to back up your word?"

"I do, Sheriff, but I think the first thing should be getting Cletus Darby here to the doc's office. He took a bad fall from his horse and busted up his right arm."

"You're right. You and Bobby take Earl and these bodies to my office. Go on in, it ain't locked, and I'll take Cletus to the doctor. He's not going to be real happy with me waking him this time of night." He took the reins from Cletus and looked up at the rider, shaking his head. "Cletus, I told you when you were a boy to stay away from that Akers bunch, but no, you just wouldn't listen."

"You're right, Harley, but can we get to the doc's? I'm hurting something fierce."

Earl had gotten some relief by pushing his fingers between the rope and his neck, opening the loop. He croaked out, "Sheriff, you gotta make this criminal take this rope off my neck. I could die if I fell."

As he started toward the doctor's office, Sheriff Nixon said to Earl, "Then I'd recommend you not fall, Earl."

Bobby had remounted. Floyd said, "Move it, Mutton." The three men rode to the sheriff's office.

Sure enough, when they got there, Floyd found the door unlocked. He opened it and walked in, looking for the lamp. There was one sitting on the sheriff's desk. It was a nice whale-oil lamp, an intricately etched globe reservoir connected to a heavy glass base. Floyd lit the three wicks, watched them catch, and stepped back. At the rear of the office, Floyd could see the single jail cell. Moving to the jail door, he pulled. Complaining loudly, it opened. Floyd motioned Mutton toward the cell. "In here."

Earl Mutton, rubbing his neck, walked through the door. Floyd swung it closed, but since he didn't have a key, he couldn't lock it. He turned as Bobby walked into the office. Behind him he heard the cell door squeak. Without turning, he said, "Earl, that cell door is between you and me. Don't you think the safe thing for you is to keep it that way?" He heard the cell door squeak again and bump, metal against metal, as it closed.

He stepped to the front door and said, "Bobby, I'm about to start a fire. Why don't you come on in and warm up."

Bobby came into the office, rubbing his hands together. "Cold out there, Mr. Floyd."

"It is. It won't take long to get this fire started, so why don't you close the door." Floyd squatted down to the fire and struck a match. The wood kindling lit, quickly igniting the larger wood. Floyd stood as the door swung open.

The sheriff moved straight to the fire, holding out both hands. "It's cold in here, too." Then he turned to gaze at Floyd. "So you're the Logan I've heard so much about. You're the mountain man?"

"Reckon I must be. Sheriff, I'd be obliged if we could answer whatever questions you have, and be on our way. I've got a family waiting in those mountains, and I need to get back."

## 23

"Well, tell me exactly what happened, and I'll see what I can do."

Floyd explained the events that took place earlier in the night, leaving out no details. Every once in a while, Bobby would jump in, but for the most part he remained quiet, listening.

When Floyd finished, the sheriff turned to Bobby. "Does that sound right to you, Bobby?"

"Yes, sir, Sheriff Nixon, that's exactly how it happened. You want me to go get our coats?"

"Yeah, Bobby, that would help."

Grinning, Bobby jumped up and ran outside. He returned quickly carrying the ventilated coats.

The sheriff took them from him and, one at a time, examined them. When he finished, he turned to Floyd. "Can you leave these coats with me?"

Floyd shook his head. "Sheriff, though they're holed pretty badly, with just a little work they'll still keep us warm. I'd sure appreciate you letting us take them with us. I still have a long ride before getting to those mountains, and that buffalo coat will come in mighty handy."

The sheriff had shoved two fingers through one hole in Floyd's coat and was wiggling them absently. "Well, Mr. Logan, you got two choices. You can stay here for the inquest, which should take place next week, or you can leave me these coats and sign a statement, after which you can be on your way. I'll leave it up to you."

Floyd thought for a moment. "Sheriff, you have me properly stuck between a rock and a hard place, but I do need to be on my way. So you have yourself a couple of coats if that's all right with Bobby."

"Oh, yes, sir. If Sheriff Nixon needs our coats, I'm willing to leave them."

The sheriff gave an emphatic nod. "Good, that's settled. Mr. Logan, why don't you use my desk and write up a statement. I'm correct in assuming you can write?"

"You are, Sheriff," Floyd said, moving behind the desk. He sat while the sheriff opened a drawer, taking out paper, a bottle of ink, and a quill pen. He slid the materials across the desk. Floyd positioned the paper, opened the bottle of ink, dipped the pen in the ink, and began to write.

The sheriff pulled two chairs over to the fire, slid one to Bobby and sat in the other. While Floyd wrote, the sheriff said, "Mr. Logan, do you know the Akers?"

Bobby jumped in. "I know 'em, Sheriff Nixon. I see 'em in town quite a bit. There's a whole bunch of 'em."

Sheriff Nixon nodded to Bobby. "What Bobby says is right. There's a whole bunch of Akers, and they're not the nicest people in the world. They're a lazy bunch, and there's not much they'll carry very far. But I can tell you this, they'll carry a grudge until they die. What I'm saying is you'd best keep a lookout for them Akers."

Floyd continued to write until he got to a stopping point and looked up at the sheriff. "Sheriff, this has been an interesting trip. Somehow, I have managed to upset a whole slew of people, and they're all promising to kill me. So this Akers bunch is going to have to do the same thing I've told everyone else. They're going to have to come out to the mountains and get in line behind the Pawnee, Ute, Blackfoot, and a few worthless slave-chasers." Then he went back to writing.

The sheriff chuckled, then said, "I understand what you're saying, but these folks won't let anyone get by with what they consider wronging them."

Floyd finished with the statement, slid it to the side, and began writing something else, which he finished quickly, and then did the same thing with another sheet of paper. He folded each, and on the outside of the first one, wrote The Logans, Limerick, Tennessee, and on the second, The Suttons, Nashville, Tennessee. When he had finished, he handed both of them to the sheriff. "If you could see these get to our folks as soon as possible, I'd be much obliged. I wouldn't want anyone to be surprised because of something I did. The Akers will have more grief than they have now if they try messing with the Logans, and I'm sure the Suttons would like to read that Bobby is all right."

The sheriff folded the two letters once more and placed them in his coat pocket. "I'll make sure they get 'em."

Floyd stood and walked from behind the desk. "Well, Sheriff, if you're finished with us, we'd best be on our way. I'd like to get on down the road a ways before pitching camp. I'm guessing you'll take care of the bodies and their horses?"

"Yep, consider them off your hands. Oh, the doc said that thanks to you, Cletus might keep his arm."

"That's good, from what I saw of this bunch, Cletus was the best of 'em. Of course, that's not saying much." Floyd turned and looked at Earl, who was now sitting on the bed, watching through the bars. "Hopefully, they'll get plenty of time to think about what they did, courtesy of Tennessee."

The sheriff glanced back at Earl, then turned back to Floyd. "You're right, Cletus is the best of the bunch. He was a good, hard-working boy before he got mixed up with Bodean. I imagine both he and Earl will be splitting rocks for quite a few years."

Earl cackled from his cell. When he had stopped laughing, he said, "Yes siree, we may be breakin' them rocks, but we'll be alive. When ole Roscoe hears about what's happened, he'll be after you like stink on a skunk."

"Shut up, Earl!" the sheriff said.

"I ain't shuttin' up, you hear? That old man will bring along Cooter and the rest of them boys. Mountain man, if that be what you are, you ain't got no chance, and if Mary Grace, Roscoe's onliest daughter, comes along, you'd best git down on yore knees and start praying. She's the prettiest, evilest, and meanest thing what's come out of that Akers clan. Hee, hee, hee." Earl started dancing in his cell. "She's pretty as can be. She'll catch that mountain man and hang him in a tree. Hee, hee, hee. She's pretty as can—"

Sheriff Nixon watched Earl for a second, then said, "Earl, I'm telling you this one last time. Shut up, or I'll see you on bread and water for as long as you're in my jail."

Earl's mouth slammed shut. He stopped dancing, and looking almost maniacal, with the dried blood on his head, face, and hands, he stared at the sheriff and Floyd, but said nothing else.

"We'd best be on our way," Floyd said. He shook hands with the sheriff and turned to Bobby. "You ready?"

Unfazed by Earl's performance, Bobby waved to him and said, "Goodbye, Mr. Mutton. Hope you get to feeling better." He turned back to Floyd, a wide grin spreading across his face. "We gonna go shoot some more?"

Floyd looked the tired young man over, shook his head and grinned back at him. "Yes, we are. But we're going to ride a ways first and then get some rest. You did good, Bobby, but why don't you hand the Paterson back to me, and I'll slip it in its holster on the saddle. That way you'll be more comfortable riding."

Bobby handed Floyd the revolver, and when he did, Floyd asked, "Have you ever ridden on a riverboat before?"

Bobby's huge grin exposed even white teeth that caught the light from the whale-oil lamp and almost seemed to sparkle as he stepped into the early morning darkness. "You mean we're going to ride a riverboat?"

Floyd, watching him, smiled to himself as he swung up into the saddle. "You bet we are. Now let's hit the trail."

The sheriff had followed them outside. He stood on the boardwalk in the damp morning air and said, "Logan, Earl may be a little crazy, but he's not stupid. What he said is true. Like I told you, watch out for the Akers bunch. The three he named—Roscoe, Cooter, and Mary Grace—are all mean, and she's mighty pretty, but they'll come after you, and they'll bring the entire clan, brothers, sons, and cousins. You could have a real battle on your hands."

"Thanks, Sheriff. I'll keep an eye peeled." Floyd swung the sorrel into the street and, with Bobby alongside, trotted west.

THE STAGE BUCKED and pitched as they raced along the *improved* road. The first day on the stage, Floyd was concerned Bobby might get sick. But the stage was greeted as everything else the young man had seen or taken part in. He was excited and enjoyed every bone-jarring mile of the ride.

They were crammed inside with four other passengers, none interested in conversation at the beginning. But after spending time with Bobby, each person became actively engaged with him. *He is an impressive young man,* Floyd thought. *I have thoroughly enjoyed these twenty-one days with him, and I'll have to admit, I will miss him.* He laughed to himself. *Although we have burned up a lot of ammunition. That boy does love to shoot.*

The coach made a sharp turn, presenting a splendid view of the town ahead. "There it is, Bobby!" the drummer selling kitchen utensils said.

"There what is, Mr. Jacobs?" Bobby said, staring out the opposite side window.

"Over here, Bobby, on this side of the coach. You can see Independence. Hurry before he makes another turn."

Bobby jerked around, leaning across Floyd and grabbing the window on the opposite side for support. In doing so, he had to reach across a young woman who was coming west to teach school.

She rolled her eyes and cast Floyd a furtive smile, asking, "Can you see it, Bobby?"

"Oh yes," Bobby said, turning his face toward hers, now only inches away. "I can see it. Did I tell you that's where my aunt lives, Aunt Judith?"

She drew back only slightly, still smiling, and said, "Why, yes, I believe you did."

The stage careened around the next curve and pitched down the slope as it headed into Independence, finally starting to slow. From the top came the call, "Independence, folks. We're coming into Independence."

Floyd glanced out one of the windows at the sky. It was still clear. The weather had been like this since they left Charlotte. He couldn't ask for better weather. *Hopefully,* he thought, *it will continue until I get home. I don't think I've ever seen a spell of good weather last this long since I've been out here.*

The stage pulled to a stop, and the door was jerked open. Floyd waited until all of the other passengers were out and then stepped down, followed by Bobby. The station manager was welcoming everyone, and as Floyd stepped out, he began, "Welcome to Independence . . . Why, Floyd Logan, welcome back. How are you?" Without giving Floyd a chance to answer, the man continued, "Can you believe this weather? It's been like this for almost a month."

Floyd, for the life of him, could not remember the station manager's name, but said, "Crazy weather."

Laughter causing his big belly to shake, the man said, "Crazy it may be, but I'm gonna enjoy it just as long as it lasts."

Bobby laughed along with the station manager.

Floyd, suddenly remembering the man's name, said, "Reese, do you know where Judith Kingsley lives?"

Still with a smile on his face, Reese said, "I sure do." He pointed across the main street to a narrow side street. "Down that street until you get to the big pecan trees. The house is on the left side, and I'm sure she'll be home. She hasn't been doing too well lately." He paused and looked from Floyd to Bobby and back to Floyd. "If you don't mind my asking, how do you know her?"

Bobby piped up. "She's my auntie, and I've come to take her home. She loves me."

"Well, that's mighty fine," Reese said. "I'm sure she'll be glad to see you, and what's your name?"

Bobby thrust his hand out to Reese and said, "I'm Bobby Sutton, and I'm pleased to meet you."

Reese, taking Bobby's hand, laughed again and said, "Well, I must say, Bobby, I am pleased to meet you too."

"Mind if we leave our things here?" Floyd said. "We'll pick them up shortly."

"Not at all, Floyd. Not at all. We'll take good care of your gear."

"Thanks, Reese." Floyd placed his hand on Bobby's shoulder. "Now, would you like to go see your aunt Judith?"

"Oh yes, can we go right now?" Bobby said.

"Let's go," Floyd said, and with Bobby at his side, they stepped from behind the stage, waited for a string of three wagons to pass, and crossed the street.

The two strode down the narrow street, Bobby stretching his legs to match Floyd's stride. Within minutes they arrived at the large house. Bobby bounded up the steps, knocked rapidly on the door facing, waited only a few seconds, and knocked again.

"Just a moment," a woman's voice cried from inside, followed by the door swinging wide. The woman's irritated expression immediately evaporated upon recognizing her nephew. "Bobby, what are you doing here? Wait, don't answer that, just come here." She held her arms open and the young man stepped into them. They held the embrace, and when they separated, tears were in the woman's eyes.

Bobby, unable to contain his excitement, began talking. "Oh, Auntie Judith, I have so much to tell you. You have no idea what an exciting trip we've had. We've ridden riverboats and stage-coaches and our own horses. We've even been shot at, and I was able to shoot these new pistols. They're called Colt Patersons. Let me tell you what happened on the first night of our trip. We—"

Floyd stepped up next to Bobby. "Excuse me, Bobby, but don't you think I should introduce myself to your aunt? Plus, it's chilly out here. You don't want her to catch her death of cold, do you?"

"You're right, Mr. Floyd. Auntie Judith, can we come inside?"

"Of course, Bobby, I am so sorry for my rudeness." The lady stepped back, making way for Bobby, who charged in, and Floyd.

"Ma'am." Floyd removed his hat and said, "Sorry about just showing up, but we would have beaten any letter that was sent. My name's Floyd Logan."

"It's so nice to meet you, Mr. Logan, and this is the best surprise I could ever hope for. My name is Judith Kingsley, and I am thrilled you have brought my nephew out. Won't you please come in and have a seat." She indicated a plush, straight-backed chair with curving and padded armrests.

He looked at the chair for a moment and glanced down at his dusty clothes. "Ma'am, I'm thinking I should stand instead of sitting on your nice furniture. Both Bobby and I are still mighty dirty from our trip."

"Oh piddle, young man, don't you worry about a little dust. Now have a seat. I want to hear all about your trip." She turned to her nephew. "Come here, and give your aunt Judith another hug."

Floyd watched the two, an older woman with health problems, and the young man with mental problems. Both radiated happiness with being reunited. Though never quelled, his need to be home with his Shoshone family now bubbled near the surface. For a moment, sadness filled his heart, knowing the distance he still must travel.

Judith released the hug and, holding Bobby's hand, led him to the settee and pulled him down next to her. Holding Bobby's hand in both of hers, she turned to Floyd. "Mr. Logan, could you please tell me how you happen to be here with my sweet Bobby."

"Well, ma'am, it all started when I stabled my horses with your brother, Fletcher. That's where I met Bobby. When Fletch heard I was traveling to Independence, he approached me and . . ."

Floyd told Judith Kingsley the whole story, leaving out the bloodier parts. Bobby interjected several times, but even with the interruptions, Floyd was able to finish fairly quickly.

"I must say, Mr. Logan, I owe you a monumental debt that can never be repaid. Thank you for bringing my nephew safely to me. He will be of great assistance in helping me prepare for the trip back to Nashville. However, I must add my warning to Sheriff Nixon's. I have known Roscoe Akers for most of my life. He is a brutal, vengeful man who never forgets an affront, real or imagined. Though you are going to those magnificent mountains I have heard so much about, he and his devil's spawn will hunt you until they find you. I hate to say this about any human being, but if you have a chance to kill any one of them and especially Roscoe, do not hesitate."

"I thank you, ma'am, for your fine advice. I'll take it to heart."

Floyd stood, continuing, "I want you to know that it has been a pleasure traveling with Bobby. He is a fine young man. I would travel with him any time, any place."

Bobby jumped up from the settee. "You're not leaving now, are you, Mr. Floyd?"

"I'm afraid so, Bobby, but I have the feeling we'll meet again. My folks are still in Limerick, so I'll make it a point to stop in Nashville to see you."

The young man's chin quivered almost imperceptibly, and he dashed across the room. Reaching Floyd, he threw his arms around the big man and gave him a huge hug. "I love you, Floyd."

Floyd hugged him back and said, "Me too, Bobby, me too." They held the hug for a long moment. Then Floyd reached up, grasped Bobby's wrists, and pulled them gently down. "You take good care of your aunt, and trust me, one day when you're working in the stable and least expect it, I'll come riding in."

Bobby's grin returned. "That'll be a good day, Mr. Floyd."

Floyd squeezed the boy's shoulder and turned to Judith. "It's nice to meet you, ma'am, but I do have to get going. I'll send Bobby's packs over from the stage office."

After dabbing at her eyes with her hankie, Judith stood and said, "Thank you, Mr. Logan, and please heed my words."

Floyd nodded, opened the door, and stepped onto the porch, slipping his hat back on. As the door was closing, he heard Bobby moving on to something new. "Aunt Judith, I met the stage manager. His name is Mr. Reese. I like him. He laughs a lot." He stepped from the porch and was struck with wind-driven sleet. He turned his head away from the wind so he could look at the sky. The crystal blue was no longer there, now covered with a gray overcast, the clouds moving rapidly from north to south. He shook his head and said to himself, the wind and sleet spitting his words back in his face, "All that good weather, gone."

## 24

Stopping by the stage office, he went through the packs, shifting his gear from Bobby's packs to his own. All the while, his mind constantly worked on the problem of traversing the prairie in this kind of weather. He knew the chance of survival was small, and the loss of his animals almost a given. His frustration rose with the realization he would be stupid to attempt the crossing now. Once finished, he turned to Reese, who was now sitting behind his desk. "When you get a chance, I'd be obliged if you'd take these to Mrs. Kingsley's house. They belong to Bobby Sutton."

"Glad to," Reese said. "Seemed like a nice boy, though a little slow."

"He is, on both counts," Floyd said, locking eyes with Reese. "He's also a good friend, and you won't find a harder worker."

The stage manager held up both palms facing toward Floyd and said, "No offense, I like him. If he's going to be around for a while, I was thinking about hiring him. He's a big boy, and I like a man with a good attitude."

Floyd turned back to the packs, buckling them closed. "None taken. You won't go wrong hiring him, but I don't know how long he'll be around. He's here to help his aunt move back to Nashville."

"Don't matter how long he's here. I need a good man who's not out to prove how tough he is, except maybe in his work efforts."

Floyd picked up the oilskins covering his rifles and checked for any holes or tears while his mind continued to work on the problem of traveling across the prairie at this time of year.

"Got you some new rifles?" Reese asked.

Floyd straightened, his frustration burning like a hot poker, and turned toward the stage manager. "Reese, you're just full of questions today. Yes, they're rifles, some old, some new. Is there anything else I can help you with?"

Again the manager held his palms up, this time leaning back in his chair. "Sorry, Floyd. Just making conversation."

Floyd turned back to the oilskins and continued his checking. He needed to be useful. *If I can't be useful to Leotie and Mika, what can I do while I'm here in Independence?* Then the thought struck him. *Salty might need some help, or maybe Hugh is still in town.*

He straightened again, turned to the station manager, who was making it a point to be busy at his desk, and said, "Reese."

The manager looked up from his desk.

"Reckon I'm a little testy today. The weather's on my mind."

Reese nodded and said, "Understandable, I'm sure it's on a lot of folks' minds. We've had almost a month of good weather, and now this." He turned to look out the window, then turned back to Floyd. "It looks like it's setting in for quite a spell."

Floyd turned to look and saw sleet no longer falling. Big wet, heavy snowflakes floated down and plopped on the ground. It indeed looked like it was setting in for quite a while.

~

Floyd sat comfortably in the saddle, his new, heavy wool coat draped over Buck's flanks. It was tied to his saddlebag and had been riding there, except for early mornings and evenings, for two weeks. The first two weeks had been miserable. Every day, every night, he questioned his decision to leave. In the Flint Hills and east, there had been sufficient protection from the wind, but as he moved farther west, the open country required a more diligent search for protection at night. As hard as it was on him, it had been harder on the animals.

Then, after two weeks out, the temperature started rising, and, except for early morning, the sky was cloud-free. In a few more minutes they would be around the southern end of the Greenhorn Mountains and back into the early morning sun. It had been a hard trip, and Floyd, as he looked back at Browny, felt sorry for his mule. The horses, Buck and Rusty, were able to have long hours during the day carrying no weight, for he alternated between them. Browny, on the other hand, had carried the loaded packs for the entire trip, and the effort was telling on him. If the mule's pack saddle would have fit on the horses, he would have also switched the packs between them. However, Browny's back was so wide that his saddle wouldn't fit the horses and would have very quickly worn sores in their backs.

He again glanced back at the mule and then at Rusty, who he would swear looked worse than the mule. Ribs stood out on all three of the animals. Floyd turned back forward and chuckled, saying softly, "You boys look like scarecrows, but I guess if I looked in a mirror, I'd see I look about like you." In fact, he knew he would. The new clothes he had bought in Nashville, which had fit him so perfectly then, now hung loose on his body. His belt, which carried his guns and knife, did as much work as his galluses, if not more, in keeping his trousers up.

But even as beaten as they all were, it was all Floyd could do to keep from lifting his tired animals into a lope, for they were within a day's ride to being home. He should be seeing Leotie late this evening. They might have to push a little, but they'd make it.

Floyd was in a shallow saddle at the southern end of the Greenhorn Mountains along the Huerfano River. The ridge, at this point, was no more than a quarter mile wide. Such a short distance, they covered it quickly. Floyd pulled Buck up before coming out from behind the ridgeline. He wanted to make sure a band of Utes didn't surprise him this close to home. He glanced to his left, his brow slightly wrinkled from irritation because of the noise coming from the river. It was a small river, but faster and wider now, due to early runoff. He'd had a difficult time getting across the Arkansas and keeping everything dry, especially the powder. However, that challenge was behind him, and his current problem was the noisy Huerfano. The river noise prevented him from using one of his most important senses, his hearing. He would have to rely on his vision and sense of smell.

He examined every bush, tree, draw, and rock where an Indian might be hiding. The only thing moving was a small herd of mule deer. He watched them for a few moments to see if they were relaxed, or as relaxed as any deer could get. They continued in the direction he was going, showing no excitement or concern. Floyd finished his examination of the country and was just about to ride out of the saddle when the faint sound of a distant shot echoed across the hills. He wasn't sure of the direction, but Buck was.

Buck, along with Browny and Rusty, were staring toward the southwest. *The southwest,* he thought. Then again, another rifle shot, followed by the even fainter sound of a pistol. Floyd checked his revolvers, the ring rifle, and his Ryland. Throwing Browny's and Rusty's leads to the ground, he turned Buck straight to the river and kicked him in the flanks. The big buckskin leaped forward. Floyd had only a moment to check the river, before the horse leaped in, and guide him to what should be the shallowest crossing. To be safe, he pulled a revolver from his saddle holster and yanked his Colt rifle from the scabbard. With the revolver and reins in his left hand and the rifle in his right, he clinched his knees around the horse as it leaped into the river.

Normally, at this spot, the Huerfano was shallow enough to walk across and barely get your ankles wet, but with the early melt, the splashed water came within inches of his saddle holsters and dunked his Ryland resting in the scabbard.

Once across, Floyd slipped the revolver back into its holster, and since the rifle scabbard had gotten wet, he held the rifle. Shots sporadically sounded ahead, but it was still far, especially with what Buck had been through over the past six weeks. He figured the shots were about ten miles distant. If Buck had been fresh, he figured he could be there in twelve maybe even ten minutes. But if he ran him that hard today, he'd have a dead horse. After about five minutes, he pulled the animal back to a ground-eating lope, and even then the horse's sides were heaving. Again, several shots, but now he was closer and could place their positions.

Before pulling Buck to a halt, he shoved the two revolvers that had been resting in the saddle holsters behind his waistband. Coming to a thick stand of pine, he yanked the horse into it, tied the reins to a small sapling using a slipknot, and ghosted into the trees. More shots were fired, and they were right in front of him, but over a low ridge. *I hope these aren't Utes,* he thought, moving toward the ridge. *The last thing we need is a fight with them. That would ruin any chance of developing a truce.* Quietly, he climbed to the top of the ridge, removed his hat, and eased his head above the ridgeline.

Down the other side of the ridge, in a shallow draw, and several hundred yards to his right, he could make out two mountain men and five horses. From his position he could see two Indians to their front, and close. Like all experienced mountain men, he knew that if he could see two, he could at least double the number, if not more. The ones he could see were approaching on opposite ends of the wash and would soon be close enough to either charge or fire into the wash.

Floyd's best approach would be to ease back down the ridge and circle around behind the Indians. He couldn't see their horses, but was sure they were in the rocks over the far ridge. That would be the perfect plan, except for the two attackers who were below on the slope and almost in position at the edge of the wash. He considered his choices only for a moment before making a decision. The closest Indian was at least two hundred yards, which would put the other one at almost two hundred and fifty. He'd had a lot of practice with the Colt Ring Rifle, but all of it had been under a hundred yards. He knew his Ryland, and with it this would be no challenge, but it sat wet in the saddle scabbard. With the Colt, he would have to adjust and hope. If the worst happened, and he missed, it would at least alert the men who were under attack. Unfortunately, it would also alert the Indians.

He could still not tell which tribe they were from, as they continued to crawl closer. He brought the rifle to his shoulder, resting it across the ridge. Centering the sights on the farthest man's back, he corrected about an inch for shooting downhill, and another two inches for distance, and squeezed the trigger. The blast echoed off the rocks and across the canyon. The man he had been aiming at leaped to his feet, spun around, and fell to the ground, motionless. Confused, the other man flattened himself, not moving. He obviously had no idea where the shot came from.

But at least one of his friends in the low brush behind him saw Floyd's smoke and fired. The ball hit low, down the side of the ridge, in the rocks. From Floyd's vantage point, he could see the man crawling to a different position. But right now, he had another priority. Cocking the rifle, Floyd, knowing the man would have to reload, ignored him and settled on the exposed Indian near the draw. At his shot, the attacker stretched his full length, stiffened, then never made another move. Before the echo of his shot had died, Floyd switched to the shooter who had fired at him, but the man was no longer visible.

There was no more movement.

He waited.

But he knew he couldn't wait too long. If his enemy located his horse, he would be in dire trouble. Minutes passed. The two mountain men started moving around in the draw, cautiously collecting their gear. Occasionally one would glance up at Floyd's position. It was time.

After scanning the surrounding area, Floyd stood, waved his rifle, and pointed it back toward his horse. The two men waved back, and he turned, running toward the pine trees and Buck. Ever cautious, his eyes continued to search the path ahead. Finally, slipping into the tall pines again, the thick bed of soft pine needles muffled his fast-moving feet as he went from tree to tree.

Through the openings between the trees, he could see Buck spot him, but his horse's head kept jerking from left to right. Floyd carried the rifle in his left hand and yanked a Paterson from his waistband with his right. Buck was nervous and he knew why. Either all or some of those Indians had circled around and spotted his horse. He knew they were laying for him. He had two choices, neither good. He could slow and try to slip the remaining distance to his horse, but he knew that was useless. They already knew he was coming. The only real choice left to him was to charge into their midst and do as much damage as possible.

Whether for good or bad, he had left Buck in a small clearing. It would give him a little room to maneuver, but depending on how many Indians, they would also have the same advantage. Leaping over a fallen log, he burst into the opening. Catching movement to his left, he wheeled, bringing the Paterson up in the same movement. Now, he was close enough to tell what tribe this Indian belonged to, closer than he had any desire to be. As he brought the revolver to bear, he thumbed back the hammer. When the muzzle covered the chest of the Apache, he pulled the trigger. The man's momentum continued to carry him toward Floyd, but strength no longer filled his muscles. He collapsed to the forest floor.

Buck reared, front legs smashing forward. A hoof struck another Apache as he charged Floyd, knocking him to the ground. But the man hit, rolled, and immediately regained his feet, joining his partner. Responding to Buck's movement, Floyd whipped back to his right, firing once, twice. Both men were down.

Smoke filled the clearing. Floyd grabbed Buck's reins and leaped into the saddle, whipping the horse around and racing from the pines. Breaking out of the trees, he spotted the two mountain men and motioned them toward him. Reaching an open knoll, he pulled up and waited while he searched the countryside for hostiles.

As soon as he spotted the two men on horseback, he couldn't help but recognize them. The two were strikingly different, one short and stubby in the saddle, the other almost unnaturally tall, Shorty and Morg. A wide grin spread across Floyd's face as the two men pulled up.

"Well, if that ain't the ugliest, welcome face this ole son has ever seen, I'll walk to Californy," Shorty said. "Man, I'm tellin' you, when all them Injuns jumped out of those rocks, I shorely thought our scalps would be hanging in a wickiup. This is the closest we've come to losing our hair since the Blackfoot dustup on the Yellowstone." Throughout Shorty's animated statements, Morg sat silent, a small smile across his face.

"Good to see you, Floyd," Morg said. "You shore came along at the right time. I'm much obliged, but what was all that shooting after you left us?"

"Yeah," Shorty said, "all that fast shooting, and it sounded like it all came from the same gun. How'd you get so many shots off so fast?"

Floyd patted Buck on the neck. "Buck, here, saved my bacon. I could see him as I was coming through the trees, and he was mighty nervous. So I just figured those boys had set me up for an ambush, and I must've surprised them. Maybe they weren't expecting me back quite that soon. But when I jumped into that clearing, they were waiting. Buck knocked one rolling, which gave me a little more time."

Shorty jumped in, "Ole hoss, they ain't give you much time at all, not from all that quick shooting we heard. How'd you shoot so fast?"

Floyd looked around again and said, "I'll tell you, but not here. I've got another horse and pack mule waiting for me, I hope, across the Huerfano."

"Well, shoot-fire, what are we waiting for?" Shorty said.

The three men headed for the river.

## 25

They made camp under the cottonwoods along the river. Here, the snow was completely gone and the ground dry. A shallow pit had been dug for the fire, horses and packs were taken care of, and now they relaxed around the modest fire as best they could.

"So, you being gone since November explains yore horses," Shorty said. "Don't reckon I've seen any as worn out looking as those three, especially yore mule. Why, I swear, if you carry a torch around to his other side, you could see it burning right through those ribs."

Floyd nodded. "Yep, they've had it tough. This last leg from Independence just about done them in. I'm sure glad that we have only one more day to go." Browny looked up to stare at Floyd, as if in agreement, then dropped his head back to the ground and continued to rip and chew the dry grass.

"You was going to tell us about those guns," Shorty said.

Floyd pulled one of the Paterson revolvers from its holster and handed it over to Shorty.

Shorty looked at it for a minute, then, puzzled, said, "There ain't no trigger."

"Pull the hammer back," Floyd replied.

Shorty did as he was instructed, and the trigger dropped in view. He slowly lowered the hammer and pulled it back again. The trigger retracted and then dropped down again. Shorty repeated his actions several times, then looked up at Floyd. "Does this thing work?"

"Really fine. All you have to do is pull the hammer back, fire, and do it again, for either four or five times, depending on how it's loaded."

Shorty tried it several more times, then handed it to Morg.

After Morg tried it a couple more times, he said, "That's a mighty fine firearm. What does it shoot?"

Floyd pulled a round ball for the Paterson from his possibles bag and tossed it to Morg. The tall man caught it and pulled out one of his, comparing the two. Finally, he looked up. "It ain't near as big."

"Thirty-six caliber."

Morg nodded. "Lot smaller than this." He held up one of his .54-caliber round balls that were used in both his rifle and pistol.

"True," Floyd said, "but with that .54, you only have one shot. If that's all I'd had today, I probably wouldn't be talking to you now.

"So tell me, boys, where have you been, and where are you headed?"

"Been trapping," Shorty said, "on the South Fork of the Rio Grande. Who would've thought it, we found a mess of beaver. This one little creek, I called Beaver Creek, was loaded with 'em. Why, I swear, it was like trapping twenty years ago. Why, we caught us four hundred pounds of them beaver. It was all we could carry. So that's the reason we decided to come on out, and those danged Apaches stole half our catch." Shorty shook his head and mumbled, "All that work."

"Yeah, Shorty," Morg said, "but we've still got the other half. That's enough to get us to Californy."

Floyd looked around, checking his surroundings. "I sure hate to see you lose all those furs. You aren't going to try to get them back, are you?"

Morg shook his head, then nodded toward Shorty. "Nope, even he ain't that crazy."

Shorty looked as if he might say something, but decided against it.

"Well, boys," Floyd said, "I reckon we'd better get this fire put out. The light's starting to fade."

Shorty squinted at Floyd and said, "Good idea. By the by, I don't suppose you'd care to join us for Californy?"

Floyd laughed and then said, "Fellas, I've got some folks I am hankering to see, and I don't think I'll be taking any long trips for quite a while."

"Well," Shorty said, "you're gonna miss out on a lot of fun."

"Maybe, but I plan on having a lot of fun right here." After dousing the fire, Floyd walked out to check the animals. The sky was crystal clear, and a few stars were chasing the light of the sun. He looked north. The Shoshone village, Leotie, and Mika were less than thirty miles away. He would see them tomorrow. His mind drifted to sweet Leotie. It'd been way too long. He could see her mysterious brown eyes and wide full mouth smiling at him, white teeth sparkling. His soul ached for her. *Tomorrow,* he thought. *We'll be together again tomorrow.*

THE VALLEY SPRAWLED open to him. He had always loved breaking into the open and getting his first view of this valley. Mountains ran along both sides, Sangre de Cristo on the west and Greenhorns on the east. The grass was still brown, covered with snow in areas sheltered from the sun. He knew that would change. The floor of the valley would again turn white before the highland winter ended. The soft glow from the cooking fires rippled across the teepees in the distance. It would be dark by the time he covered the remaining few miles to home.

The animals, who were near exhaustion, quickened their gait. For they too knew feed, rest, and home were near. His mind drifted over the past four months, eliciting a chuckle. More trouble than he could've ever gotten into here in the mountains had dogged him back east. *But maybe I helped a few folks, and I got to see mine.* His heart swelled with the thought of his parents, his brothers, his sisters, and his nephews and nieces. *Callum and Wallace,* he thought, *are going to be headed out here when they're old enough. I just know it.*

Then he thought of Ezra and Liza. *What a good man Ezra has grown into, and I'm certain that Liza had a lot to do with it. Both good friends.* With the thought of Ezra and Liza, Reuben and Keri Foster slid back into his mind as well. *I sure hope those folks will be safe and happy.*

The final miles fell away, as if in a moment, and he was riding into the village. They were all gathered there, in the evening firelight. The entire village had turned out. Standing in the very front were Pallaton and Nina, Kajika, and Jeb with Ayana, she holding their new baby.

Floyd felt a warm glow suffuse his body, for in the very front, next to their son, Mika, stood his beautiful Leotie. She was the reason he had made this long journey, and she looked fine, strong, healthy. His worries, his premonitions had all been in vain, and he was home. He reined Rusty to a stop and stepped to the ground. Here was why he had braved the trials of this long journey. He stepped forward, placed his arms around her slim waist, and drew her to him.

After a long embrace, she leaned back, rested her hand on his scarred cheek, and gazed into his deep blue eyes. When she spoke, her voice caressed him. "Welcome home, my husband."

## AUTHOR'S NOTE

Thank you for reading *Mettle of a Mountain Man,* the third book in the Logan Mountain Man Series.

If you have any comments, what you like or what you don't, please let me know. You can email me at: Don@DonaldLRobertson.com, or you can use the contact form on my website.

www.DonaldLRobertson.com

I'll be looking forward to hearing from you.

**BOOKS**
**Logan Mountain Man Series**
**(Prequel to Logan Family Series)**

*SOUL OF A MOUNTAIN MAN*
*TRIALS OF A MOUNTAIN MAN*
*METTLE OF A MOUNTAIN MAN*

**Logan Family Series**

*LOGAN'S WORD*
*THE SAVAGE VALLEY*
*CALLUM'S MISSION*
*FORGOTTEN SEASON*

**Clay Barlow - Texas Ranger Justice Series**

*FORTY-FOUR CALIBER JUSTICE*
*LAW AND JUSTICE*
*LONESOME JUSTICE*

**NOVELLAS AND SHORT STORIES**

*RUSTLERS IN THE SAGE*
*BECAUSE OF A DOG*
*THE OLD RANGER*

Made in the USA
Las Vegas, NV
16 July 2024

92397076R00152